To Catch the Conscience of the King

To Catch the Conscience of the King

Martin White

Martin White
2016

First Printing: 2016

ISBN 978-1-326-55399-9

Published by Di Butrio Books

www.dibutriobooks.co.uk

Dedication

To my parents, Jack and Phyllis White, gone sadly, but still an inspiration

Contents

Contents

PART ONE: HEREFORD

Chapter 1

Under Hereford's old Wye Bridge, at the southern end where the town privies discharged to the fast flowing current, ordure had spattered on the wooden stanchions, decade by decade, so that now they were festooned with a thick film of excrement, bearded about with lank weeds and thriving colonies of furry mould. There was a foulness, which in the foggy winter air seemed to coat his lungs and throat with a sour viscous membrane.

Stephen's nostrils wrinkled and his stomach heaved. He turned and scrambled back up the bank. What with the mud and the injury to his foot, he almost lost his balance and slid backwards a couple of times; and then, when he regained the pathway, he managed to tread on the hem of his habit pitching himself forward. As he struggled to his feet, his hood slipped to his shoulders revealing a thin, pale, but handsome face with rather globular eyes.

"What a place for a meeting!" he thought, feeling the bite of the wind round his close cropped tonsure.

The odour from the town jakes was still poisoning his lungs and he retched twice, feeling bile burn the back of his throat, before gulps of frosted air began to revive him. No way would he descend that bank again. Besides, he could keep watch here. Though the path was at a lower level than the old bridge itself, he would see anyone approaching – whether from east or west.

He pulled up his hood, and straightened his cape and habit. The touch of rosary beads began to settle his nerves, and when he clasped the plain crucifix about his neck, its very smoothness seemed to calm him. He whispered to the Virgin Mary, and felt the pounding of his heart subside and the rasping of his breath ease just a little.

To his right, as he gazed east along the river bank, he could see what might be a beggar ambling away, where the path ran opposite the bishop's palace and the cathedral of St Ethelbert; but there was no one else – no one who appeared they might be searching for him.

When he looked westwards, still no one appeared on the pathway, but he was struck by the density of the throng now passing over the bridge. From there, he could hear a swelling commotion – quite a hubbub of excitement. As well as tradesmen about their business, and villeins herding cattle towards the Market Place, there seemed an unusual number of other townsfolk of all classes jostling amongst them, hurrying along, forcing a passage north in the direction of the centre of the town. They must be the sight-seers: men and women intent on viewing the day's great trial and execution; droves of children too – boisterous and rowdy at the prospect of a gory spectacle. As he watched them, it seemed the very air vibrated – maybe from the tramp of so many feet on the bridge, maybe from blood-lust in so many hearts.

Suddenly a hand grasped his shoulder making him jump. Beside him stood another monk, his gaze likewise directed towards the surging crowd.

"Poor Hugh le Despenser! See how they've all come to gawp at him!" the stranger murmured.

Like Stephen, the newcomer was a Dominican, and wore the Order's white habit and black cape and hood. Beyond that any resemblance ceased. The stranger was older – perhaps in his forties: twenty years older than Stephen. He stood a full cubit higher, and, whereas Stephen was slight of frame, this man was well built, with broad shoulders and a bull-like neck. His features were large and rather course: bushy eye-brows shaded deep-set eyes, and grizzled tufts poked out from his hood just above the ears. Yet the voice muttering words of pity for King Edward's favourite had a refinement Stephen would not have expected, given his appearance, and he could tell the newcomer spoke French with the accent of the court – indeed, of the University, where Stephen himself had studied.

This had to be Brother Thomas Dunsheved, special envoy to King Edward II and chaplain to the pope – the man whom Stephen's prior, Brother Walter, had instructed him to meet down below the bridge near the privy outfall. This was the man from whom, he understood, he was to be given information pertinent to the welfare of the Order – information which the prior was eager to receive.

"It's a sad day to make your acquaintance, Brother Stephen," the stranger resumed. "A day when the king's greatest servant is to be butchered before a mob, and the king himself is in grave danger... But this is the age we live in – and this is why we're meeting!...Come, we have little time for our business, and I especially must be on my way. While everyone else heads for the Market Place, let's make our

4

way along the river bank. I've things to tell you no one else must overhear. Come on. Make haste..."

Dunsheved began striding out along the footpath away from the bridge, whilst Stephen struggled to keep up. This was not easy, for he could not match the other man's lengthy steps, and in any case his maimed left foot, the two smallest toes of which had been missing for several years, caused him to limp and lag behind.

"I looked for you a moment ago," Dunsheved added with a chuckle, "down there where the privies give on to the river, but I guessed from the stench you'd have sought better air! No one but a whore desperate for trade would loiter there! – I suppose Prior Walter thought we'd have such a rendezvous to ourselves at this time of day! Or perhaps he has a more wicked sense of humour than I'd imagined!...Still, enough of that, for, Brother Stephen, you must now listen and note. I've much to tell you."

Stephen reflected that he had not yet uttered a word himself, but it was clear the older man had no intention of trading pleasantries. Indeed, as Dunsheved hastened on, he launched without further explanation into an account of the momentous events which had in the past few years beset the nation. These were matters familiar to Stephen, as to the world at large, and he needed no reminder of King Edward's struggle with his barons, his victory, and the following period, when, with the help of the Despensers, father and son, he had imposed his will on a recalcitrant nation.

Trying his best not to fall further behind, Stephen wondered why, if time was short, Dunsheved had set out upon a history lesson. It seemed like a prologue, but to what? Maybe the man was so much the royal envoy, so much the man of affairs, that he fell to lecturing even when he had no crowd or court to address! Stephen felt breathless, both from exertion and increasing exasperation.

As they drew level with the palace and cathedral on the far bank, however, he listened with more interest, for now Dunsheved was touching on more recent events: the rift which had grown between King Edward and his queen; how Isabella had gone abroad to her father's court in France, and then had stayed there, refusing the king's commands to return. These were matters rumoured throughout the land, though as often denied by those who took the sovereign's part.

Dunsheved recounted how two months previously the queen and her ally, Mortimer, had invaded England from the east, bringing with them a force of foreigners, vowing both to restore her rights and those of the barons, and to rid the country of the Despensers. They had then pursued the king and his forces across the country. Wherever they arrived they had taken power and replaced the king's representatives with their own. Again Stephen had heard as much before, though he had found it all hard to credit – at least till he had himself arrived in Hereford the day before, and had learned that Mortimer and the queen were in residence in this very city, and were issuing commands and proclamations, as if acting on the king's behalf.

What had happened during the weeks which followed the invasion had remained a mystery for Stephen, though he had heard much wild speculation. Some said the king had fled the country, and that the older Despenser had been tried and executed: the same fate that was about to befall his son. If such was true, Stephen, like so many of his countrymen, was eager for confirmation, and to know how it was such a revolution could have taken place. So now he strained to hear, as Dunsheved went on with a tale to which, it seemed, few but he were party:

"When the king fled from London – incredible as this may seem, Stephen – very few of his supporters, men whom he and the Despensers had promoted and whom they relied on, rallied to his cause. I was with him for much of that time, and shared in his anguish and disappointment, as hopes withered and those he'd called friends betrayed him.

"I'll explain in a while what happened after the king went to the West Country, so you may make it clear to Brother Walter and to others in the Order the process of his downfall and how desperate his situation has become. But be aware, Stephen, that I also have instructions for you – important instructions for you to carry out – and on which may depend what hopes the king has left. That's why I sent to your prior at Gloucester begging his assistance. I can only say how fortunate it is you were already here in Hereford on priory business. Doubly so, as I've heard you're one of Walter's most trusted brothers!"

Dunsheved went on speaking, whilst stumbling and slipping in his haste along the muddy track. It was harder and harder for Stephen both to keep up and to hear all that was being said, for at times Dunsheved spoke almost under his breath, even though no one else was in sight.

"When King Edward arrived at Chepstow, just before St Luke's Day," he continued, "with Queen Isabella's army only a few days' march behind, and with his own troops melting away, he and Lord Hugh realised the bitter truth that, for now at least, no further support could be mustered in England. So the king's remaining party – myself included – set sail in a small cog, hoping to make for Ireland where new forces might be raised. But Fate was cruel to us, and a violent storm forced us to make land near the town of Cardiff.

"Even then not all was lost, for Lord Hugh holds many lands in that part of Wales, and Edward himself placed much store on the Welsh, whom he always calls his countrymen! But again our hopes were dashed. We rode from Cardiff to Caerphilly, and then to Margam Abbey near Neath, and all the while more and more of Edward's officials and the few soldiers who remained to him were slinking away – mostly, needless to say, under cover of night!...Then came another blow, when a commissioner sent to the west of Wales found that even in that region not one person was willing to join the king and support him!

"It's for this reason you must impress on Brother Walter that nothing is to be hoped for at the present time, either in England or in Wales, or in terms of battles, armies or rebellions! And, to tell the truth, I doubt things would have been much different if we'd made our way to Ireland."

"I can barely believe this," said Stephen, making a desperate spurt to draw level with Dunsheved, and at last able to interrupt. "Surely, with all the power and wealth of Lord Hugh and his father..."

"I tell you, the cause is lost!...At least for now!...Besides, there's worse." A look of pain crossed Thomas' face as he paused to take breath, now that Stephen was at his side. "What the rumours say, I'm afraid, is true: not only was Hugh le Despenser captured – now to face death here in Hereford – but so too was King Edward himself!"

"But..."

"Silence! And listen!" But before Dunsheved could add any more, a burst of laughter and chattering from around a bend in the path ahead announced the arrival of three townswomen making for the bridge. Their faces were flushed with the cold winter air and, Stephen guessed, with the prospect of the day's entertainment. At once Dunsheved drew aside, bowed his head in prayer, and began telling the beads of his rosary. Stephen followed suit.

As they passed, the women in fact gave them no more than the merest of inquiring glances, and once they were out of earshot, Dunsheved was off again, intent on his tale:

"To be brief, Stephen, for time is pressing, from Neath in desperation the king set out once more for Caerphilly, planning to follow a mountain road by way of Lord Hugh's castle at Llantrisant. But in driving rain and on open heath land we were surprised by Henry of Lancaster's search party. All, apart from myself, were captured. The prisoners were held first at Llantrisant itself – so much for Hugh's power and wealth! – and then at the fortress in Monmouth.

"For eight days now I've been trailing them: attempting to discover what the queen's plans are, both for Lord Hugh – whose fate we now know – but also for our lord, her husband, who is entirely at her mercy and that of Mortimer!" Dunsheved had at last slowed his pace, as though these words weighed him down. He turned to face Stephen, his expression twisted in bitterness.

"For Lord Hugh, the day is lost. I pray God the king himself does not suffer a similar fate."

"But that's unthinkable, Brother Thomas – surely!..." began Stephen. "You tell me the king is in the queen's custody, but you cannot think she'll do more than reform his counsel – replace his old counsellors and friends with her own: with Lord Mortimer, for example. You can't think she plans to usurp his throne, let alone have him killed! He is her husband, her lord – her head in all things!"

"I do not know what to think, Brother Stephen! If Isabella had any regard for wifely obedience, would she have led a force of invaders into the land?...Haven't you read the chronicles? Don't you know the evil queens have done in the past? And aren't you aware how hugely ambitious my dear Lord Mortimer truly is?...Perhaps you imagine he's merely her loyal servant and adviser, rather than what he's now become: her paramour and corrupter!" Dunsheved all but spat these words at Stephen, and, having now raised his voice, checked to ensure no one was near enough to have overheard him.

8

There was nobody in either direction along the path, though on the other side of the river, Stephen could make out a man untying a coracle at the rear of the bishop's palace. Both monks froze, watching till it became clear the man was unaware of their presence, and was heading away from them downstream on the current.

They resumed walking, and Dunsheved explained how at Monmouth he had learned that Edward had been deprived of his Great Seal, and that the prisoners were to be separated: Despenser, Chancellor Baldock, and Simon de Reading being taken north to Hereford, for trial before the queen herself; Edward being taken elsewhere – whether to London or to some other stronghold, he could not at first find out. Since he could do nothing to prevent Despenser's destruction, he had continued tracking the soldiers guarding the king, as they made their way north-eastwards from Monmouth through the Forest of Dean till they stopped for the night at Ledbury.

"There God smiled on me, Stephen! Lord Lancaster had appointed one of our fellow Dominicans as the king's temporary confessor, and through my own cunning I managed to make contact with him, and through him with the king! That's how I discovered the king's destination: Lancaster's own castle at Kenilworth – for a few weeks at least. Also, at my suggestion, the confessor obtained letters addressed by the king to Lord Hugh, which I undertook at all costs to deliver before Despenser reached Hereford."

Dunsheved then explained how, to bring the king's letters to Lord Hugh's hands, he had the evening before bribed one of the guards at the Priory of Aconbury, just a few miles south of Hereford, which was where the prisoners had spent their final night.

"I can only imagine the sad content of those letters," said Dunsheved. "The declarations of love and gratitude they must have contained!" He sighed, then added:

"It was at Ledbury the previous night that I'd despatched a horseman to Gloucester, to your prior, Brother Walter, begging for someone to meet me, so I could arrange what next both I and the Order – given its allegiance to King Edward – should do. I was most relieved to learn, when my messenger returned, that you, Brother Stephen, were already here in Hereford...So it comes, my friend, that we're stumbling our way together along the frosty greasy bank of the River Wye! And hence..."

9

"But surely, Brother Thomas, in light of all you've said, there's nothing which can be done! If the king's a prisoner and the whole country has turned against him, what power has the Order of Preachers..."

"Edward and his forebears have been the greatest benefactors of our order since its foundation here in England! We must hold our nerve, Brother Stephen. Hold our nerve, then act when the time is right!..." Dunsheved had ceased advancing and now seized Stephen's shoulder. "Do you think it's an easy thing to depose a king? Have you heard of such a thing happening in this realm before? What will the Parliament say, what will the Church...?

"We must bide our time! We must see if we can make contact with the king, plan how he may be freed, and then spirit him abroad for safety...For, looking to the future, if Mortimer himself can escape the Tower of London, as they say he did, flee to the continent, and then return at the head of a victorious army – all within a few years – why may not Edward do likewise!...Time...Time is what we need!"

Dunsheved paced back and forth, speaking more to himself now than to Stephen:

"Our enemies will quarrel...There's no doubt of that, now there are spoils to be divided – Mortimer, the queen, Lancaster, the whole rabble!...And if the crowds cheer Isabella and her henchman now, will they do the same in twelve months' time? – when they're all at each other's throats, or when taxes have risen to pay for some new Scottish adventure, or when the Almighty, in retribution for the casting out of his anointed king, has sent new plagues and tempests to destroy the crops and land!

"But in the meantime, Stephen, in the meantime...!" Dunsheved gripped both of Stephen's shoulders, his spittle spattering Stephen's cheeks. "As I say, we must make contact with the king, make sure he faces no immediate danger. This I'll do. As soon as I leave you, I'll resume my pursuit of Edward and those guarding him to Kenilworth. There I have spies. If we discover any plot to do away with him, I'll have no alternative but to mount a raid on the castle – my family's lands at Dunmore are close – and we'll rescue Edward or die in the process.

"But, if such desperate measures are not necessary, Stephen, if there is more time for us to hatch a more subtle and more foolproof plot, that, Stephen, that is where I must rely on you!"

A certain excitement had been growing in Stephen's breast as he had listened to the tale of danger and cunning just told to him, but this now turned to alarm and then to panic at the thought Dunsheved was about to inveigle him into his plots and scheming. He felt himself straining against the older man's grasp, almost struggling to escape him.

"First, Stephen, you must relate all I've told you to Brother Walter. It's he who must make sure that the Order understands what has happened and how desperate the king's position is. But I want you to do two things more. Firstly – and I know this will be a grievous thing to witness – you must attend Lord Hugh's trial and execution. – I cannot do this, for I must return to Edward himself! – You must note all that's said and done. This is intelligence we'll surely need, though I've small doubt that Hugh will be hung, drawn and quartered before the day is out.

"Secondly, Stephen – and Brother Walter's letter assures me you're an able and resourceful fellow – you must travel with the queen's party when she departs from Hereford. She's to travel first to Gloucester, then on to Wallingford for Christmas. Again you must find out all you can, worm your way into the counsels of her friends, if possible – again so as to advise Brother Walter. Above all, seek to discover what they have in mind for Edward: whether after his stay at Kenilworth he will be taken to London, or whether they intend to imprison him somewhere else, and to what end. This is vital knowledge for both myself and Brother Walter, so that we may plan, make our preparations – so that successfully we may smuggle Edward abroad. Above all else…"

"But Brother Thomas, how am *I* to do this? I am a scholar and preacher, only lately down from the University, not a knight or man of action like yourself! How am *I* to worm my way into counsels – let alone those of the queen's friends? And how can I attach myself to her party?...I could hardly seek to ride with them! As a friar of our order, I'm forbidden to ride on horse-back, as you know... Besides, you may have noticed, I have a disability which prevents me…"

Anger flashed across Thomas' face. He let go of Stephen's shoulders, so that the younger man staggered back towards the edge of the bank:

"This is no time for weakness, friar. No time for niceties! We must save King Edward, our order's benefactor! You're a capable man chosen by Fate to play a role in King Edward's rescue! – the ablest of all his forty monks, Brother Walter tells me. Now act accordingly! Promise me you'll do as I've said..."

By now Brother Thomas had again seized Stephen's arm and was wrenching it round in his powerful grip.

"I'll try my best," bleated Stephen. "Believe me, Brother Thomas, I will do all I can..."

"Do! Or may you rot in Hell!" came the snarled response.

Suddenly Stephen was free again, staggering backwards, almost toppling over the edge towards the river. His arm was throbbing. He watched as Dunsheved turned on his heel, scrambled away from the path and disappeared across a patch of scrubland. Then everything round him seemed to lurch, as he tried to make sense of what he had just heard – most of all, of what he had just been ordered to do.

The day before he had been on a minor errand from Blackfriar's House at Gloucester to the Order's small sister house at Hereford. Even when he had received a written message from Walter telling him to meet Brother Thomas Dunsheved below the bridge two hours after Prime, he had been mystified, but not fearful.

Now the world had changed, and it was as if, without warning, he had been cast into a chasm of danger and uncertainty. His nausea returned. He felt a cramp in his guts, and had to scuttle down to a bed of reeds, where he relieved himself.

Still squatting, he looked back along the opposite bank to Bishop Orleton's Palace, where, he had learned, the queen and Mortimer had been staying since the winter weather had set in. The cathedral towered above it, its bells – along with those of all the other churches in the city – now clanging a frenzy of peals, no doubt signalling the approach of Despenser's hour of trial and execution. If truth be told, Stephen himself had few feelings of loyalty or affection where Lord Hugh was concerned. King Edward was beloved within the Order, but Hugh's reputation was one of cruelty and rapacity. Yet to see him tortured and then butchered was not something Stephen had ever wished or expected to endure.

Back on the footpath, he fell to his knees on the frosted grass and spent a few moments in prayer, his lips pressed on his rosary beads. He offered praise to the Virgin for the many times She had helped and guided him through past tribulations: from the days of childhood loneliness after his mother died, during his uncertainties when first a novice, and on to the black times when he was a student at Oxford. He implored Her again to vouchsafe him Her assistance.

A little calmer, though still shaking inside at what was now expected of him, Stephen stumbled back along the river bank to the old Wye Bridge, and passed under the gateway at its southern end. As he joined the rowdy throng heading in the direction of the Market Place, he grasped his crucifix, and kept his head bowed, his eyes fixed on the ground, as the Order's rule demanded.

Chapter 2

Amidst the throng, noise assailed him from all sides – chatter, argument, anger, the sound of cart-wheels trundling, cattle in distress. Yet he still heard the shout when it came – the mighty cheer which rang out some way behind him, perhaps from beyond the city wall. Then there was the blare of trumpets from further away. Some in the crowd stopped and turned round, whilst others kept forcing their way northwards, jostling and cursing. The trumpets rang out again, but this time louder. Now everyone halted. There was excited whispering, then gleeful shouts of the name "Despenser", and then again "Despenser, Despenser. The traitor's arrived!"

The flow on the bridge reversed, as bodies twisted round and began thrusting, pushing, heaving against the backs and shoulders in front of them. Stephen found himself squashed between two drovers, then pinioned by the jabbing elbow of one of them up against an apple-cart, as its driver somehow manoeuvred his nag round in a semicircle. He was crushed, almost stifled in a profusion of reeking limbs, bellies and buttocks pressing in on him.

Then something yielded. It was as though way up ahead a dam had burst, and the mad pressure of body on body eased. The crowd began to move forward, hastening back over the bridge, up the slight incline of St Martin's Street past the hospital and church, and on towards the city wall. There, as all now guessed, Despenser and the others to be tried and executed must be arriving. Stephen heard the rumour run from tongue to tongue that the prisoners had come north from Monmouth, escorted by the queen's ally, Lord Henry of Lancaster.

As he hastened forward with everyone else, he thought of the hangings he had seen in the past – usually of thieves and murderers, and both in Gloucester and in Oxford. Often on those occasions he had rejoiced that by such means some semblance of God's order could be maintained on earth. Today, though, the prospect of an even grislier spectacle made his stomach turn and his limbs tremble – the more so, since he was charged now with witnessing and reporting it for others.

Yet dread began shading into the tingle of anticipation, as he became infected with the crowd's excitement. There was a scent of blood in the air, and – in this pack of baying humanity – something like the thrill of a stag hunt. He grasped his rosary beads as an anchor, fearful his soul might be swept up in the frenzy all around:

"Hail Mary, full of grace," he mouthed. "The Lord is with thee..." But he could not go on, for in this human tide neither mind nor body seemed quite his own. He was keeping pace with the apple cart, holding on to the timber struts and roping along its rear for safety, but even this became more difficult when the throng began funnelling, squeezing together again to pass through the ramparts of the city walls up ahead. Somehow he managed not to let go.

When two young urchins scrambled up before him on to the apple sacks which the cart contained, he was on the point of scolding them, but then he noticed that neither the driver nor anyone else seemed in any way to mind, so on impulse he did the same himself. So it was that when the cart came to a stop by the old drybridge which was beyond the ramparts, he had an excellent view out over the heads of the crowd and across the open pasturage to the south of the city.

He could see at once that a small posse of horsemen bearing Lord Lancaster's colours had approached Hereford by way of the old Roman road over the hills from the south. They had halted perhaps one hundred yards from the drybridge. At their head was a solitary nobleman, who was mounted on a magnificent grey destrier, and this Stephen guessed to be Earl Henry himself. In the distance, a further posse approached at a slow canter, whilst in the foreground, a troop of foot soldiers held back the crowd to keep free a wide space in front of the earl. Stephen shuddered. In this arena he guessed the first rites of trial and punishment would be performed.

The second group of riders now came closer into view, and made their way into the open space. In their midst were three bedraggled figures bound and roped together, all mounted on the thinnest mangiest donkeys Stephen had ever seen. These had to be Despenser himself, Baldock (the king's chancellor), and Simon de Reading (one of Despenser's vassals), and as the crowd reached the same realisation, cheers turned to jeers, then to screams and cat-calls, and then to a frenzied roar.

With a wave of his mailed fist, the earl signalled two of his retainers to dismount and approach the captives. They seized on the prisoners' ropes and yanked them down from their mounts, so they fell sprawling on the stony ground. Others then dragged them back to their feet and stripped them to their undergarments. Next, brimming steaming piss-pots were passed to the guards by eager members of the crowd, and a libation poured over the prisoners' heads.

Stephen had always heard Despenser to be a man of stature like the king himself, but, even assuming the tallest of these three to be Despenser, the wretch before him looked gaunt and weak, as if starved for many days. Urine drenched his hair and beard, and had dislodged a crude crown made of nettles. Despenser sank to his knees, his face creased in despair, before being hauled up yet again by the two retainers, this time for a sack-cloth tunic to be forced over his head. On its back was a coat of arms reversed and upside down, which, nevertheless, Stephen recognised to be that of the Despenser family. On its front was pinned a piece of hide bearing writing, which Stephen was not close enough to read, but which, for the crowd's benefit, and to the sound of gleeful cackling, one of the two now read out in the common tongue:

"He has cast down the mighty from their seat and has raised the humble and meek", and then "Why do you glory in evil, oh you, who are mighty in villainy".

As he heard the first sentence, containing as it did words from the Magnificat, Stephen crossed himself, and began reciting more of the Blessed Virgin's speech, hoping to edify those around him, but his voice was drowned, and his tongue stuck to the roof of his mouth, as raucous cheers from crowd and soldiers alike saluted the two retainers as they bowed and remounted their horses.

The cacophony redoubled as two women carrying panniers now forced their way past Stephen's cart. They were ushered through the cordon of foot soldiers and began smearing excrement over the prisoners' faces. Stephen gaped at the way these women seemed oblivious both to the stench, which must fill their own nostrils, and to the brown slime, which now coated their own hands and arms. And all the while the crowd cried out for more ordure, more cruelty, more degradation.

When the prisoners were befouled from head to toe, a further command rang out from Earl Henry that his soldiers clear a way through the crowd. Coercion proved unnecessary, though, for the people shuffled aside, eager to begin the great festive procession, which the troops with their prisoners would now lead back towards the river, then round the city to the place of trial. The driver had now reversed the cart and had towed it back on to the drybridge, and Stephen could just see the prisoners, no longer riding the emaciated donkeys, but staggering down St Martin's Street under a shower, not only of insults and curses, but of rotting flesh and vegetables, and every other manner of detritus which the crowd could hurl in their direction.

It was at that moment the apple-cart jammed against a gatepost in the wall, and Stephen eased himself down into the crush of bodies, and let himself be herded in the same direction as everyone else. The pelting and screaming continued the whole length of St Martin's Street, and, once the river had been crossed, along Wyebridge Street and all the way up to the Church of St Nicholas. There the Earl's contingent turned left, leading the rabble out through the Friar's Gate and beyond the city's western walls. Stephen guessed this was in order to avoid the network of narrow streets and alleyways south of the Market Place, and to make a grand approach to the Guildhall up along Blythbrook Street, and then through the Eign Gate and along the High Street itself.

Shock at the prisoners' treatment had for now purged the crowd's hysteria from Stephen's blood, and had brought back an aching awareness of the task with which he had been charged. As the soldiers headed left for Friar's Gate, he therefore seized his chance to escape Hugh's tormentors. He veered right along King's Ditch and Brode Street, and then plunged into the dinginess and fetor of Behyndthewall Lane and Narrow Caboches Lane. There he hoped to collect his thoughts, and through prayer prepare his mind, if not his stomach, for the worse brutality to come.

The sun had pierced the late autumn mist just as the crowd had approached St Nicholas, but along the sinuous streets Stephen now followed it could not penetrate the shadows cast by upper storeys which butted almost one against another across the street. And though he was grateful to have escaped the hordes of revellers, in this gloom he found himself jostled and pushed – this time by traders and other townsfolk still about their normal business. Prone as he was to lose his balance when others barged into him, he found himself stumbling against buckets of foul smelling rubbish and offal, slipping into the

17

open sewer, and more than once almost tripping over lepers who, as ever, crouched beside the thoroughfare, their suppurating limbs swathed in filthy rags.

Finding this no place in fact either for prayer or quiet reflection, he hurried on, pulling his hood tight about his face to avoid the miasma of the lepers' fetid breath. As he drew nearer the Market Place, however, he slowed his pace, more and more reluctant to complete his journey. Out in the public square, he would have to confront the multitude again, and then witness fresh bestiality visited upon the prisoners. For neither experience did he yet feel prepared.

When, despite his tardy footsteps, he at last approached the end of an alleyway which gave upon the Market Place, he halted in the shadows. He could see the High Cross and the Guildhall, both now bathed in midday sunlight, as well as many booths still open and profiting from the day's extra customers. Large crowds already milled about, even though the prisoners and their accompanying horde had not yet arrived along the High Street. He noticed too that to the left of the Guildhall, and linked to it by a wooden walkway, was a high dais on which benches were arranged in a semi-circle, and in front of that was a smaller lower stage-like structure, roped around like a sheep pen. Here, he felt sure, Despenser, Baldock and de Reading would be arraigned.

If he was to carry out his instructions – hear all that was said and make report of it to Walter – he needed to be as near as possible to that dais, even though this would bring him close to all the cruelty and beastliness of the trial itself. His guts churned. Yet, how was he to secure that vantage point when so many citizens were already bunched around the dais, no doubt ready to elbow away anyone fighting their way to the front?

He retreated a few paces up the lane, and took refuge between two water butts. Their stagnant contents had spewed a thick green slime over the adjacent wall and ground. He clutched at his crucifix and implored God for guidance. As he often did when he sought strength, he conjured in his mind's eye the Saviour on the Cross, pictured His gaping wounds, imagined a cup proffered by the Virgin Mary, filled with Christ's precious blood. From this he envisioned himself drinking. This was for his salvation's sake, but also for the miracle he now craved.

18

Now he began reciting the Lord's Prayer and the Salve Regina over and over again, and as he did so he rocked back and forth, matching his body's movement to the rhythm of the words. Body and mind fused in supplication, he swayed to and fro more and more violently. He pounded his fists upon his chest, willing himself, driving himself, punishing himself onwards, knowing in his inmost core that when he stopped this motion – when he hurled himself against the ground, smashed his face into the wall – his prayers would be answered: God would show him what to do.

Chapter 3

His face smashed into the wall, and for an instant lightning flickered through his brain. Stunned, he slid down the greasy surface, before his hands, scrabbling at the water-butts either side, arrested his fall just before his knees hit the ground. His breaths came short and fast, and the dank wall in front of him lurched back and forth, as pain took hold.

Was he injured? His head must be cut or bruised, but for the moment he was aware only of his tongue, which he had bitten on impact, and which now began to sting and throb. He wiped his right hand against his lips and saw an opulent red, as if he had drunk from the cup proffered by the Virgin.

And then meaning came to him. His tongue – his tongue, or rather its peculiar skill – his ability to preach – that was it! Wisdom was revealed once more through his body's mortification! Here was the answer he had sought. He must preach! – no more, no less – the task at which he excelled. What else should a Dominican do, being of the Order of Preachers! This was God's answer; this was God's will; the Virgin had interceded. Then and there in the Market Place he would preach – then and there where the trial would take place. He would do so. He would do so, and all would be well.

Stephen heaved himself away from the butts and staggered back up the alleyway, almost tumbling out into the gentle sunlight of the square. There was a sick feeling in his gut at the pain still pulsing in his mouth and now also in his forehead, but he would not be dissuaded from the purpose revealed to him. This was God's way, this was the Spirit working on him and through him – as it had done with Mary's help, oh, so many times before! God wished him to preach, and Mary would assist, would lead him out into the Market Place, and would find a place fit for his sermon, where also he might hear and see those things he must report to Prior Walter.

As he advanced, he kept his breathing shallow, and his eyeballs hovered part-hidden beneath their lids. He now felt, rather than saw, how the whole world was spinning about him. He stumbled several times and, flailing about with his arms, raised his voice, tremulous through lack of breath, raw though his tongue still was.

"Repent, sinners," he began in the common speech. His tongue impeded him. "Repent, all you who hear me." He collided with a boy selling peascods from a tray, knocked into a merchant's stall sending reams of fustian unrolling across the cobble stones, then staggered further into the Market Place. As he did so, people drew back, allowed him space, till he fell to his knees a short distance from the dais. The jolt of this broke the tension racking his body, helped him gulp down deep draughts of cold air. Then, as the ground seemed to steady and the tall merchants' houses to cease their gyrations about him, he raised himself once more, confident now of God's purpose, inspired, yet not knowing what he was about to say:

"Repent, sinners. Repent, all you who hear me. Let the humble repent. Let the mighty repent. Let all who draw breath beneath God's firmament repent." His tongue pained him less, though he could still taste blood.

"Above all, let he who was mighty repent – indeed, the mightiest: the one cast down from the greatest pinnacle of power and riches! For today the Lord God has indeed shown strength with his arm, scattered the proud in their hearts' imagination, thrown down the mighty from their seat, and exalted the humble and meek." Now there were cheers all around, though Stephen hardly heard them, and from all sides the crowd converged on this new spectacle – this new entertainment – though leaving a wide circle free round Stephen as he staggered back and forth.

"And for those thrown down, those who have not repented, nor yet done penance – yes, for all those who die unshriven – the gate of Hell surely gapes. Do you not glimpse into its depths? Do you not smell its sulphurous air? From its gateway leads a bitter road, lengthy beyond measure, dark, dismal – insufferably so. It is a pathway through forests full of torments, and deserts full of pain. It leads along rivers of boiling blood, round lakes of frozen tears.

"You who enter Hell – you must pass through these most hateful places, through others no less loathsome, and for all eternity. For every minute of that journey, every stride along that way your sins will be punished, your senses tortured by the Devil's agents, for the luxury and iniquity of your lives. Think of the sharpness of the augurs they will drill into you, and of the knives with which they will strip the flesh from your bones – all in punishment of your loathsome deeds, thoughts and words! Imagine the stench of Hell in your nostrils and its bitter gall in your mouths. Feel the leaden weight of its very air, which will crush your lungs and break your backs.

"Think on these matters; grieve for these torments; and above all else repent, repent, repent!" There were now tears flowing down Stephen's cheeks, and his voice cracked with emotion. Some in the crowd too broke into uncontrollable weeping and fell to their knees, tearing their hair and beating their breasts. Stephen paused, suddenly aware of these anguished sounds. He stepped forward, made the sign of the cross, placed his hand in blessing on several heads. But the turmoil of words and images his mind would not abate, and he continued with his sermon:

"Let not the ruler who has reigned many summers, let not his right hand, nor his left; let not the baron, nor his knight, the bishop, the monk; let not the merchant, freeman, franklin; let not the villein, nor the humblest beggar think that they may leap Hell's chasm, before repentance and due penance. For that chasm, that cleft, that mouth is vast. It yearns to suck the marrow from your bones, the blood from your veins, every juice from your body, and still to leave you whole and prey to yet more pain – yes, even to the burrowing of monstrous worms deep within your inner parts. Therefore, repent, I say. Again, I say, repent!

"And do so now, my listeners. Now! You must do so now! Make haste – do not delay! For whosoever is absolved, but dies before paying his temporal debt to God, his sins being mortal, that person shall still suffer the panoply of Hell's torments. If his sins be venial, nevertheless, he shall suffer the cleansing fire of Purgatory. Such fire is healthful and shall lead to Salvation, but how much hotter is it than any fire here on earth, for it must burn away sinfulness, it must melt away imperfection, till the sinner's soul is as pure as beaten gold! Only then shall that soul be meet for everlasting life in Heaven.

"Do not think, therefore, you may avoid these things. Only God's saints find the gateway to His glory without fire and purgation. Think not that the mouths of Hell and Purgatory gape for others, but not for you. Think only that with true contrition, with full confession, and with due repentance you may abridge your time in Purgatory. Think also, if you fail in this, of the torments worse by far which wait for you in Hell. Repent! Repent. Again, I say, repent!"

22

The chill of the breeze wafted against his cheek, there was a scent of wood smoke in his nostrils, and a hubbub of voices reached his ears. He breathed in the moment, realized himself the focus of many eyes, sensed the Spirit depart, leaving him becalmed, peaceful, as though he had slept, or fainted, or had died the little death and returned to life. For a few moments he held the gaze of his listeners, then looked away, aware of the mutterings of prayers, the many signs of the cross being made, and the chink of silver pennies being cast at his feet.

Dunsheved and his demands now came back to him, but, as the older monk's face and those of Despenser and Prior Walter hovered in his consciousness, he felt a calmness he had not known since the day had dawned, and he praised God, Mary and all the Saints for Their munificence, and he gave thanks that he was now but a few yards from the dais, as had been his objective.

He picked up the scattered coins and pushed his way towards the side of the dais closest to the prisoners' enclosure. There he would be certain to hear the words both of the prosecutors and of the accused. No sooner there, though, than he became aware that two men had fixed him with their gaze and were hastening towards him. From their attire they were noblemen. One was tall, perhaps thirty years of age, fair haired and bearded. He was armed, and bore on his chest the device, which Stephen, as a man of Gloucestershire, recognised as Lord Berkeley's: a silver chevron and ten crosses on a red ground. His companion was similar in age and dress, though shorter and of dark complexion.

"Well preached, sir monk! Your words have branded the hearts and minds of your listeners!" It was the taller man who spoke. "I give you a groat for your troubles, and for my soul, and request your name!"

"God be with you, my lord," replied Stephen, inclining his head. "My name is Brother Stephen de Birstin of the Order of Preachers, and my priory is at Gloucester, where Brother Walter is my prior."

"Then we are countrymen, friar. I would ask what brings you to Hereford, but I know Walter, and know he has fingers in many pies! From your speech, I guess you're also no foreigner to Gloucestershire. Were you raised there?"

"My father was Sir Geoffrey de Birstin, my lord. My oldest brother, Sir William, now holds my family's manor house near Tewkesbury."

"So you are of gentle birth, friar, though without wealth enough for a living outside the Church! I know of your brother, and believe Sir John Maltravers here, my kinsman, has met him several times." The other now spoke:

"I have indeed, sir, and liked him well enough. And so, for his sake, for your excellent sermon, and also for my own soul, of course, I give you here another groat!" Sir John sniggered at his own pleasantry, as did his companion, whom Stephen had by now realised must be Lord Thomas Berkeley himself.

Stephen was still thanking his benefactors, when a sound of jeering and shouting, which had become noticeable as they were speaking, swelled to a roar coming from the western end of the Market Place. The great throng which had accompanied the prisoners round the city now emerged from the High Street, to the beating of drums and the blaring of horns and trumpets. Merchants who were still trading hastened to shutter their stalls and stow away their produce, whilst the crowds of citizens already in the square surged towards the dais, and Stephen once more found himself pushed and jostled, though he and the two noblemen stood firm and maintained their favourable vantage point.

With the agglomeration of people already present and the multitude arriving from the west, it took some time for the prisoners to be herded past the High Cross and to be thrust cowering up the steps and into their pen, though Stephen could see soldiers shouldering people aside to clear a way for their approach. They were bespattered with mud and excrement, though here and there about their bodies, as Stephen noted when they were closer, blood seeped through the filth from wounds inflicted by the more solid projectiles which had been hurled at them.

As the prisoners were again made to kneel with their heads bowed, a party of nobles began to emerge from the Guildhall and processed along the walkway to the benches set out on the dais. None of them were known to Stephen, other than Lancaster, but, since these were the members of the tribunal charged with trying Despenser, their names were now announced to the crowd: the Earls of Kent and Nor-

24

folk, Lord Henry of Lancaster, Sir Thomas Wake, and Sir William Trussel, the last being the court's spokesman. Stephen looked in surprise at the two whom he took to be the Earls of Kent and Norfolk, for they were the king's brothers and yet were here to sit in judgement on the king's greatest favourite.

Then above on the balcony of the Guildhall a woman appeared dressed in a scarlet cope edged with fur and glinting with jewellery. She wore no wimple, and her hair and brows were bound about with gold. This must be the queen herself. Behind, but looming over her shoulder, was another nobleman, whom Stephen guessed at once to be her ally and alleged lover, Sir Roger Mortimer. His clothes were of black sable, and his expression grim, despite the fixed smile he turned from time to time upon the crowd. Cheering broke out, which the two acknowledged, before Mortimer took his leave and went down to join the other lords on the dais.

Sir William Trussel now called the prisoners to attention. He spoke in Norman French as custom required, and whilst this was comprehended by Stephen and many others, it was not the language of the multitude, and so there were many pauses in the proceedings whilst Trussel's words were rendered into the common speech by several self-appointed translators close to the dais; and those words in turn were passed back in waves of whisperings from the front to the back of the assembly.

Trussel disposed first of Baldock, who, as a priest, was declared to have Benefit of Clergy, and was therefore marched away to be handed over to the Church for judgement and appropriate punishment.

Then the names and titles of Hugh le Despenser were read out, almost inaudible against the screams, taunts, and shouts of "Traitor", which pulsated from all around the square. Stephen tried to catch the words as the list of charges against Despenser was pronounced, each item producing cheers of approbation as soon as the crowd grasped or guessed at what was being alleged. Close as he was to the dais, however, it was difficult to glean every detail, and, as charge mounted on charge, he soon lost track of what had been said. Later he could recall little, other than that Hugh was said to be a traitor and an enemy to the realm; that he had without due cause imprisoned many nobles, who were named – Lord Berkeley's name producing roars of affirmation from the two lords still standing at Stephen's side; that he had indeed procured the death of two – the Earl of Hereford and Lord Lancaster's elder brother; and that he had "come between the king and the queen" and hindered their relationship. At these last words, so great was the sound of jeers and cat-calls, so foul the exhaled breath of the crowd, and so uncomfortable the press of their bodies against him, that Stephen felt a hollow trembling in his guts, and a dizziness about his temples, till the comforting touch of his rosary beads steadied his mind.

As he tried to concentrate on the proceedings which followed, it seemed to him that nowhere did there come any division between what was alleged and what was judged to be true. No evidence was produced, and no opportunity given to Hugh to refute what was said of him; and no sooner had his crimes been enumerated, than Trussel proceeded to read out his allotted punishments. He was to be hung as a thief, for the noble property he had appropriated. He was to be disembowelled for the discord he had caused between king and queen, as well as between others. And he was to be hung, drawn and quartered, because he was a traitor to the realm.

Once this announcement was made, Stephen felt the crowd surge with an emotion unlike any he had experienced before. It was a venting, not so much of joy, as of a lust for blood, spiced with an ugly exaltation. Burghers, nobles, townsfolk (both men and women), were leaping up and down, shouting, screaming, their faces twisted with hatred, once more pelting the prisoners with anything they had to hand, spitting in their direction, and spitting over each other in the process. Whether any trial or judgement was being conducted with regard to Simon de Reading, Stephen had no idea, for all further words were drowned, all sense of order trampled beneath the now dancing feet of large sections of the crowd. He could see also that the soldiers were having difficulty dragging forward the ox-hide sleds and the frightened horses which were to draw Hugh and Simon on a fresh tour along the city streets – this time to the place of execution itself.

Above on her balcony Queen Isabella raised a goblet of wine, toasting the assembly. Below the members of the court began to leave the dais and return to the Guildhall; and to his right Stephen was aware of Lord Berkeley and Sir John arm in arm forcing a way through the throng in the same direction.

Now with such furore all around and quite despite himself, he began to feel that same frenzy which had invaded his senses earlier, when the prisoners had first arrived outside the city walls. Despite his prayers, despite his most fervent wish, despite the silken play of beads about his fingers, he could no longer fight, as his own blood seemed to pulse with an excitement not its own. There was a pounding in his head, then in the crowd around him, then in the very air of the afternoon, as the words rang out from his and every other throat:

"Death, death, death to the traitor. Death, death, death to the traitor."

And as Stephen leaped and clapped in time with all those around him, he was quite unaware of the wild rattling of his rosary beads dangling from his waist, and of his crucifix as it bounced and jolted its own dance of death about his neck.

Chapter 4

Soldiers had moved forward to keep the crowd back from the prisoners and from those who were binding them hand and foot to the ox-hide sleds. Between helmeted heads, and despite the jumping spitting mayhem, Stephen kept his eyes fixed on Despenser and on the sleds as they were next tied to the linked harnesses of the four horses. Redoubled yells, this time of encouragement, came from the crowd – from his own mouth too – as four retainers now mounted the horses and, on their commander's signal, began dragging Despenser and de Reading away for their final journey. They circled the High Cross, then headed out through the north-east quarter of the city in the direction of the castle, where rumour spoke of a vast new scaffold with double gibbets erected for this grand occasion.

Many at once pursued the horses with their sliding swerving burdens of meat and bone, but Stephen had enough presence of mind and recollection of Dunsheved's instructions to join those taking a more direct route to the place of execution. He was part of the throng which swarmed from the square into the noisome warren of streets which lay to the south. Along the two stretches of Caboches Lane, he found the press of humanity even denser than earlier in the day, with all the pushing and prodding, the fights and fracas which this involved, so at first progress was slow. But once in Canons Street, he joined with the many others who then broke into a run and soon reached Castle Street by way of the Cathedral Close.

Just as he arrived at the drawbridge, a great roar of voices came from the north. It signalled the arrival – in advance of expectation – of the two bloodied bodies jolting their way over the cobble stones and gutters of Hungreye Street. The sound drove those round Stephen to barge forward in a mad scramble for the best viewing-places, and Stephen was swept along over the drawbridge and out into the castle grounds.

It was then that the day's momentum seemed to stall. Though the prisoners were now close by, those who knew of such things claimed they must remain with their guards outside the walls till the queen and lords had made their own formal entry. They, it seemed, were still some way off in slow procession from the Guildhall. There was nothing to do, therefore, either for Stephen or indeed anyone else, but to wait and watch as the vast green before the keep filled up with more and more spectators.

The wave of obscene excitement which had borne Stephen all the way from the Guildhall now began to ebb away, and for this he felt grateful. No longer part of the vengeful swarm, no longer gasping for breath amongst a frenzy of bodies, the reality of what he had already seen, and of what he would now have to witness, took stark and appalling form in his imagination – the more so as he approached the huge new scaffold in the north-east corner of the castle, just a short distance inside the wall. As he stood in front of it, his sweat-bathed limbs felt the bite of the cool afternoon air, and guilt at his own complicity in the day's events likewise chilled his mind.

To avert his thoughts from the butchery to come, he fixed his gaze on the array of military contraptions positioned either side of the gatehouse: trebuchets and mangonels glowing pale gold as the sun slipped westwards. Yet the acerbic smell of fresh cut timber filled his nostrils, and drew his attention back again and again to the skeletal whiteness of the scaffold itself. Above it were the two gibbets: one of extraordinary height (perhaps the height of ten men); the other to its left much shorter. From both, ropes dangled down to the main wooden platform, where nooses swayed in the breeze. Behind them, and against the castle wall, a ladder ascended to just below the cross-piece of the higher gibbet, where a further platform had been bolted, and Stephen guessed this would be used after the final drop, even whilst the prisoners gasped their life's last breaths, for the hangman to inflict his ultimate tortures.

These dark speculations caused him to pray both for the souls and for the bodies of Hugh and Simon, to beg forgiveness for their sins, and to implore the Virgin for some miracle which would diminish their earthly sufferings. Small comfort was it to recall that the more painful their deaths, the less penance might await them in Purgatory. He turned his head away, closed his eyes, and mouthed a prayer for strength to endure what was to come.

When again he opened his eyes, he was surprised to notice something he had missed before: a further structure away to the right of the scaffold. It comprised another raised stage, set with chairs and a table, and in part sheltered by a canvas canopy forming a pavilion. Since servants were laying out platters and goblets, which glinted bright gold and silver in the fading light, he could only conclude the table was being prepared for the royal party. There the queen would eat and carouse with Mortimer, whilst Hugh and Simon, rather than any minstrels or jugglers, provided their entertainment.

"No words of wisdom for us now, friar? No prayers of thanks for God's mercy so manifest in today's proceedings?" So absorbed had he been that Stephen had failed to heed two horsemen cantering up from behind. As these words broke into his thoughts, however, he turned and saw that it was Sir John Maltravers who addressed him, the same wry amusement as earlier playing about his lips.

"God be with you, my lords," he began, but before he could think of any additional response, Maltravers had raised his hand:

"Do not trouble yourself, Brother Stephen. I speak only in jest. This is no time for preaching – we are here for the sport, and, besides, we have no care for the soul of Hugh le Despenser. I owe my exile to him, and my brother-in-law his imprisonment!" Both lords chuckled. "But perhaps back in Gloucestershire we may again have the pleasure of your engaging turn of phrase! We shall shortly be spending time there, for we return with the queen's party in two days' time...Maybe you will preach for our benefit at the High Cross in Gloucester, or at Scriven's Conduit near your priory? Or perhaps one day you will grace my lord's great hall at Berkeley – whenever you feel like earning a few more groats, or selling a couple of indulgences, that is!" Still smiling, but paying no further attention to him, Maltravers and Lord Berkeley then spurred their horses on towards the pavilion.

Stephen followed them with his gaze, feeling somewhat indignant at Maltravers' tone. He now noticed that other nobles were also arriving, making their way from the drawbridge to the pavilion, and crossing close to him right in front of the scaffold. His heart began to thump, as he sensed the day's climax approach. Now the crowd began moving forward, eager for the queen's arrival, pressing close all around him, till soldiers wrestled amongst them and cleared a way for the royal party to pass.

Almost at once raucous cheers broke out from the gatehouse, and soon Stephen was staring as the queen and her consort went by. Beneath her hooded cope she was dressed in silks and satins, which were of white and palest cream, but there was nothing gentle in her expression. An eager glint fired her eyes, and a smirk of satisfaction laced her lips. The saturnine Mortimer walked a full six paces behind her, but when she mounted to the pavilion, Stephen noted that he alone was privileged to offer his assistance.

Once the queen and her party had been seated, and were being served with what looked to be a lavish meal, the prisoners were at last hauled into the castle. Stephen doubted much more daylight remained, for though the sky was now clear of mist and cloud, the sun was low in the western sky. Some of the guards already carried lighted torches, and more would be lit as the sun sank further, and shadows began to cavort on the castle walls.

The prisoners now staggered on to the scaffold platform, the last rags of their clothing barely clinging to their limbs. They were made to kneel before a confessor, though whether they were aware of what was said to them Stephen doubted. They were so weak their legs and knees could not support them, and Hugh faltered from side to side, whilst Simon buckled and fell forward upon his face. Stephen prayed they might already have confessed their sins and done as much penance as opportunity could allow, for he could see little benefit in the ministry being offered.

His concern for their souls was not, however, shared by the crowd, for the prisoners' suffering seemed only to inflame their lust for vengeance. A deep-throated chorus of yells and curses broke out, and then turned to shouts of encouragement as the hangman himself appeared. He was large, was dressed all in black, and wore a mask. He and an assistant mounted the platform, and, once he had made a deep bow towards the royal party, he brandished an axe and several butcher's knives for all to see. The queen and the lords and ladies in response raised their goblets, then returned to their feasting, throwing only an occasional glance over their shoulders as the final ritual commenced.

A second priest now mounted the scaffold and began chanting in Latin, but his words were drowned in the roar of voices which demanded the hangman be about his business. Knowing the power of the texts themselves, Stephen repeated aloud the Nunc Dimittis, and then the words of the requiem mass, all the while clasping his crucifix to his breast to fend off the hysteria rekindling around him. This time he would resist its rhythms, its malign joy, its raucous voice screaming from his own mouth. He would bear witness, would pray for

Hugh's soul, would keep his mind inviolate: a fitting conduit for God's Mercy.

Then the butchery began. Weary of the bleatings of the priests, the hangman seized Despenser, and placed the noose of the longer rope round his neck. He dragged de Reading from the floor and placed the shorter one round his. Then the nooses were tightened, and bit into the begrimed and bleeding flesh. All the while the crowd's roar increased. The hangman now wound on a pulley, jerking Despenser from his feet and up over the scaffold, upwards, swinging backwards and forwards, upwards again, his limbs flailing till he was left twisting high above in the sun's dying rays. At the same time De Reading was hoisted on the lower, but no less deadly gibbet by the assistant.

Stephen gaped as the hangman now mounted the ladder at a speed belying his bulk. Leaving de Reading to gasp his last alone, he hauled in the shitting, pissing, but not yet dead, body of Despenser to the platform way above. He loosened the noose, and, leaving his victim slumped for a moment, seized a torch from the castle wall and ignited a brazier. Below his assistant lit an even larger blaze in a pile of faggots on the ground beside the platform. Two pools of light now flared in the gathering dusk, and, as the sun shed its last blood-red beams, Stephen felt he beheld Hell's Inferno.

The hangman next took one of his longest knives, and waved it at the throng below. Dragging the almost lifeless Despenser to his feet, he gestured with a flourish towards the man's penis (now improbably erect through asphyxiation), and to cries of "Sodomite! Sodomite! Kill the king's seducer!" sliced clean through the genitals and threw them down to the fire below.

With speed and relish, he now slit Despenser's abdomen from the navel to the thorax, pulled apart the two great flaps of flesh, and began to grub out the intestines and other organs. A gory shapeless pile of viscera slithered from his hands on to the platform, before he started scrabbling in the cavity he had crafted, tying pipes and arteries to prevent the last drops of Hugh's existence from escaping far too quickly. Then he hurled the viscera into the blaze below, where they hissed and spat, giving off the foulest odours. As they fell and then fried, great gouts of fluid splashed all over his assistant. Others spattered the spectators making them scream for more.

Meanwhile, Stephen wept and pulled his hood about his face, shielding himself against the sight and smell of Hugh's destruction, but in no way could he bar its sound. For then the body that was all but a corpse – the shattered, ruined, butchered entity that had been, but barely was any longer, Hugh le Despenser – uttered a cry that not even a dying animal might have vented. And Stephen knew that in that agonised rasp, that wail of loneliness, Hugh's soul, such as it was, had slipped away, leaving him aching with its echo, leaving the hangman, too, deprived of a beating heart.

The crowd's baying ceased. The day's savour soured, and, as the hangman hacked open Despenser's chest, ripped out the now motionless heart, and held it aloft, he received only a few desultory cheers, before he took up his axe and descended to complete his handiwork. The body was lowered by ropes, and the hangman chopped off the head, shook it at the heavens, and then mounted it on a pike. What remained of Despenser was then sawn into quarters to be displayed across the kingdom. But by now the crowd had begun drifting away.

Stephen made his own way back towards the small Dominican friary where he had been staying and where he was to spend this and the following night. He stopped at St Ethelbert's Well to offer more prayers for Lord Hugh, his mind too numbed to think of how he might discharge Dunsheved's additional instructions in the days to come.

In the distance he could hear the festivities continuing unabated at the royal table. They would go on, it seemed, till a frost began glistening on the deserted scaffold, and the revellers retired to Bishop Orleton's Palace, oblivious to everything but their own satiety.

Chapter 5

He slept little that night. On the narrow truckle-bed, which he shared with another visitor, he could not break the rote of the day's memories burning their way deeper and deeper into his mind; and when from time to time he dozed, he could not banish Dunsheved's lips as they hissed at him, making demands he could barely hear and which he knew he could not fulfil. His belly ached with panic.

The day that followed, though, was one of respite. He fasted till early evening, went to pray at the cathedral tomb of St Thomas de Cantilupe, and attended services in the small chapel attached to the priory where he lodged. Though he spoke to no one – not daring to mention his meeting with Dunsheved, and unable to describe what he had seen later that day for fear he would break down in tears – he sought solace in the flowing plain chant of his brothers' voices, the rounded vowels of Latin text, and the pungency of incense. When, sanctified by scent and sound, he went upon his knees before the Virgin to beg Her guidance, he found that he could breathe more easily, and sensed the balm of the eternal, rather than the sting of present wounds.

At the evening meal he kept his mind upon the mysteries of the mass, and imagined the touch of the Madonna's robe, rather than grapple with the morrow and what it might require of him. But it was there, as he sat bolt upright amidst his fellows, amidst the bustle of the refectory and the reading of godly texts – there, as he still allowed himself no more than a few crusts and a cup of ale – that he sensed a growing certainty within: a conviction that, if he did as Dunsheved ordered, he would succeed – he would gain access to the queen and discover what she planned!

This certitude expressed itself in words: words which whispered at his ear – more persuasive than any uttered by Dunsheved. They spoke of the Market Place, told him again to use his preacher's skills, and, if he did, that all things would be well. And it was a woman's voice he heard – he was sure of it – a voice, which must be Hers. His mind raced. That he could succeed in his task had seemed such a vain hope. Yet was not the Virgin speaking to him? Was it not Her counsel he now received?

When the meal was over, he hastened to the chapel where he rejoiced in prayer, lighted candles before the Virgin's image, and thanked Her for Her special care of him, both now and in the past. He recited a litany of Her benevolence, recalled Her first whispers to him in the soughing willows on Severn's bank, how She had told him then that to be a priest would be a blessing not a sacrifice; how through Blackfriars' bells She had promised succour and success, if he did as Walter wished and went to Oxford; how later, in his blackest of days, he had heard Her voice in the draught-guttering candles of his college chapel, offering ease from loneliness, delivery from temptation's alleyways.

And had these things not come to pass?

He attended Compline, retired to bed, was confident of peaceful dreams. Yet he passed a second night in a purgatory of painful recollection and dismal fantasy. Hugh's limbs flailed about. His body opened and its guts spilled into Stephen's gaping mouth. Then later Berkeley and Maltravers joined with Dunsheved to pursue him, as he hid among offal tubs in the noisome streets south of the Market Place.

When the Matins bell rang and he joined the other monks for the first service of the day, those dreams' squalor still caked his consciousness. It took the glacial air of the small chapel, the sight and touch of the Virgin's image, and the comfort of Her remembered words to cleanse his mind. After the service he waited only till dawn before taking his leave, and hobbling his way towards the bishop's palace, where the royal party was lodged.

In the chill light of the new day he could envisage no way to begin his undertaking (now blessed by the Virgin), other than to go and wait outside the palace till the entourage appeared. How then he would join it he was unsure, but he knew She would help him and would make his way clear. Maybe the Spirit would move him, as it had in the Market Place. Maybe, if he saw Berkeley and Maltravers, they would invite him to preach as the company journeyed south. Perhaps, if he did no more than stand in prayer as the procession passed, the queen herself – by the grace of her heavenly counterpart – would stop, call him forward, and, as he knelt before her, choose him as her chaplain! Wish built on wish, hope on hope, till a febrile certainty shone from his eyes as he passed under the Norgate.

Once near the palace he spent an hour or so limping the length of Brode Street, hugging his cloak about him, and cursing the hoar frost which made his sandaled toes tingle, then ache, then burn. (How the absent two throbbed even more than those which remained.) He bought a loaf and some cheese to eat later on his journey, and busied himself with his rosary and his prayers.

Outside a noisy hostelry he paused to purchase ale, and was just gulping it down, when a blast of trumpets rang out from beyond the palace gate-house. He left his flagon half-drunk, and hastened to the far end of the street, where a throng was already cheering as first a troop of horsemen passed by, then – also on horseback – Mortimer, Kent, Norfolk and most of the great lords he had already seen at the Market Place. Amongst them were Berkeley and Maltravers, though on this occasion neither cast his eyes in Stephen's direction. Next came a brightly decorated coach, which was open at the sides and in which Queen Isabella sat with one other noble-woman; behind them a troop of servants and household servants all on foot; and at the rear marched yet more soldiers and retainers.

As the coach passed by, Stephen stood on tiptoe to see over the heads and shoulders in front of him. For only a brief moment did he glimpse the queen, though, if anything, he was even closer to her than he had been at the castle. She was wrapped in furs, her face and beje-welled hair just visible beneath a loose-fitting hood. He had an impression of beauty – or what he knew passed for beauty amongst womenfolk: pale skin, small regular features, a tall forehead, a full mouth. But then she had gone, and she had not noticed him.

Slightly dejected, he then strove for the trance-like state of two days previously, but, though he pinched and beat his flesh and tried to goad himself with prayers, he remained standing where he was, his spirit unmoved, his tongue mute, the back of the royal coach receding into the distance.

The cathedral bells began to toll, their clangour signalling the queen's departure to the whole population, and soon they were ans-wered from many towers and other churches round the city. As the procession made its way up Brode Street, along King's Ditch, and at last south to the Wye Bridge, crowds again hurried to view this latest of the great spectacles visited on Hereford since All Saints' Day. Many cheered and waved, and some formed a growing phalanx of revellers, beggars and children following on behind the royal party in the street itself.

Uncertain what else to do, Stephen decided to join this gaggle. He told himself this was the Virgin's will, though had to admit he had no sense of Her approbation, no glow of conviction in his gut. Then doubts began, as the lewd and base conversation of the rabble all around assailed his ears. Soon it became clear too how very far he was from those to whom he wished to speak – or at the very least to listen. For the most part on horseback, those individuals were at the head of the procession, and even when they stopped, as they often did, to let the others catch up, Stephen did not see anyone he recognised. He must pray, avert his gaze from the worldliness about him, picture for himself the Manger and the Cross, and above all trust in the Virgin's words.

Once past the Wye Bridge, most of the townsfolk fell away, leaving Stephen very near the back of the parade. He followed on as those in the lead now reversed Despenser's mournful approach to the city, picking up the Monmouth road from the old drybridge to a little beyond the pastures. There, at a fork in the way, a different road was taken, continuing eastwards for an hour or so till the procession once more crossed over the river near Mordiford. Then a break was made, so that those who like Stephen were on foot could catch up, and also dinner could be taken by the roadside.

Since Stephen himself would eat nothing more that day till evening – only one main meal a day being allowed by the Order during the winter months – this pause meant that he could move along the now sedentary host to seek company which was more congenial, if not more pertinent to his mission. Eventually he sat down close to the servants of the royal household, but then could see no way or excuse to intrude amongst the nobles, let alone the royal party itself. Besides, it was at this point that he first sensed something amiss with his innards, and for now at least, somewhat distracted, he hesitated to strike up conversation with anybody.

Once the procession had resumed its journey, and as the afternoon progressed, Stephen told himself he had been wise to bide his time. Perhaps when the next halt was called, by the Virgin's grace, he would find himself close to Lord Berkeley or to the queen herself. Then the Spirit would move him, and he would begin to preach by the roadside. Inhibition would fall like earthly raiment from his limbs, and the Holy Word would surge from within him. He pictured the wonderment of his hearers – from the lowest servant to the highest in the land – as they fell upon their knees weeping tears of joy and gratitude. The sound of silver pennies would chink again on the highway, and he pictured himself relieved of his burden and at peace.

But this did not happen. Doubt and apprehension returned, and, as mile followed mile, he remained unnoticed, uncertain what next to do, his worries aggravating – perhaps they were causing – the growing discomfort in his belly. A dizziness also began to befuddle him. Through his hood the cold was striking his bald pate – maybe that was the cause; or, there again, maybe not.

At the village of Much Marcle, progress was halted once again. News filtered along that the queen was being greeted by Bishop Orleton himself, who had travelled north with the Great Seal of State of which King Edward had been relieved. The pause was short, though, and there was another weary march before as dusk fell they arrived at Ledbury. There Stephen's dizziness increased and the pain in his guts reached such an intensity that it became clear neither in fact related to his mental agitation. Alarm as to their true cause bore in upon him along with his other woes.

That night, lodged with many others – but none of rank – in one of the inns on the narrow lane from Ledbury's market place to St Michael's Church, he again slept little. As he shifted from one side to the other, trying not to disturb his bedfellows, Dunsheved's whispering lips seemed to swell, then gave way to Hugh's gaping wounds, to the great maw in his chest venting its last desperate howl, and then to Isabella lying in her carriage, her furs thrown back, a pile of viscera within her lap; and he felt himself falling into a burning chasm of horror and depravity.

Fever grew, causing his body to sweat, and his brain to seem to swell within his skull. At the same time panic that his illness might be grave cramped the pit of his stomach. A raging thirst afflicted him, yet when he tried to quench it with ale, this only stoked the confusion of lurid thoughts which crammed his mind. Once before dawn he staggered to the window, threw back the shutters, and gulped down some frosty air, and as he did so the remembered voice of sanity told him to have no further truck with Dunsheved or with his intrigues. To spy on the queen, to worm into her circle: what hope had there ever been he could achieve such things? And now, now he was ill, it was all no more than fantasy!

Yet, had not the Virgin promised?...

Quite how Stephen completed the journey to Gloucester the next day, he never fathomed. Sometimes he seemed back amongst the rabble following Mortimer's retainers, sometimes a straggler fighting to keep up. He recalled faces turned away from him, hoods pulled tight across mouths. Later he remembered sweltering beneath his habit as dark clouds approached from the south and a light snow began to fall on an already frosted landscape. He recalled – or did he? – a horseman at his side, a horseman called Maltravers, whom he seemed to know – or maybe not – and who spoke of his native land of Dorset, called on him to preach, offered money and sustenance, then spurred his horse away scowling as Stephen stared back at him, blank with puzzlement.

In the boggy wastes north of Gloucester, he fell further behind. His fever abated a little, for which he thanked and blessed St Genevieve, but an aching tiredness and a frequent need to vacate his bowels of the poisonous substances within made him pause for rest more and more. The towers and spires of Gloucester's abbey and churches, indistinct at midday against the snow-dusted Cotswolds, were scarcely clearer as the sun edged between cloud and the western horizon. He summoned a last spurt of energy, or desperation, to gain the safety of the town walls before nightfall, even though thirst burned his throat and racked his whole chest and belly.

He no longer dared turn his thoughts, even the few which were still rational, to the Blessed Virgin, for he had betrayed Her trust, and failed in Her mission. He had presumed he had heard and understood Her purposes, when it was manifest that he had not. Illness had been sent upon him, perhaps as punishment, at best as a test whereby now he might redeem himself.

When at last he crossed over the five arches of Gloucester's great West Bridge, a steady drizzle had replaced the earlier snow, but the roadway's slabs and cobbles retained their icy sheen. He struggled past the shops and houses which nestled on the bridge, managed to pass though the small gate at its eastern end before it was locked, made his weary way over a second bridge spanning a drainage ditch, and then by way of Foreigners Bridge crossed over the Severn's final arm into the town itself. As he did so, he felt a strange comfort in the familiar dank odours of the river bank, and in the distinctive smell of mould wafting on the mist from under the arches of the three bridges, such that he could have wept with relief, had any moisture been left within him.

He climbed the slight incline of Ebbruggestrete, past the Guildhall and the Boothall. Street traders were packing their wares, closing up the great hinged flaps over their shop-fronts, whilst others had already departed, perhaps at the time of the royal procession, which must have passed this same way several hours before. A few merchants greeted him, but he could not place their faces. At the High Cross with its eight ornate waterspouts, he collapsed to his knees, taking deep draughts, quenching his thirst like a dog.

When he was able to stagger to his feet again, he turned right in front of the Tower of St Michael, and toiled his way along Southgate-strete, then right again past the iron forges on Satireslone to Broadsmith Street. From there he at last gained access to his priory at Blackfriars House.

Without attending the final services of the day, without washing his feet or eating anything from the refectory, without thinking of anything else but slumber, he hauled himself up to the dormitory where he lay down at once on his bed, and fell into a deep and dreamless stupor for the first time in four long nights. He did not hear the raucous sounds of the festivities celebrated by the queen, Mortimer and the other lords at Gloucester Castle, but a stone's throw away. He remained oblivious too when his fellow monks retired to their own beds an hour or so later – even when his friend, Brother James, whose bed was adjacent, tried to rouse him, whispered his name in his ear, held a candle near his face, dropping hot wax like gouts of gore on the mattress of straw beneath.

PART TWO: GLOUCESTER

Chapter 6

"God bless you, Brother Stephen," a voice whispered. "The Lord be praised. Have you come back to us at last?" Stephen sensed he was no longer treading the scorched road through Purgatory, as he had been since death. His parched lips could frame no answer, and his vocal cords were too taut and sore to function. The owner of the voice which had whispered to him, however, had begun stroking his hair and now placed a finger on his lips:

"You've been ill, my friend, gravely ill, and you mustn't try to speak now, nor move, nor do anything, but only rest and recover. Peace and quiet are the greatest gifts of the infirmary...It's your Brother James, and I'm here to care for you, as I have been doing these past ten days." The short, squat, middle-aged man with yellow stumpy teeth, who now came into focus and who was sitting at his side, he now recognised as his friend. James helped him to drink a little ale, paused with a smile of affection, then departed for a while, saying he would give the prior the glad tidings of Stephen's recovery. Once he had gone, Stephen faltered once more on the threshold of his dream, but neither flames nor the smell of sulphur returned, and it seemed to him the burning of his skin and throat had lessened.

For several moments he struggled to focus on features of the white-washed room in which he found himself, till its strangeness dissolved and he knew that he was in the long airy chamber of the infirmary behind the east range of the priory. At one end was a fire and at the other an altar, and lined along the walls were a number of beds. Towards the altar end he could just make out two which were occupied by slumbering forms.

He was himself lying between clean woollen sheets, under a cover of clipped sheep-skin, and there were pillows and cushions about his head. With a start he realised that beneath the sheets he was wearing nothing but his tunic, a girdle, and his braies, and for a moment he panicked, wondering where his other clothes and possessions might be. Feeling the presence of his crucifix about his neck, however, he relaxed, and with trembling fingers clasped it, before lapsing once more into a doze.

In the days that followed, Stephen spent many hours sleeping, though his dreams were peaceful now, and no longer sweated their way through regions of fire and brimstone. During waking moments James told him of the illness that had afflicted him, and explained the various cures to which, unconscious, he had been subjected.

James recounted how news had reached him in the infirmary of Stephen's return from Hereford, but also of his immediate ascent to the dormitory. He had been perplexed and a little hurt that Stephen had not sought him out at once to tell him of his journey, and, whilst he had busied himself with the day's final duties and had then attended Vespers and Compline, where again Stephen had failed to appear, his mystification had only increased. When he and the other brothers had at last taken the night stair, however, they had found Stephen already sound asleep and incapable of being roused, either by gentle shaking or by the urgent whispering of his name. Without waking, he had in fact drawn his hood tight across his face, as though to shut out the flickering of the night-light. James had lain upon his own bed nearby, and had kept watch for much of the night, listening with growing concern to the unusual wheezing of Stephen's breathing.

When the Matins bell had rung two hours before dawn, James had again tried to rouse Stephen, shaking him with more vigour and speaking his name aloud, before hastening down to the chancel. It was when Stephen still failed to join him within another few minutes, that he could no longer doubt something serious to be amiss and, with the prior's consent, had hurried back to the dormitory, where he had found Stephen perspiring and attempting to remove both his cape and his tunic, quite contrary to the Order's rules. In the light of the night lamp, he had also observed the bright red pockmarks which had started to invade Stephen's face and limbs.

Once Matins was at an end, James had sought immediate instructions from the frater medicus, Brother Drogo, who had confirmed that Stephen should be removed at once by stretcher to the infirmary, and further that James should give him every attention, and should notify the prior himself if his condition worsened, or if he made any strange utterances, or – God willing – if he should escape the fever which now consumed his body. James revealed that Stephen had indeed cried out many times and had seemed to speak in horror, but at what none could interpret, even the prior, to whom full accounts of Stephen's physical condition and of his utterances were supplied every day.

Though fearful for his friend's condition, the task of caring for Stephen had been one which James vowed he had been eager to undertake, and he detailed how he had drawn and tasted Stephen's blood, taken his pulse, how he had rubbed Stephen's nether parts to obtain samples of his urine, and had applied such herbs and poultices to his inflamed limbs as the savour of those fluids dictated. On several occasions, he was not abashed to say, he had used with skill, but utmost gentleness, a hollow wooden pipe attached to a pig's bladder in order to squirt healthful salts, soap, honey, and mallows through the fundament deep into Stephen's bowels.

James had battled long and hard against the illness for mastery over Stephen's body, and had employed his deep knowledge of herbs and secret substances to rid Stephen's limbs of an excess of what he pronounced to be the melancholy humour. At last he had prevailed, the balance of bodily fluids had been restored, and the demon, that underlying cause of the disease, had been cast out. This had occurred towards the end of Advent's first week, and from that point onwards Stephen's fever had lessened, and the pockmarks about his face and body had begun to fade.

If his friend's descriptions made Stephen's pulse race in consternation, they also made him smile almost in exasperation to think of the care which had been lavished on him – care greater, he suspected, than was normal, either for sick monks or for any guests of the priory who became ill. To think so was to cast no aspersion on James' general devotion to all his patients, which Stephen was sure was both thorough and selfless. It was just that he knew James' feelings for him as a friend would have driven him way beyond the customary bounds of duty. Even when Stephen enjoyed good health, James would often embarrass him with his rather unctuous solicitations for his welfare, and his eagerness to prescribe potions and tinctures for the very slightest of sniffles.

As Stephen had previously learned, James' early life as a novice of the Order had followed a very different pattern from his own. Of humble background, James had entered the Order at the age of eighteen to become a lay brother, and in consequence he had never himself left the priory to pursue studies elsewhere. Rather, under Brother Drogo's guidance, he had become adept in matters of physic and had taken prime responsibility for the care of the sick. His knowledge of medicine had in fact become far greater than was usual in the case of infirmarers, or even of men such as Drogo himself who had included medicine amongst their studies at the university. Before Stephen had himself set out for Oxford, friendship had been kindled. After his return, James had done all he could to blow new life into its embers, even though he often seemed in awe of Stephen's learning, and would assert, despite Stephen's blandishments, that one day Stephen would become prior.

*

Once Stephen had regained some strength, and they could sit together by the door leading from the infirmary to the herb garden, he was pressed by James to tell him of his journey to Hereford. He felt free to describe in measured words his original errand, the city with its great cathedral, its bridge, its market place, and its many alleys with their filth, garbage, and foul miasmas of leper-breath. James had no doubt that these had entered through his pores, disrupting the balance of the humours within his body, and generating his recent illness.

Of Thomas Dunsheved Stephen said nothing, and of the fate of Hugh le Despenser he was guarded in his speech, though it transpired that James, like most of the brothers, was well informed both as to the course of the trial and to the protracted horrors of the execution. Until he had consulted with Brother Walter, however, Stephen felt he could not know which further information either should or should not be repeated to James or to anyone else. Brother Walter in fact himself began visiting him daily, but would not permit him to speak of his ordeal until it was clear there would be no serious relapse in his condition.

It was on the third day following his recovery of full consciousness, when James had permitted Stephen to be helped from the infirmary to the cloister in order to take the air, that the prior found him near to the lavatorium propped up in a great wooden chair and wrapped in several shawls, his face merely blotched now, the greyness fading beneath his eyes.

"In Heaven's Name, you must be feeling better, Brother Stephen – sitting out on a December day like this! Are you sure you wouldn't be better by the fire in the infirmary?"

"Brother James tells me I've been festering there for more than two weeks already, father. To me it feels like months, though I've no

46

clear memory of any but the last few days. So I thought a change of air might help me. To be honest, I prefer the nourishment of fresh air to the meaty diet which Brother James keeps pressing on me – and since this is my favourite place to sit and tell the rosary…"

"You must not let the air give you a chill, or the damp get into your lungs."

"But I don't find it too cold, father. Besides, I love this kind of weather in the winter, when the frosts disappear for a week or two and the winds and rain blow up from the south-west!…"

"Some would think that a little odd, my son!"

"No. Really, father! The winds bring the sea-gulls in from the estuary, and I love to watch them squabbling on the cloister roof, or swooping down when I throw out a little crust. Somehow this weather makes me feel nostalgic! It did when I was at Oxford. There's something almost homely in it that makes me think about the place where the rivers meet near my family's home, about steady rain on green fields, sheep on the hills and cattle in the meadows, gales rattling roofs and shutters when you're safe in your bed – about Gloucestershire, I suppose!…"

"God be praised. You are better, aren't you! Only two days ago, my son, you couldn't string two words together, and here you are prattling on just like you used to! I'm so very pleased, Brother Stephen… and if it means you're now capable of unburdening yourself…if you feel strong enough to tell me the details of your meeting with Thomas Dunsheved…then come to my lodging after Prime tomorrow. For we must speak privately of course – and certainly not in front of Brother James and the other patients in the infirmary. If you've the strength to walk to my lodgings, I shall know you are well enough to talk of certain grave matters. If you've not, then, eager as I have been to hear your news, those matters must wait another day or two!"

"Oh, Brother Walter, please let me talk now of Dunsheved! He was so insistent I carry out certain tasks on his behalf, and in all of them I seem to have failed! He also said I should give you a full account of Despenser's end, though I know from what James has told me that the story seems common knowledge now, at least in many respects."

"Brother James was a fool to talk of such matters whilst you were still ill!" said Walter. "And Brother Thomas Dunsheved can also be a fool at times – albeit of a grander sort! You should not reproach yourself if, due to illness, you have not done all he told you to!...But – when you are able – it is of course important that I at least know what he said...Please, therefore, if you can, Brother Stephen, do come to my lodgings after first light tomorrow." The prior smiled and held out his hand so that Stephen could lean forward and kiss his ring, though at the same time he placed a gentle hand on Stephen's shoulder to ensure he did not try to struggle on to his knees.

When Brother Walter had departed for the chapter house, Stephen gazed out once more across the cloisters towards the chapel nave. Rain was lashing down now, leaking a little through the timbers of the slanting roof, droplets splashing up at him from the flagstones, and he knew that before long he would have to call for assistance to return to the infirmary.

He said a prayer of thanks for the prior, for his great wisdom, and also for the generosity he had always shown from the moment Stephen had entered the priory as a child. It was the prior who had encouraged him in his studies, had first sent him to the Dominicans' provincial school, and then had used his influence to ensure Stephen progressed to the Order's hall at the university. He reminded Stephen of his own father – or what little he could remember of him – not only in respect of his kindness and understanding, but also of his manner and his looks, given his large, but stooped frame, his thin grey-gold hair, and his extreme short-sightedness.

Stephen pondered too what had just been said of Thomas Dunsheved, suddenly at a loss how to interpret the conversation on the riverbank – the conversation which ever since had rehearsed itself over and over again in his mind during many a conscious hour, and indeed many an unconscious one. And, as was so often the case, thoughts of Thomas Dunsheved led on to thoughts of Hugh, and of those barbarous events which, however hard he tried, Stephen could not erase from his memory.

Seeking to return once again to holy contemplation, he crossed himself, recited the creed, and then began to tell the beads of the rosary. As was the custom at Gloucester, he began with an "Our Father" on the first large bead, then said a "Hail Mary" on each of the following three smaller beads – one for faith, one for hope, and one for charity – but he could not go on, for now an overwhelming tiredness interposed itself, and he rang the small bell he had beside him to summon those who would help him back to his bed.

As he waited for their arrival, a certain sadness took him, for his prayers to Mary again revived a further thought which had been nagging at him during the days of his recovery. Though his return from Hereford was clouded in his memory, he still recalled how he had joined the queen's procession convinced that the Virgin would help him perform what Dunsheved had required. Yet this had not happened. And since the Virgin could in no way have misled him, the fault, the very grievous fault, lay in himself, in the Pride of his imaginings. This he would confess, though as yet he had not sounded the true depths of contrition. Then would come the blessing of penance; though only a healthy body, one fully recovered from disease, would be fit for the punishment to which it would then be his joy to subject it.

Chapter 7

The next morning when the Matins bell rang Stephen tried, but did not succeed, in making his way to the chancel. By the time he had staggered from the infirmary, through the eastern range, and into the cloister, he was already in no state to cover the remaining short distance into the church itself, and Brother James was then obliged to help him back to his bed. After Prime, when Stephen again stated a wish to visit the prior's lodging, James would not hear of it, and said that, after attending further prayers, he would consult both the prior and Brother Drogo to decide what additional treatment might be necessary before Stephen could be allowed once more to venture out on his own.

When James returned to Stephen's bedside he broke the news that, with Brother Drogo's consent, he had decided no longer to defer applying a particular branch of his skill from which Stephen was bound to benefit, and which would provide a means to strengthen limbs which had wasted and to sooth any lesions of the skin which still erupted. It was a cure he had been longing to employ since first Stephen had begun to revive.

"This therapy was practised by the Romans, and is most helpful both to the outer and the inner man," he explained. Then he tapped his nose, and a strange winsome smile crossed his face. "Besides, since too much talk is frowned on in the infirmary, and since to perform the treatment we must go down to the lavatorium, it will give us more chance to chat together at our leisure!" Stephen began to suspect he was to be pressed again for further details of his time in Hereford.

Two novices were then summoned and given orders to go down to the refectory, where they were to obtain pails of hot water which they should use to fill a large wooden tub which was kept in the lavatortium. Stephen protested that it was his custom to bath at the start of Lent, on the first Wednesday after Assumption Day, and not otherwise, and that to do so in the depths of winter might cause him an ague. Some time later, however, he found himself being stretchered out of the infirmary and into the cloister by the novices. When they arrived beside the now full wooden tub, James was adding fistfuls of ground herbs and spices to the water before tipping in a sackful of dried rose petals. Stephen tried again, pleading that to place his damaged foot in such hot water would reawaken his past injury and cause the wound to throb, but James insisted that a bath would in fact ease any malady in Stephen's limbs and would help his body resist any further generation of the black bile, recently so harmful to it. Besides, he assured Stephen that, due to the current alignment of Jupiter and Mars, it was a propitious time for bathing as a cure for many ailments.

The white woollen habit and black cape and hood which Stephen had managed to put on when he had risen before dawn were now removed, and, dressed only in his braies, he was prevailed upon to mount three wooden steps which had been placed beside the tub, and with James' help, for his legs shook and were about to give way, he lowered himself into the water.

At first it seemed too warm for him, yet to raise himself up above its surface made his upper torso freeze and shiver in the cool air from the cloister. As he adjusted to the warmth, however, he could not deny that he felt soothed and calmed, and, as the intense aromas rising from the water all around filled not only his lungs, but his head as well, he felt the deepest relaxation and an overwhelming torpor creeping over him. He was not aware when James poured more warm water into the tub, nor when he stood behind him pricking out lice from the hair round Stephen's tonsure, and then elsewhere upon his person.

He must have drowsed for some time. Indeed he must have been in a deep slumber, for it was only a creeping chill from the water around him which at last impinged on his consciousness and roused him to a little more than somnolence. To his mild surprise, he saw that James had joined him in the tub, and was now also asleep, his head tilted back over the edge of the tub, so that his breath wheezed and spluttered about his larynx. He also became aware that somehow James' rather bulbous left leg had become entwined round his own right knee. He had to give it a little shove, and, after opening a bleary eye, James smiled, then withdrew the errant limb, breaking wind as he did so.

"There, Brother Stephen...Said a bath would do you good!... You'll find your limbs more supple now... walking'll become easier." His words drooled from his lips and their sound was strange, as if heard through water, or from the far side of a dream.

Stephen had again almost fallen asleep when James began hauling his own ungainly shape from the bath, causing waves which

51

splashed in Stephen's face and spilled out of the bath on to the flag-stones. James dripped his way down the three steps, and then gathered up some towels and fresh undergarments from the ledge by the row of basins:

"Now, let me wipe myself down, Stephen...Then I'll help you dry yourself."

"Kind of you, as ever," said Stephen, his own speech sluggish, as he tried to enunciate his words. "But I can manage on my own... I'm sure of that." He began raising himself in the tub, and then realised that, whilst James still wore his braies, as was the monks' custom when bathing, his own were now down around his ankles. "Yet, pass me a towel, James...It seems I'm no longer decent!"

It took some time for Stephen to dress himself. He could only think that his illness, or maybe the mere effort of climbing out of the tub, had made his head swim, as though he had drunk strong wine. Several times he needed to cease fumbling with his clothes and to rest, sitting on the long stone bench in one of the cloister bays. Meanwhile James rang a bell to summon the two novices again, so that they could begin the lengthy task of emptying the water from the tub, bucketful by bucketful, into the runnel beneath the basins.

Later on that morning, back in the infirmary, James sat at Stephen's bedside. Again they both dozed. Then James stirred himself to attend mid-morning prayers, and, when he returned, gave a desultory check to the two other patients, before returning to Stephen. Once more they fell asleep. It was not in fact till food was brought for Stephen, a little before midday, that the two friends attempted conversation, their tongues at last loosened from lethargy; their heads clearer. James did indeed press Stephen again for details of the events in Hereford, though he kept his voice low for fear the other patients would overhear.

"Is it true the queen toasted the crowds when the judgement on Despenser was read out, and that she and her lords feasted whilst he was butchered to death?"

"It is indeed, my friend, though it pains me to say so."

"She was so full of vengeance, then, that she exulted in public at her enemy's downfall! I'm shocked to hear a woman could nourish such violent hatred and emotion. In this she surely displayed the sin of Anger."

"I admit I was at a loss to comprehend it myself, James. But woman is too weak a vessel to withstand powerful passions; even though, from what little I saw, I fancied the queen was forged of some steely French mettle!...Only she and her confessor know why she believes she, rather than God Himself, should be avenged on those who have wronged her... But it's said she suffered greatly at her husband's hands. She was deprived, you know, of all her lands and riches thanks to Despenser and his father, and they stood accused also of procuring the deaths of several of her knights, and of ill-treating some of her ladies..."

"But they say too that the king was no good husband to her, that Despenser himself had taken her place in the king's bed, and that for vengeance she had become Lord Mortimer's mistress!...Can such things be true, Stephen – that the queen is an adulteress and the king a sodomite?" Spittle oozed between the stumps of James' teeth, down over his pendulous lower lip, and on to his chin, as he leaned towards Stephen, eager for explanations. In his excitement his voice had become quite loud, and Stephen placed his finger against his own lips, before going on in a whisper:

"Again I cannot say, James...But we must speak quietly of these matters!...I hear what people say of the queen...and of the king...but I know only that when the judgement on Despenser was read out it was said that he had come between the king and queen hindering their relationship..."

"But they gelded him like a bull. That must surely signify..."

"That was not part of the judgement! He was to be hung, drawn, quartered, and beheaded...and his bowels were to be ripped out...Maybe the hangman himself, for the sake of favour with the crowd..."

"Or with the queen; for they say she procured the same vengeance on the French lords who bedded her sisters-in-law!"

"I know no more than that it was not part of the punishment read out by Sir William Trussell..." But James was no longer listening:

"Just to imagine this could be so!...That Despenser and the king himself...Does it not shock you, Stephen, to imagine such things: that a man can sin against his own kind, make his friend a woman, seek his pleasure in the foulest place?...Oh, Stephen, just think of it: that a man can so revolt against Nature that he will lie on a dung-heap and take seed through his arsehole and into his belly? Think of it! ..." But Stephen did not wish to think of it, for it was a subject which filled him with fear and perplexity, and one with which he had sworn to the Virgin Mary he would not sully his mind. There was a silence.

"My friend," James resumed. "Rest assured, I'll use this as an example: an example to preach to the sodomites on the Barelonde!...What do you think of that?...By the king's ruin they shall see what catastrophe awaits them in this world, as well as in the next. They shall see that, when their blackness is uncovered, when Nature is..."

"Calm yourself, Brother James! Calm yourself...We know little of these matters, other than what rumour whispers. You'd do well to say nothing of such things!...against the king in particular, even though it seems his power is overthrown...And do not forget his many kindnesses to our order!...Besides, my friend, what 'preaching' do you mean?...You're a lay brother, and you know you should not..."

But by now James was oblivious to his words, and was pacing beside the bed, his pig-like eyes twinkling between thick folds of flesh, an almost rapt look upon his face. At that moment, though, there was a tolling of the bell for midday prayers, and, without a further word, and without any of the lethargy which had affected him earlier, James scuttled away to the chancel, muttering to himself through his slavering lips.

Trying to blot their conversation from his mind, Stephen lay back against his straw pillow and, as he often did whenever his brothers were engaged in one of the services of the day and he could not be present, he recited the words of the mass, even raised his voice in a little plainsong. Yet the thought of James and his "sermons" kept returning to him. Preaching was the duty of friars who were ordained, not those who were lay brothers like James, and who had more menial responsibilities. James would be disciplined by the prior, if his preaching were discovered, and rightly so – Stephen could not deny that. As to the subjects James wished to preach about, he could not credit what he had heard. He had long known it was James' particular fascination to go wandering about Barelonde, but he had thought it for the purpose of meeting and offering herbal cures to those unfortunates who spent time there, either through perverse inclination, or because for their sins or diseases they were hounded out of the main streets of the town. To know that James purported ministry to them of a spiritual, as well as a practical kind was disconcerting.

Barelonde itself was an open waste land off Longsmythystrete, which stretched between Blackfriars Priory and the castle. Musters took place there in times of conflict, but in general it was the town's rubbish dump, where there were piles of animal bones and entrails, broken crockery, rotting meat, and human faeces. It was a place of stench and squalor, frequented by thieves and lepers and, if James was to be believed, by sodomites too.

Once Stephen had accompanied James when he ventured out into this wilderness, and he had seen how the very degradation of the place seemed to inspire his brother to paint the most lurid pictures as they spoke together of Hell and Purgatory. He had himself on that occasion attempted to preach to the wretches they encountered, though his audience had melted away, and he doubted his words had made much impression on the paltry few who stayed to listen. Perhaps it had been this sorry experience which had given James the idea that sermonising to these outcasts was something which was needful, and something which, for some deluded reason, it was *his* mission to undertake.

Stephen must have again drifted into sleep, for suddenly he found himself awakening with an acrid stench about his nostrils. As his eyes opened, James' face was close to his own, the smell filtering through the half-open lips from the tooth stumps beyond.

"I was just checking if you were awake," James said with a solicitous smile. "It's just before Compline and time for me to sprinkle the holy water." As he set about this task, James paused by each of the occupied beds in turn to say a short prayer and to scatter droplets from the aspergillum. When he had finished, he turned once more to Stephen.

"I think I'll spend part of my time tomorrow out on the Barelonde – especially after our conversation this morning...Oh, Brother Stephen, I long for the time when you've recovered, and you'll be able to come with me again, perhaps to assist me in my ministry to the ones who dwell there."

As sleep reclaimed him, Stephen felt it best to keep his peace for now at least.

Chapter 8

Joy mounted in Stephen's breast when next morning helped by James he was able once more to attend the Matins service. Most of the forty or so friars who lived at Blackfriars were present, and, though it was not yet light, he could sense the looks of encouragement and goodwill for his further recovery which enveloped him as he entered the chancel.

Though he chose to take little account of such matters, Stephen was aware of his brothers' high regard for him. From time to time he had heard himself praised both for his devotion to the calling and for his learning, which, it was said, already outstripped that of all but the most senior of them. He knew such talents to be gifts from God, and due, of course, to no merit of his own. The unspoken warmth of his reception on this occasion, however, made him smile to himself, and helped him endure the rigours of standing and kneeling during the service which followed.

After almost three weeks' absence it was also a special pleasure for him, as he mouthed the morning's ritual responses, to gaze once more on the Madonna's – his Madonna's – statue in the niche above the prior's chair. In the flickering of the torches placed on the chancel walls, he could see the glint of gold-leaf stars on the painted firmament above her head, and indeed of the crown of stars encircling her brows.

"And there appeared a wondrous thing in the heavens; a woman clad with the sun, and the moon beneath her feet, and on her head a crown of twelve stars." As the words of Revelation passed through his mind, he fancied he saw the gleam of Her very eyes; and then sensed – and knew this could be no mere imagination – a hand touching him with a balm for the body, more powerful than any potion within James' skill to devise, however adept his friend might be. And at the same time he imbibed a balm for his soul, a forgiveness for those false and proud imaginings – that reprehensible love of self – which had shamed him on his way back from Hereford, before illness began the punishment of his presumption.

Several times during the service, when he looked away from the Madonna's face, he felt Walter's eyes upon him, and knew that they must speak together as soon as Matins ended. Therefore, once the sermon had been delivered by Brother Drogo, who was Doctor of Theology as well as frater medicus, and once the other friars had gone down into the nave to pray with the congregation, he made his way at a gentle pace the short distance along the cloister to the prior's lodgings. He had declined any further help from James, though, as he knocked at Brother Walter's door, he could see his friend still hovering by the well within the quadrangle.

Though Walter occupied two fairly large chambers in the priory's west range, the first contained little other than a desk, a table and a few chairs. (The door to the second – no doubt the prior's bedroom – always remained closed whilst visitors were present.) Beside the desk was an small cupboard which contained manuscripts and a number of books bound in vellum, and from this it appeared Walter had just taken a letter which he was reading with the benefit of a lighted reed and the wood-rimmed spectacles he had purchased in Paris whilst on the Order's business the year before. The prior smiled, closed the cupboard door, and motioned Stephen to pull up a stool beside the desk, whilst he finished reading the letter, as if to refresh his memory.

When Walter put the letter aside and sat down behind his desk, he said a prayer of thanks for Stephen's recovery, and then explained that, to avoid Stephen's over-tiring himself either in mind or body, he would himself recount what he had pieced together from various reports of Despenser's trial and execution. His only request was that Stephen correct any details which seemed to him to have been misreported. First, however, it was necessary they discuss Stephen's meeting with Brother Thomas Dunsheved and the instructions given him, though again the prior would assist by stating what facts he had already gathered.

Walter explained how he had heard from Dunsheved, as the latter shadowed the soldiers guarding the king on their journey northwards from Monmouth. Desperate to know more, he had taken advantage of Stephen's then current errand to Hereford to arrange a meeting at which Dunsheved could pass on the most recent news, and any advice concerning Edward's likely fate and what the Order might do about it. Brother Walter now apologised for his failure to pre-warn Stephen of the true nature of the meeting, but he had not wished to burden Stephen with the dangers which might be involved till this became unavoidable. He had explained little, therefore, when sending instructions for Stephen to rendezvous beside the old Wye Bridge.

The prior now revealed that in the past week he had received a further letter from Dunsheved – the document he had been reading. It contained matter and suggestions which Brother Walter found perplexing, because its author assumed he already possessed the information which had been passed to Stephen. It was now pressing, therefore, for Stephen himself to give a full account of what had been said three weeks previously, though again the prior insisted, if he became over-weary, he should at once desist till strong enough to proceed. Only then would Walter wish to consider what moves, if any, to take, and would only do so after consultation with other senior members of the Order.

As Stephen began his account Brother Walter made no interruption. He looked pained at the tale of Edward's flight into Wales, his ignominious capture and his imprisonment, but queried no more than the occasional detail. Later, as Stephen recounted how Dunsheved had demanded he insinuate himself into the queen's counsel and had rebuked Stephen for his reluctance, Walter's look softened to something of a wry smile. He picked up the letter again as Stephen, leaving the matter of Despenser's execution for later, concluded with an account of his desultory attempts to implement Dunsheved's wishes on the journey back to Gloucester.

"So that is what Brother Thomas told and commanded me," said Stephen, "and that, father, is the extent of my failure! My illness was of course to blame later in the journey, but I should have made more of my opportunities before! If only I'd been able to win the confidence of Lord Berkeley and Sir John, whom the Blessed Virgin had most certainly placed in my way, I might indeed have been able to..."

"But, my son, what in fact would you have found out, had you won their confidence? Do you think the queen and Lord Mortimer discuss their darkest plans with the likes of ourselves? It was grossly unfair of Brother Thomas to suggest such a thing, and I doubt, if he'd been in your place, he'd have achieved any more than you have done! No, Brother Stephen, you did well enough in observing and reporting what you have. Be assured, no man could have been expected to do more." The prior had stood and had moved to Stephen's side of the desk, where he placed a consoling hand upon his shoulder, till the look of anguish began to fade from Stephen's eyes.

"Besides, my son, as Brother Thomas has now told me in his letter, the king is still at Kenilworth, and it seems likely he will remain there at least until the Parliament has met, which, I hear, cannot be till well after Christmas. As he does not seem to be in immediate danger of death or deposition, we do have time to consider if and how we may intervene, and – to speak the truth – if and how we may have to intervene to prevent Dunsheved making a fool both of himself and the Order!" Brother Walter returned to his seat, and spread his hands upon the table.

"Since it is not impossible that you, Stephen, will have more dealings with Brother Thomas, I should perhaps also explain a little about him. He is indeed an able man, a renowned preacher in his own right, but someone who has devoted his life to matters of state, rather than of religion. He was an envoy for the king to the papal court – some say to secure the king's divorce from Isabella – but whilst he was in Avignon he did not hesitate to further his own interests, and became a papal chaplain in the process! When he returned to England, he was so full of airs and graces, so enamoured of riding a great horse – which he claimed to do under special dispensation – and of filling his belly with meats forbidden to us, that he earned considerable disfavour within the Order, and indeed incurred the king's displeasure for many months. As you know, King Edward is a devout man, who sets much store by the observance of religious form and regulation!

"Brother Thomas Dunsheved is manifestly – perhaps always was at heart – a man of the world, rather than of the cloister. And yet he is a dreamer too. His letter to me is full of broad hints that he and members of his family are planning to spring the royal prisoner from his trap, though what arrogance or foolishness possessed him to put such a thing in a letter, when he had already told as much to you, I cannot think!"

"But if the king is no longer a friend to Brother Thomas, why does Thomas now conspire on his behalf?" said Stephen. "Surely someone like him might profit from the great changes in our land!"

"A dreamer, he may be – sometimes an adventurer, and a reckless one at that – but whatever the issues after his return from Avignon, he, like all in our order, knows King Edward to be a man of piety and our greatest patron – as was his blessed mother, Queen Eleanor, before him. Dunsheved did well for himself, too, whilst the Despensers held power, and that will be known to the queen's party. They must also be aware of his alleged mission to the pope, and will hate him for it...Even if the queen no longer loves her husband, she will no doubt regard talk of a divorce as an attack upon her power!"

"So, do you think that Brother Thomas really will attempt to release the king?" queried Stephen.

"I have no doubt that he and his family will try something of the kind. From his point of view it's a fortunate coincidence that King Edward is held at Kenilworth, not many miles from Dunmore Heath, where the Dunsheveds are powerful, but my fear is they will act precipitately. The king's safety and liberty are things we in the Order of Preachers must work and pray for, and indeed I will give what counsel and assistance I can to Brother Thomas, but I am reluctant for the Order to become too obviously involved, in case he does something too rash, it all comes to nothing, and we incur blame." Brother Walter's shoulders sagged and he looked weary. There was a short silence, before Stephen again interrupted:

"Brother Thomas seemed to think that I, as well as he, had a role to play in King Edward's fate. What he meant I'm unsure, and what little he made clear I've failed to achieve. Do you have any instructions for me, father, now that my health is better?"

"Brother Thomas tends to talk that way," said Walter. "In his book we are all of us always at some point of crisis – there is never more time in which to reflect on a decision, Fate has always decreed immediate action, and has chosen Thomas (or whoever he is speaking to) as its chosen instrument!

"But be assured, my son, I and others in the Order will do all we can to preserve the welfare of our sovereign, and should we discover a way to take effective action, it could be that I will call on you again, as the most able of the younger friars to assist... For now, though, do not trouble yourself over Brother Thomas and his plans. I wish you fully to recover and to resume your normal duties, both as a preacher and as a scholar in the scriptorium...Now let us turn to the sorry matter of Despenser's trial and execution."

The prior then began to inform Stephen of all that rumour had delivered him on that subject, and this accorded for the most part with

Stephen's own recollections. Indeed the prior had received from Gloucester's sheriff a written list of the charges brought against Despenser, and so Stephen's inability to recall all that Sir William Trus-Trussell had read out before the Guildhall was of no significance. Only when it came to an account of Despenser's execution could Stephen add much to what Walter already knew, and then it was a matter of detail (every instant of the atrocities within the castle walls remaining vivid in his memory) or of correction (for rumour had it that Hugh, as Edward's paramour, had railed against those who would punish him, and had been unmanly to the end).

Once Walter had explained how Despenser's head had been sent to London, and that the four quarters of his remaining corpse were now on show above the gates of Bristol, Newcastle, Dover and York, a silence fell between to two men, which it was hard to break. Each bowed his head in prayer till, crossing himself, Brother Walter rose to his feet and blessed Stephen, who on this occasion managed to kneel to kiss the prior's ring.

"Thank you, father, for your advice to me today" said Stephen. "You've raised a burden from my shoulders in explaining more to me of Thomas Dunsheved."

"It is you who should be thanked, my son, for you have discharged what I have asked of you, and in doing so have endured not only illness, but grievous sights it would have been better for you to avoid. I will speak of these matters to others in the Order, and in due course will let you know of any further service you may provide."

When Stephen emerged from the prior's chambers, he found Brother James still loitering by the well, and, though he felt relieved by the prior's reassurances, his legs now seemed so very weak that he was grateful for James' stout arm around him, and his whispered encouragement, to assist him on his way back to the infirmary; though, if James hoped to be rewarded in any way, let alone with an account of Stephen's interview with the prior, he was disappointed.

Chapter 9

By Christmas Stephen had recovered sufficiently to return at night to the dormitory, where James was hardly less attentive for his well-being than he had been in the infirmary. During daytime he also resumed his studies in the scriptorium, where he began labouring once more at his translations from Latin and Greek, and resumed his reading and contemplation of the works of Aristotle and St Thomas Aquinas.

The scriptorium occupied the first floor of the priory's south range. Along its centre a series of tables and cupboards contained books, manuscripts and presses. Areas of study were provided along the two sides of the room, north and south, where at each shuttered, but unglazed window there was a carrel with enough space for a desk and stool set sideways on. Beside each desk the window frame was cut away at an angle to maximise light for study, whilst each monk's privacy was ensured by a thin stone screen between his carrel and the next, and by a curtain which could be drawn across its entrance.

Stephen's carrel was the third to the left, as one approached from the stairs, and from this he could look out over the kitchens. Although it faced south, at this time of year the meagre daylight permitted no more than a few hours work per day, and even then Stephen would often close his shutters against rain or snow and work by candle light, for fear of damaging the valuable manuscripts on the desk before him, to say nothing of his own still fragile health. Yet his spiritual well-being benefitted from his studies – of that he was sure. As he re-entered the world of the "Summa Theologica" and other writings of Aquinas, the palsied core of his confidence in himself, in his abilities, in his very powers of reasoning, took in new nourishment and ceased to tremor.

Shortly after the Feast of the Epiphany, Stephen resumed saying daily mass, and began giving regular sermons again at the nearby church of St Mary de Crypt, where he had licence to preach whenever he wished. It was a church he loved, for its small proportions and the cool darkness of its interior, notwithstanding its rather crude representation of the Virgin Mary. Her breasts were bared, ready to bestow the milk of Her mercy on the faithful; and from this he would avert his gaze, even though he knew that the Mother of God had in fact granted this very blessing to St Dominic, when revealing to him the rosary's mystery a century before.

He spent many hours too in discussion and disputation with Brother Drogo, who, as Doctor of Theology, had done much to prepare him for his studies before he left for the university, and who was ever willing to debate the finer points of theology, whether in the scriptorium or whilst they walked together round the cloister. Drogo was of Walter's age, but appeared younger. Black brows over piercing eyes gave him an intense, almost intimidating look, and he had a vigour both of mind and body which well suited his teaching role within the priory.

All in all, it seemed to Stephen that his old life was returning to him, and he thanked God and the Blessed Virgin that this was so. Yet in some ways he felt changed from the young friar who so recently had left for Hereford, quite unprepared for the snare life was about to set for him. Now, when he went out into the town, he could no longer bear the sight of a head upon a pike, or of a burdened gibbet. And at night he would often wake sweating, a stench of burned flesh in his nostrils, sure something warm and viscous had splashed against his cheek, or hissed and fried amongst the cinders. Sometimes too he would dream that he was weeping for some overwhelming grief he could not define, and indeed would wake to find his cheeks and pillow moist. On such occasions James would have woken too, roused by his sobs, and would seek to calm and comfort him with a gentle touch against Stephen's brow, or cheek, or shoulder.

When some three weeks after Epiphany Stephen's brother came to visit him on his way back to Tewkesbury from the Parliament in London, Stephen learned that King Edward had been deposed, and that within a few days his son would be crowned in his place. Incredulous and sorrowful as this news made him feel, and unworthy as he knew such reasoning to be, he could only conclude that any hopes for Edward's rescue, let alone his return to the throne, had now foundered. Hence he, Stephen, would have no further role to play either in Edward's fate or in Brother Thomas Dunsheved's plots and intrigues; and for the present he heard nothing which implied anything to the contrary from Brother Walter.

*

Snowdrops had begun appearing in the cloister quadrangle a week or so later. It was a day when a south-west wind spoke to the gulls of lofty rocks and plentiful shoals away in the Channel, and their excited cries tore at Stephen's concentration, both in the chancel and the scriptorium. For him it seemed a day to halt his studies for a few hours, an opportunity at last to yield to Brother James' wheedling requests that he accompany him once more out into the Barelonde. Perhaps they would distribute a little food, or some of the potions James had been brewing. Perhaps they would offer spiritual solace, and Stephen would preach again to those unfortunates whom the infirmarer regarded as his own special charge. Whatever else, Stephen could now satisfy himself whether or not James was behaving in a way inappropriate for a lay brother.

When they had ventured into the Barelonde previously, during the parched summer of the previous year, Stephen had been overcome by the putrescent stench of the place; and eventually, when his attempts at sermonising had come to nothing, he had fled back to the cloister, his hood pulled tight across his heaving chest and mouth. Even James had achieved little on that occasion, other than to send a few beggars and a wave of rats scurrying cross the pits and piles of the pockmarked terrain. Yet James had claimed to him recently that such failure on their part had been an exception, that there in the midst of the wasteland he had regularly comforted and, by his example, helped to save lost souls, or at least bring them to a few days' grace, before they were sucked back into the slime of their iniquity, as he termed it. Stephen should come once more, not only to see what a sea of vice lapped at the doors of the priory, but also to understand how James, lay brother and poor scholar though he was, had made it his especial task and achievement to plumb its depths and halt its tide.

It was therefore with a great gap-toothed smile that James greeted Stephen, when he arrived in the infirmary a little after Terce and proposed that there could be no better day for a foray into the Barelonde. They set off almost at once, leaving a novice to take over the steeping of mallow leaves in ale, a task which otherwise would have occupied James for the rest of the morning.

Outside the priory, they kept for a while to the inner side of the town wall, which ran from Blackfriars towards the castle at the southern end of the site. Away to their right, they spied smoke rising.

"There, there are the devils!" exclaimed James, and at once began hurrying in that direction, slithering his way through mud and ordure. Stephen followed as best he could, though his lameness, as well as his recent illness, meant that he soon lagged behind. As James drew near the centre of the site a large flock of crows rose from whatever carrion they had been devouring and wheeled sideways on the breeze towards Longsmythyesstrete.

"Come, Brother Stephen," he shouted back. "Did you see that? Always a sign The Evil One's at work! That's my experience!"

"They're only birds, James – birds, not soldiers in the Devil's army!" Stephen hoped James could hear him, and also that he could catch up now James had paused; but his friend ignored him, took out his crucifix and began brandishing it aloft, as he scrambled onwards again, leaving Stephen bemused at the frenzy which seemed to possess him. Stephen followed on, hitching up his tunic to avoid the pools and puddles amongst the garbage, though he felt filth squelching between his toes.

Eventually, James halted at the top of a bank, surveying whatever lay in front of him. Stephen struggled towards him, breathless, and again tried to capture his attention:

"What is it, Brother James? What's over there?" But James, though he himself still panted, was now also chanting words from the Latin mass.

Stephen drew level with him, and at last descried the origin of the smoke they had been pursuing: a number of large mounds of brushwood and rubbish which had been ignited, no doubt by those who worked nearby, for the sake of a little warmth. Through thick eddies, he could make out perhaps twenty figures in rags rooting amongst the town's detritus for any morsel they might eat, putrid or otherwise. Several were looking up, already alerted by James' babbling, and Stephen did not need the rasping of their voices, the clack of their rattles, or the clang of bells about their necks to know that they were lepers. His stomach turned, as he recalled the fetor of their breath, and he imagined a stench more noisome still emanating from their nether parts; for he knew leprosy signified fleshly sin, and if the lepers and James' sodomites were, as he suspected, one and the same, an over-powering reek would surely cause him to swoon, if he dared approach them.

No such scruples affected James, and the older man now began to slide his way down the bank towards the fires, still gasping for breath, but clearly intent on launching an harangue:

"Be gone, sinners. Be gone, from my temple…says the Lord…I shall make a whip out of cords! And it shall be bitter for you…I shall overturn the tables…where evil is transacted! For all you before me are the fornicators, the adulterers…and the men of Sodom…who give yourselves to luxury and bear the signs of your degradation. For it is God's will that you shall rot and putrify like corpses – even while you yet live; that your fingers, toes…yes, your other extremities…shall become rotten and dissolve; that your noses shall melt into your mouths; and that your voices…shall become as those of wild beasts… And all this shall be a sign to those who would sin in like manner…Now, you shall go forth into the towns to show them what you have become…and shall no longer desecrate my Father's house!"

Whilst he ranted, James still held his crucifix above him, making his way forward, sometimes slithering, sometimes almost falling down the tip's incline towards the spot where the four nearest lepers huddled together. Whether because they thought they were beset by a madman, or whether through fear of the burning branch which James now grabbed from their fire and began brandishing at them, they began to retreat, uttering hoarse curses, dragging themselves on limbs which were hardly limbs, desperate to find some new pit or sewer in which to hide from this latest misery inflicted on them.

"Whatever are you thinking, Brother James?" cried Stephen, trying to follow him down the slope. "What nonsense are you talking? This is no temple, no house of God, from which to cast out these poor creatures. Our Lord touched and healed the leper! If you cannot do the same, at least be merciful and let them stay in this wretched place, when they've nowhere else to go!…Besides it's not for you to preach…" But James seemed not to hear. As Stephen lost his footing, slid on his back, rolled, and slid again, James simply beamed back at him with a look of greatest satisfaction. Then he threw the branch back into the fire, and gestured about him:

"This is my temple, Stephen. This is where I come to do the Lord's work…Didn't I speak well? If I can be no great scholar like my young friend, I can at least build Zion here!" Struggling to his feet at the bottom of the incline, and spitting what he hoped was only dirt from his mouth, Stephen gaped at James. If he had seemed eccentric in the past, now he was truly demented. Stephen knew his friend's knowledge of the gospels to be faulty, but what he had just seen and heard went way beyond superstition and any pardonable ignorance.

"You may share my kingdom, if you like," James went on, his lungs still wheezing as he bent forward, hands resting on his knees. "Come, let's keep ourselves warm by this fire. Those devils won't return till after dusk, nor will the sodomites, so we've the place to ourselves."

"But James, even an ordained priest is not sent to chase sinners from the earth, but to preach to them and save their souls. It's not a patch of wasteland that God wishes the Church to win for itself, but men's minds...and for His glory! Surely you don't think this is what Brother Walter would have you do?" Stephen had approached within a few paces of James, but now halted, still shaking dirt and ash from his robes.

"I serve God as I know best," said James, now standing upright. The corners of his mouth twitched, and he looked a little vexed. "This is my way...And let neither you nor any other man hinder me...Oh, come, come, Stephen..." He smiled again, and now stepped forward and seized Stephen by the arm. "Don't be cross with me, and don't condemn me out of hand. Let me serve as I can. I tend to the sick and I tend to this patch of God's earth – that's my life's new mission. I thought you'd be pleased..." There was silence as they looked at each other, Stephen unsure if he should stay and reason further, or if he should at once flee to the sanity of the priory. But then James moved closer:

"We're friends, you and I. We are, aren't we! I only thought to share with you what I do here ...only wanted you to be impressed..." He reached out his hand to touch Stephen's arm. "Since you returned from Oxford, Stephen, you've become my dearest friend – my dearest friend in all the world...True friends should respect each other's differences, shouldn't they? – as I respect your great learning, which is quite beyond my understanding. Can't you accept that my way is different – can't you accept it in the name of friendship?"

"But, James, you're in such error..."

"But for friendship, Stephen, friendship!...Let's be brothers in Christ, yes – but in life too – like David and Jonathan, or...or like

67

Launcelot and Galahad..." By now James had Stephen by both shoulders, his stale breath panting in his face, saliva seeping at the corners of his mouth. "Let's seal our brotherhood with a kiss...only a chaste kiss. Come..." Stephen was now struggling to be free, but James' grip became tighter, and he tried to hug Stephen to him. "It's so long since I've had a special friend, Stephen...Someone to share things with, some loving soul...You remember Brother Martin, who died while you were at the university...he was such a friend to me...In the summer we used to come out here on the wasteland. He and I, we used to play at games, sometimes used to wrestle...though, of course, that's perhaps not something you..."

Whether it was or was not, wrestling was what the two friars were doing as he spoke; and it was the stronger heavier James who in little time prevailed, forcing Stephen to topple over beneath him. The stench of the ordure on which Stephen landed was no worse than the acrid taste of James' lips and tongue which now forced themselves upon his own.

"Stop this, James. Enough!" spluttered Stephen, trying to wriggle from under his friend's belly. "This must not be!...Get off me! Go. Go to Brother Walter at once. Confess yourself..." But James' fist was now over Stephen's mouth and he began thrusting his bulk at Stephen's groin.

Then James let out a cry – half groan, half strangulated sigh – and fell forward, his whole weight crushing the air from Stephen's lungs, so that it was almost impossible to breathe, let alone sob, as he yearned to. When James at last gave in to Stephen's attempts to push him away, he rolled aside and, without looking at Stephen, lay on his back, a dark stain oozing through the cloth of his habit below the waist-band.

Stephen dragged himself to his feet, stumbled, willed his illness-weakened legs to move, staggered forward, almost slipping into the glutinous slime of a stagnant pool. James called after him, but he managed to move and to pick up pace, as his legs began once more to function. Then he found himself floundering in a pit where stench rose in almost tangible form from the carcass of a cow, whose rotting flesh shimmered and pulsated with a rich crop of white maggots. He hauled himself out, scrambled on, and crawling, reeling, found his way back to Satireslone; then, bedraggled and stinking, hobbled back to the priory, slipping unobserved into the lavatorium.

All the while his heart pounded, and did so, even after he had washed in the spring water which was channelled beside the monks' basins, even after he had hidden himself away behind his curtain in the scriptorium. His whole body quaked, not only at the thought of what James had just done, but also at the morass of memory which now mired his mind. So many images bubbled like marsh gas, belching a foulness which made him gasp for breath – images he had held down, drowned so deep. There was the thrusting between his legs in the attic above the school-room...his cousin's cock, sour, choking, as he knelt behind the dovecote... and then at Oxford... at Oxford...

His mind reeled, and he felt sure he must faint. Then in the wan light of a November dawn he watched a mallet swing, smash upon a chisel head, and felt again a searing pain as two toes were severed from his foot. He felt the excruciating agony of penance – its throb, its ache, and then its ecstasy as blood washed a little guilt away. It was a mutilation he would have inflicted again and again till all his toes were gone, had it proved necessary; but in the event it did not, for as dawn hardened on the stable wall, a subtle glow had filled his sight, and the Virgin had appeared to him. By Her grace She had cleansed his soul, had drawn a veil across memory: a veil which now was riven in two.

*

In the weeks which followed Stephen made no mention to anyone of what had happened, let alone to Brother Walter, though he knew it his duty at the very least to let the prior know that James was, contrary to law and scripture, purporting to preach in God's Name. Keeping to himself, he spent even more of his time in the scriptorium, though was unable to lose himself in his task of translation, for the writing in his manuscripts would only dance and writhe before his eyes yielding none of their secrets. Neither was there relief to be had when he prostrated himself before the Virgin's image in the chancel, for he no longer felt fit for Her presence, or deserving of Her grace, now his soul was once more naked.

He uttered no further word to James, nor did he cast any look in his direction, whether in the chapel or the dormitory, though each sleepless night they lay within the uneasy radius of each other's breathing.

Chapter 10

Bitter rains fell during Septuagesima and then during Lent – rains, sometimes sleet, borne on strong winds from the north-west, dragging veils of grey over the hills of the Forest of Dean away to the west and of the Cotswolds to the east, pounding on the wooden roof of the cloister and the scriptorium shutters, slanting into the quadrangle to bruise and flatten crocuses. The turbulence seemed reflected within Stephen himself. His mind wandered during prayer, even at this time of solemn observance; and, as he pored over his texts, his eyes would glaze, and he would find himself listening to the anger of the storm, his gut knotting tighter and tighter.

From Ash Wednesday onwards he took to spending more hours away from the priory, seeking those who would listen to his sermons in the tangle of alleys around Aylesgatestrete to the east of the High Cross: the quarter the Jews had occupied till they were expelled in Queen Eleanor's time. Some of their buildings still stood empty and derelict, cursed – it was said – for all eternity, though others had been taken by immigrants from the Forest and from further afield. The new occupants would come out into the street – even in freezing rain – eager to listen to what he preached of Hell and Purgatory, open mouthed as if they had not heard the like before; unwilling, though, to spend hard-earned farthings on the price of an indulgence.

He felt himself invigorated with this new mission, almost wild in his enthusiasm for it, and wondered if Brother Walter might permit him to take leave of the priory and to preach at large amongst the villages of delvers and charcoal-burners from which these foreigners came. There he might lose both himself and his memories, tramping from hovel to hovel through the groves and thickets of the wildwood. Was it not the Order's purpose to fight heresy, to defend and preach the catholic truth in those dark and distant places where ignorance lay like thick mould upon the earth?

There was, of course, something else prompting his absences from the priory: his need to avoid James. If he could not escape the spectres James had raised – which Stephen's prayers to Mary had so far failed to vanquish – he must evade the man himself, with his now spurned lust and his bewildering presumption. James, in fact, never ventured into the scriptorium, and meal times were no problem – their customary places were well separated, and no discussion was in any case allowed at table – but it was Stephen's impression that as he made his way about the priory James often followed him at a distance, particularly when he had to pass through the cloister which ran nearest the infirmary. Furthermore, in the chancel James' eyes were always on him, their sparkle gone, replaced now with a look of cold balefulness; and at night in the dormitory, as they lay in their habits, back turned to back, he would be aware his own wakefulness was shared, his own animosity reciprocated, as they lay in an uneasy twilight.

Yet neither the black blight cast on his life by James' behaviour, nor his unwonted enthusiasm for ministry, nor even the abiding horror he still felt for what he had seen at Hereford months before, explained fully, even to Stephen himself, his need to wander the streets of Gloucester in this time of squalls and sudden downpours. When storms drenched his robes, making them bitter against his flesh, or when he felt the bite and sting of hailstones, he felt chastised, then suddenly cleansed of the ill humours with which his soul, rather than his body, seemed afflicted. It was a purgation such as none he had craved since his palm closed round a wooden mallet, his fingers fumbled with a chisel, and he placed a trembling foot on a block of wood years before in Oxford.

*

Six days following the Feast of the Annunciation, and a week and a half before Easter, Brother Walter summoned Stephen to his lodgings. As he entered the prior's study Walter was already seated behind his desk. He said words of benediction and motioned Stephen to sit down.

"My son, it's many weeks since we spoke concerning the king – "Sir Edward" as we now must call him! – and of our brother, Thomas Dunsheved. I have news for you of both of them, but before I say anything on that subject, I wondered if I might enquire a little after your health. Would you say you are fully recovered now?"

"It is kind of you to ask, father, but my health is good and has been so since before Lent began," replied Stephen. The prior paused:

"And yet you still do not seem your normal self...if I may say so. You seem a little distracted and, whilst I make no complaint, Brother Drogo says that your regular carrel is often left empty for more hours of the day than used to be the case. He also mentions your frequent absences from the priory...Is there anything troubling you, Brother Stephen?"

"No, father, nothing troubles me, though I dream often of those things I saw at Hereford, which is far from restful!"

"I had more in mind your waking hours, Brother Stephen. Does the 'Summa' of the Blessed St Thomas Aquinas no longer spark your keen intelligence, or is there some other reason why you are now so often out on the streets preaching – a godly pursuit, of course – but we have many young friars who can strive for souls in the Old Jewry, though few of your capacities as a scholar. It could not surely be that you no longer seek a life of contemplation?...Or perhaps our brother, Dunsheved, has infected you with his need always to be out and doing! If that's so, it surprises me, for I had thought you and he as different as chalk and cheese!"

"No, no, indeed that's not the case at all, Brother Walter...I can only say that at present I feel unsettled, as if nothing in my life can be quite the same, now I've seen the glint of hell-fire in men's eyes. It makes me feel I must do more than sit for hours in the scriptorium...Maybe I might make a mission to the Welshmen of the Forest..." There was a long pause. "It's what I witnessed in Hereford, father, rather than anything said by Brother Thomas..."

"But is there not some other reason, my son?...It is nothing new for you to preach, whether at St Mary's or on the streets of Gloucester. Indeed you've a great talent for it! But the amount of time you now spend doing this...and the streets which I hear you visit...Is there any other reason you seem to forsake the priory for long hours of the day?...I must ask – has it, by chance, anything to do with Brother James?...Brother James, who nursed you so devotedly through your illness, who indeed was God's instrument in your cure, and with whom you seemed so close till recently?...It's been remarked by several of the older brethren that a gulf seems to have opened between the two of you in recent weeks."

"I have no complaint to make against Brother James." Stephen was surprised at the speed of his own rejoinder, and he felt his cheeks colouring. There was an expectant pause before he resumed: "Although he has in the past been a most dear brother in Christ to me, particularly since my return from Hereford, I have to say it's become

73

clear to me that we are very different sorts, he and I: he in the infirmary, I in the scriptorium. We don't in fact have that much in
common...other than our love of God, of course, and our wish to do
His will...and sometimes I have to say his understanding of the gos-
pel..."

"Then you do, Brother Stephen, in some way make complaint..."

"No, father, I apologise. It's not for me..."

"It is not for you, my son...But is there something else?...Has he
in some way importuned you? He has not somehow tempted you into
some uncleanliness?...I have reason to ask this, over and above your
own recent behaviour." Stephen paused again, feeling wretched:

"I have no uncleanliness which is unconfessed, father, neither at
the behest of Brother James, nor of any other...I can say no more of
him. He will no doubt confess to you or to one of the more senior
friars, if he feels that mortal sin has entered into his life." There was
another pause, and then Walter bowed his head and was silent for a
while, as if in prayer, whilst Stephen was fervent in his wish the interview would end. At last Walter spoke again:

"I note what you say, my son, and am glad to hear it. I would
wish, though, that in your remaining time here you would try to make
amends with Brother James. I had hoped your fellowship together was
proving a beneficial influence over his troubled life. For – and I speak
in confidence – he is one of those for whom not only has the vow of
chastity proved heavy, but one who has turned to the male rather than
the female in his sinfulness. I do not betray what has been told to me
in confession. This has been common knowledge amongst the older
brethren, and a matter which, whilst you were at Oxford, came before
a meeting of the chapter. In fact, it was only under the strictest conditions that Brother James was permitted to continue as a member of
this community...A younger monk, Brother Martin, was somewhat
implicated at that time...but, regrettably, was found drowned in the
Severn before the matter could be investigated."

Stephen's mind reeled as he heard these things, though something
Walter had said almost in passing prompted a different concern –
something which both alarmed him and, he felt, excused him from
further comment on the prior's revelations concerning Brother James:

"Brother Walter, you asked that I resume my former fellowship
with Brother James 'in my remaining time here'...Am I to be sent

74

away? Do you have another mission for me – perhaps amongst the delvers of the Forest?"

"My son, this was in fact the main reason why I wished to speak to you, though first I wished to test your frame of mind, to know whether your spirit was still afflicted with the effects of your illness, or by some other secret grief. What you have said encourages me to believe you are sufficiently recovered. Indeed, in what you describe as your current 'unsettled' state, you may be the more ready and able to undertake what I have in mind!" Stephen's pulse began to race and his mouth felt unpleasantly dry as Brother Walter went on:

"I must first explain that in the period since we last spoke of these matters, Brother Thomas Dunsheved has in fact done as I feared he might, and has made an attempt to release our royal master from imprisonment at Kenilworth. Everything was botched and came to nothing, as one might have predicted. Despite this setback, however, and through God's grace, new opportunities concerning Sir Edward have now arisen in which we of the Order of Preachers may play a useful part – with or without Thomas!

"Just two days ago I learned from the Augustinians of Llanthony Secunda that Sir Edward is to be moved in secrecy from Kenilworth to Berkeley, that his journey will bring him here to Gloucester, and indeed that he will spend the night of Palm Sunday, five days hence, at Llanthony outside the wall – not a stone's throw away! I have this from the canon, Brother Michael atte Hull, who has already despatched his nephew, William, to inform the Dunsheveds, in case, which seems unlikely, they're still in ignorance of this.

"Now, it is Sir Edward's brief stay at Llanthony which provides our opportunity. Call it Fate, if you want to emulate Brother Thomas; I prefer to say it is a divinely inspired coincidence!

"Let me explain. For some time now, Stephen, I have been in touch with the commissioners, and they with the head of our order, concerning the royal confessorship. You'll know that for many years all confessors to the king and his forebears have been provided by our order. Friar Robert Duffield held that post till the time of Queen Isabella's uprising, but then he disappeared, and it's feared he is dead. Meanwhile Sir Edward of course has had no permanent confessor, and even the queen, with a little prompting from ourselves, has come to accept recently that this is not a satisfactory state of affairs. Suffice it to say, she has now agreed that a new confessor should be appointed. Sir Edward's visit to Llanthony gives us the occasion to present our candidate for the post – both to him and to his captors – and with Isabella's blessing! And that candidate, if you agree, will be yourself, Brother Stephen!"

Walter's words pierced like steel. As he gasped and fought for breath, Stephen could find no words with which to reply.

"Now, do not tell me you cannot do this, Brother Stephen." (Walter had reached across the desk and was holding Stephen's arm.) "You have been licensed by the bishop to conduct confessions. Furthermore, you have all the scholarship, and the precise way with words which is required. You are, indeed, more qualified than many others who act as confessors to great lords and their ladies. Besides, it will be a further important mission for you; and I'm not convinced, despite your protestations, that you do not hanker for the sort of challenge which was presented to you at Hereford, but in which you felt you had failed!...You will live at Berkeley Castle near Sir Edward's chamber, and you will visit him daily...You will have the opportunity to pursue your studies too...They say Lord Berkeley has a fine library, and, of course, it is no great distance for us to send you any manuscripts you may require..."

"But, Brother Walter," Stephen interjected at last. "I had not looked for such a posting, and I do not wish to leave our priory here in Gloucester, unless, as I said... Is there no other who could undertake this?"

"There is no other as suitable as you are, Brother Stephen!" Brother Walter smiled and patted Stephen's hand. He then placed his finger-tips together and looked more pensive:

"In fairness, Stephen, there is another aspect to this which I must now explain, and which makes it the more logical that it should be you who must undertake this task...We of the Order would wish that, as well as tending to Sir Edward's spiritual needs, you should also keep us notified of all aspects of his captivity and all matters concerning his well-being. To that extent we are requesting that you should be something of a spy! If occasion arose, we might then also need you to assist our agents in securing Sir Edward's liberty! There's no one other than yourself that I could rely upon for such an undertaking."

"It is not without danger, then."

"It is not without danger, my son, but these are dangerous times, and a great king, who was loyal and generous to our order, is in need of our assistance."

Stephen felt snared in a trap, and, whichever way he strained, he knew he would not escape its bite.

"I must pray, father. I will ask the Blessed Virgin what I should do."

"Do so, my son, and let me have your answer at Lauds tomorrow."

Stephen rose and walked towards the door. Then a thought occurred to him:

"If I do as you wish, father, it hardly seems I will have time once more to become reconciled to Brother James."

"True, my son, though I would request that you attempt it. If, for whatever reason, you were never to return to this priory, I would not wish this to be a matter you had left undone."

Chapter 11

As soon as he left Brother Walter's chamber, Stephen knew deep within himself – even if he did not yet acknowledge it – that, whatever self-doubts and fears now racked his stomach, in the end he would do what was being asked of him. Though for hours he might prostrate himself before the Virgin begging Her guidance, though he might lie consumed with worry beside the sleeping – more likely sleepless – form of Brother James, he knew that when Lauds sounded the following morning he would visit the prior again, would kneel, confirm obedience, and accept the cup being proffered him. And so it was, though he did not spare himself those long hours of supplication and anxiety.

During the next few days he busied himself in the scriptorium, trying to finish work which had occupied him since his recovery, but also trying to decide what few manuscripts he could place in his meagre baggage, and which documents he could leave behind to be sent on after him, once he was settled at Berkeley. As he did so, he tried to appear nonchalant, to be concerned with nothing other than the commonplace, for his mission was a secret from all but the most senior of the prior's colleagues. He suspected the Doctor of Theology must be one of these, but Brother Drogo gave no such indication, as he sat at his high lectern between the two rows of carrels, making an occasional nod towards Stephen as the latter went about his business.

Whenever he encountered Brother James that week, Stephen no longer scurried past, or increased his pace to evade him. Instead he strove to pause and smile in his direction, though he feared that the anger that still boiled within him locked his face into a boggle-eyed rictus, and that James would interpret this as hatred, perhaps lunacy. In fact, on the occasions when this occurred James did no more than avert his gaze and walk on past.

Try as Stephen might, he could not bring himself to make any other overture, to speak, make his peace, or in any way prepare James for his own departure, which he suspected would wound the infirmarer's feelings even more than had their recent falling out. It would be an injury, though, which he could neither prevent nor heal, nor was it something about which at present he could even care, despite Brother Walter's promptings and his own duty to comply with them.

When he examined his conscience as to why this might be so, he was surprised to feel no overwhelming disgust at what James had attempted, at the poke of his coated tongue, the savour of his spittal, and the weight and thrust of fat thighs against his own. It was rather James' presumption and the memories his actions had stirred, which kindled and rekindled an ire within his soul, precluding any form of reconciliation.

*

After Vespers on the evening of Palm Sunday Stephen and Walter slipped from the priory, took the pathway to the castle along the inside of the town wall, and then passed over the bridge leading to Naight Island, where there was an orchard owned by the monastery of Llanthony Secunda. They exchanged few words. Stephen carried a leather satchel slung over his shoulder, in which were a few furled manuscripts, but nothing else other than a pair of clean linen braies. He also had with him a staff to help him on the journey he would soon be making from Gloucester down to Berkeley.

As they passed through the orchard in the fading light, the fruit trees still displayed the bleakness of winter, their leaves and blossoms bound within their buds. Yet there was a freshness in the air and a hint of daffodils and blackthorn, as if spring had dared to breathe, but not yet stretch its limbs. With those scents in his nostrils, Stephen's spirits rose as he told himself this was a time for hopes, for new beginnings, for challenges to be overcome in Christ's name. But the breeze had a chill to it too. He thought how buds often blackened with a late frost or when snow scudded in on a north-east wind.

The path led down to Sevarnestrete, which within half a mile brought them to the monastery itself, where many years before Augustinians, fleeing attack upon their house at Llanthony in the Marches, had settled and built a sister institution. Walter led Stephen under the ornate but fortified gatehouse, past barns and stables, where soldiers in Lord Berkeley's colours were tending to horses, whilst others stood guard. Crossing a forecourt, they arrived at the west door of the church, and there, as arranged previously, a young friar awaited them. He led them to a meeting chamber adjacent to the Lady Chapel, where Canon Michael atte Hull greeted them and offered refreshment, since it was now dusk and the day's Lenten fasting was at an end.

"It's been agreed that Brother Stephen will be presented once Lord Berkeley and Sir John Maltravers have finished dining with our father prior in the misericord," explained Canon Michael. "Sir Edward himself is of course confined to his chamber, but I hope they'll allow him to share some of the better dishes from their table! At least we have the opportunity for a short while to discuss in private how our own plans may be taken forward. Brother Walter, you must explain your latest thinking." The canon motioned them to sit where ale and cakes had been set aside, and closed the door to the chamber before joining them.

"We are hopeful," said Brother Walter, "that given Brother Stephen's status as a scholar, no objection will be raised if we at Blackfriars supply him on a regular basis with manuscripts and other materials for his study. Whenever such a delivery is made to him, it should be possible for him then to return other documents he has finished with by the same messenger. Now, our hope and intention, Canon Michael, is that these will include texts in which Brother Stephen will have recorded in the Greek tongue the information on Sir Edward and his welfare which we require! Likewise, if we ourselves wish to convey secret messages to Brother Stephen, I or Brother Drogo will render them into Greek and include them with our own despatches."

The canon looked a little quizzical:

"For this to succeed, Brother Walter, much will depend on the regime to which both Sir Edward and Brother Stephen are subjected. You can imagine how raw has been Lord Mortimer's temper since the attempts to release Sir Edward from Kenilworth, even though they proved unsuccessful. It seems he has chosen Berkeley Castle instead, not only because it is held by his ally and kinsman, Sir Thomas, but also because it is remote – out there in the marshy wastes of the Vale – and it should therefore be secure from external attack. But he will demand the strictest internal security as well, and I've no doubt the physical conditions under which Sir Edward has so far been held will be tightened. Lord Thomas and Sir John will be under instructions to prevent any contact between the former king and the outside world, and to maintain the closest scrutiny over those that serve him – in whatever capacity. Indeed, I hear the royal physician, Pancio di Cotrone, has today been removed from him and placed under arrest! It's really a miracle that the appointment of a new confessor has been agreed to at all. Were it not for the queen's intercession, I doubt Mortimer would have approved any additional retinue at the present time."

Whilst the older men spoke, Stephen felt his own doubts redouble. He found no appetite for the daryols and simnel cake laid out before them, though he sipped at a cup of ale, staring down at his sandaled feet and wondering if his own views would at any time be canvassed.

"Brother Stephen," (the canon turned suddenly to him, though not to request his opinion) "you are soon to meet our former sovereign. As you'll be aware, we must now call him 'Sir Edward of Caernarvon' at least in public, though I'm sure that in the privacy which your role as confessor will permit with him, you will afford him the dignity to which we consider he is entitled.

"Now, I must counsel you additionally that, even as 'Sir Edward', it seems that certain behaviour and respect is expected by him and permitted by his captors. You should be bareheaded in his presence, and should kneel frequently – once on entering his presence, then again when you have walked to the centre of the room. Then, if beckoned forward, you should kneel three times again at a respectful distance from him. You should not speak unless he speaks first to you. You should bow on each occasion when you do speak, and you should never look away from him or turn your back, and of course should never sit unless he allows it." Stephen nodded, feeling at school again.

"Nevertheless, my son," said Walter, "do not be intimidated unnecessarily by such earthly forms. Remember always that you are his confessor, and therefore have a godly role to perform to which even a king is subject. And in that role you must always speak God's truth. Respect, but do not flatter. Honour, but do not fail to censure where his soul's progress is at stake!"

Stephen had confessed several noblemen in his time, and knew well what was required of confessors by the Order's treatises and penitentiaries. He was more eager to be told the likely duration of his service at Berkeley and whether he would continue as royal confessor should Sir Edward be moved to another prison. Before he could press Brother Walter on these matters, however, a loud knock was heard at the door and a soldier requested their immediate presence at Sir Edward's chamber.

This, it turned out, was back within the gatehouse, where they had earlier seen soldiers on guard. Having mounted a staircase to the second floor, the two Dominicans were ushered into a large room where candle-light played upon elaborate wall paintings. Immediately they bowed their heads, and knelt upon the threshold, leaving Canon Michael outside the door, which was now locked behind them. There were three other men within the chamber, two of whom Stephen had recognised at once to be Sir Thomas of Berkeley and his brother-in-law, Sir John Maltravers. The third was a tall man dressed all in grey, the glint of a gold band about his hair. He was standing by a chimney breast, his back turned, contemplating the large fire in the grate. Sir Thomas stepped forward:

"Let me greet you, Brother Walter. You may stand – Sir Edward allows it. And so may you, Brother Stephen de Birstin, whom, if I might venture to say, the winter has made somewhat thinner than when we last met in Herefordshire!"

"God bless you, my lord," said Stephen, rising to his feet, then hazarding a further bow, whilst remaining where he stood. "I regret to say I have been ill, since I had the honour of speaking with you and with Sir John…And I'm sorry also that it has not so far proved possible to preach before you here in Gloucestershire, as you kindly suggested."

"That is a sad omission," said Sir John stepping forward, a supercilious smile upon his lips, "for how well we remember your vivid words before the trial of Sir Hugh!"

The figure at the chimney breast straightened at the reference, and now turned, a furious look fixed on Berkeley and Maltravers. As well as being tall, the man had a powerful frame, and, though of middle years, his fair hair and beard were thick, curled, and lustrous.

"Is this whom you bring me as a confessor? – one of your own creatures, who had the audacity to preach before the murder of my brother, Despenser!" The voice was light for a man of Edward's size, and it shook with his sudden rage.

"This is no 'creature', Sir Edward, but, as you see, one of the Dominican Order, who are said to enjoy your favour," snapped Sir Thomas. "Brother Walter is the prior of the Order here in Gloucester, and will vouch for what I say." Sir Edward glared at him, then beckoned to Walter. The older man, perspiration glistening on his face, stepped forward, bowed, stepped forward again, and was in the process of bowing a third time, when Sir Edward exclaimed:

"Speak, man. For God's sake, speak!" and strode towards him. "I know you for an honest man, Brother Walter. Tell me whether this monk is one whom the Order indeed approves, and not one of Mortimer's spies. Upon your faith, I require it!"

"God's grace be upon you, my lord," began Walter. "This young friar most respectfully is proposed by the Order itself to be your confessor. He is of noble family, the de Birstins holding lands near Tewkesbury. He has studied six years at the University, and, since his return to us, the priory has benefited greatly from his scholarship, as well as from his skill as a preacher and orator. He indeed has the blessing and approval of the Order's commissioners, and the queen has agreed his appointment."

"Worse and worse! So that vixen is involved in this! I'll not have him near me! Let him leave now!"

"Sir Edward, please! Such tantrums do not become you!" The words were spoken with force and venom by Sir John. "This is Brother Stephen. He is no spy or lackey, but a fine priest and scholar. He will be your confessor, for you have no say in the matter!"

"Then I will not confess!"

"Then your soul will be damned for all eternity, if it is not so already!" said Sir John.

Sir Edward turned on his heel and, had he not been a prisoner, he would no doubt have stormed from the chamber, but he could do no more than stride back towards the fireplace, where he stood with his back to them. Then his shoulders, to Stephen's surprise, started to shake as he surrendered to a fit of sobbing.

"Brother Stephen," said Lord Berkeley, "I do not think we need detain you longer this evening. Rest assured, you are to be Sir Edward's confessor, and you will accompany our party when we leave for my estates in the morning. Regrettably, in your new role you will not enjoy the state and attendance of your predecessors, for these are changed and straightened times! Canon Michael will now show you to the dormitory where a bed has been provided.

"Brother Walter, we are grateful to you and to your order. God bless you and all at your priory till we meet again."

Sir John had crossed to the doorway and held it open for the two monks to depart. Neither was sure if they should remain facing Sir Edward as they left, but, since it was his back which remained turned towards them, and since it appeared no such niceties were being observed by the two lords, they sidled out to where Canon Michael was waiting, a look of consternation on his face. It was clear he had heard through the door all that had just been uttered.

As they descended the staircase to the ground-floor level, and were out of earshot of those on guard, Canon Michael whispered that all was in God's hands now. Stephen expected him to say more, but all three then lapsed into silence. Outside the gatehouse, Stephen took leave of Walter, kissing his ring, and then being kissed on both cheeks by the older man. Again no words were spoken, and Stephen sensed from Walter's expression a fear that already their plans were unravelling.

PART THREE: BERKELEY

Chapter 12

On the Monday of Holy Week Stephen spent many hours, not walking southwards from the town armed with his staff as he had anticipated, but in a three horse carriage pulled along behind Berkeley's mounted retainers. Due to the Dominican prohibition against riding a horse, Maltravers had decided this was the only means by which Stephen could make the journey, whilst keeping pace with the rest of the party. Once they had left Llanthony, they went by way of Sevarnstrete to join Brisstowes Hye Wey south of the town walls, and then followed the ancient road as it ran through the flat lands of the Severn Valley, before meandering away from the great river and towards the steep Cotswold escarpment.

Stephen was not alone in the carriage, for he had to share it with Odo de Bodrugan, one of Berkeley's retainers. Odo was suffering from a fever, and for much of that day vomited and fouled himself and then cried out in Cornish, or bellowed obscenities in the common speech. To calm his agitation at this, as well as to drown his fears over what the next few days would bring, Stephen recited the prayers and meditations of his rosary, giving the fullest form he knew to its various decades and mysteries.

This led him to reflect again on the Virgin's appearance to Dominic more than one hundred years before, when, accompanied by three queens and fifty maidens, She had explained the use of the rosary. She had then pressed milk from Her breasts for Dominic to drink. (Stephen pictured the Virgin's statue at St Mary de Crypt, and wondered if he would ever honour Her there again.) As the wagon swayed and jolted over the rutted highway, he made a solemn promise: if nothing else, at least to use his time at Berkeley to rededicate his life to Mary, for he had felt himself estranged from Her, almost adrift, the more so since Barelonde; perhaps, if he was honest, ever since his return from Hereford.

When Stephen wearied of his beads and recitations, he could not bring himself to peer through the awning of the carriage and be diverted by the rich farmland of the vale with its many groves of fruit trees. Instead, he kept his eyes either closed or fixed on the bucking heaving floor of the carriage, whilst he suffused his mind with images of the Nativity, of the Passion and of the Cross, and most of all of

Christ's Wounds, whose severed folds he imagined himself fingering in joyful ecstasy, as if he were St Thomas the Apostle. Then Hugh came to mind, and he retreated once more to the sanctuary of formal prayer.

*

Towards evening the party at last arrived at Berkeley Castle, and made its weary way through the outer bailey, under the main gatehouse, and on into the inner bailey at the castle's heart. There Lord Berkeley's horsemen dismounted, and servants appeared, some to uncouple the horses from the carriage in which Stephen had been travelling, others to do what they could for the now unconscious Odo. One of them explained to Stephen where he would find the room allocated to him, but that there was no time to inspect it then and there, for all were bidden to attend the great hall where supper was about to be served. (At this point he saw nothing of Sir Edward, though he later discovered that on arrival the former king had been bundled off to his quarters, which were up a narrow flight of stairs which ran from the floor of the inner bailey up to the first storey of the keep.)

Inside the great hall Stephen found he was to be seated, according to the order of precedence, amongst the more senior retainers and officials, well removed from the castle's functionaries and menials. Flattered by this at first, he would find over the days which followed that the course and hearty exchanges in which these men indulged, and which reverberated round him as he attempted to eat in silence, were both an embarrassment and an irritation. Many times he would long for the peacefulness of mealtimes at Blackfriars, where – in accordance with the Order's rule – the only sounds to be heard had been those of knives on trenchers, and of holy texts being read aloud to divert attention from the sensual pleasure of food and drink. Later, though, he would realise that this heady banter at least provided him with some feeling of connection, through gossip about the castle, with its other occupants, and, through rumour, with events beyond its walls.

As to the food provided on this day of arrival and then subsequently, the restricted diet of Holy Week in fact suited him well enough, being for the most part bread, ale and fish. After Easter, though, he would find that only on formal fish days could he eat his fill, no concessions being made by the kitchen to the dietary scruples

88

of just one Dominican. Fish days themselves were something of a miracle, for not only did the castle benefit from plenteous supplies of lampreys, eels, plaice, stouks and flounders brought in on the spring tides of the nearby estuary, but it was well provided too with both salt and freshwater fish from large stew ponds constructed in the castle grounds by Lord Berkeley and his predecessors.

After the meal that first evening, much recovered from the discomfort of his journey, Stephen went in search of his new accommodation. He had expected to be housed quite close to the royal prisoner, but instead found he had been provided with a small chamber in the eastern range of the inner bailey, in fact facing the keep and close to the kitchens. Intoxicating cooking smells pervaded that part of the castle, and it occurred to him that this might serve him well, when later he undertook fasts, for it provided a ready means of self mortification.

As to the room's appearance, it was small and unadorned, just as Stephen would have wished. It had the smallest loop hole for a window, and through this, when the shutter was opened, he would in due course discover a narrow view out over the valley to the green wooded slopes around Dursley and Stinchcombe. On the opposite side of the room set in the rough stone wall was a small fire-place, though from the absence of any kindling it appeared that by this time of year the lighting of fires for warmth was already viewed as an extravagance.

The largest piece of furniture in the room was a wooden bed-frame. It was strung with taut ropes supporting a thick mattress, which Stephen found to his amazement contained feathers, rather than the straw to which he had always been accustomed, and on this were laid sheets of linen, rather than of wool. To the frame was affixed a candle in a small holder. This provided the sole means of light, other than that which filtered through the loop hole. There was also a rail attached to the other side of the bed-frame on which clothes could be hung, though, since Stephen had no garments other than those he was wearing, and the spare undergarment in his satchel, and since the rules of the Order required him to sleep in his habit, this was superfluous to him.

The only other furnishing was a rug and a small cupboard, which may have been intended for linens, but neither did Stephen possess any of these. It did have a lock, however, the key to which had been left for him, and it occurred to him straight away that this might prove useful as a store for the few books and manuscripts he had brought with him, together with any papers of a more sensitive nature received in due course from Brother Walter.

Not far from the door to the room he found the nearest garderobe, which again hinted at a luxury to which he was unused. The stone blocks of its seat – so mortifying on a winter's morning – were boarded over and then covered with a soft green cloth. A green cushion was placed in the aperture to prevent malodorous drafts when the facility was not in use.

*

On that first evening at Berkeley, having arranged his mnimal possessions, and having observed Vespers and Compline, Stephen retired to bed and slept soundly – for a while forgetful of his impending tasks at the castle, both official and unofficial. The bed seemed extraordinarily comfortable in the absence both of rough straw and the watchful form of Brother James.

In the morning, though, any feelings of having rested soon evaporated before a returning panic at the uncertainties ahead, and a conviction of his own unworthiness to deal with them. He at once pitched the feather mattress off the bed, leant it against the wall, and put in its place the thin rug of blue tapestry which had so far lain upon the floor. He also folded the linen sheets and placed them within the small cupboard. Not even in the infirmary had his flesh been so cosseted as it had been the previous night, and he feared that such luxury would encourage the sin of Sloth, rather than the fortitude which his mission would require.

But how, now that he had arrived in Berkeley, was his mission to begin? As that first day progressed, no one summoned him, no one gave him any instruction, nor in any way seemed to heed his existence; and so matters continued during two long days. He kept the church hours, told his rosary beads, tried not to let his mind be sucked back into the mire of Barelonde, and went to the great hall for his dinner and supper. Otherwise, though, he was bereft of purpose, having no access to Sir Edward, nor even to Lord Berkeley's library, where in other circumstances he might have recommenced his studies.

On the morning of Maunday Thursday, however, a servant brought a message that Lord Berkeley and Sir John awaited him at the inner gatehouse. Breathless after three flights of steps, he was ushered into a large chamber above the portcullis to find the two lords seated on the far side of a large oak table. They did not invite him to take the stool which stood between the table and the door. Neither did they give him formal greeting.

"I hope your lodgings are adequate, Brother Stephen," said Lord Berkeley, leaning back upon his chair.

"God bless you and give you good day, my lords...Indeed they are," Stephen replied. Lord Berkeley stood up and sauntered to Stephen's side of the table, where he perched on the table's edge, very close to where Stephen was standing.

"Brother Stephen, we must talk of your duties here at the castle. I know I need not stress what is commonly known: that Sir Edward, though our former king, has been judged unfit to rule, for his many crimes and other ill deeds committed against the country and against his former office. He is an enemy to the realm, Brother Stephen, and that means that, whatever your function here, he is your enemy too.

"He is to be kept imprisoned where he may create no further mischief, and where other evil-doers may make no contact with him. I myself and Sir John Maltravers here have been entrusted by the queen and Lord Mortimer with the task of keeping him secure as long as both he and we shall live. It is a task we undertake joyfully, and one we shall execute with utmost rigour!" Berkeley's expression had become fierce, almost challenging, but he now attempted a smile, as he inclined his head even closer towards the friar.

"We think well of you, Brother Stephen, and we are pleased you have been chosen to be Sir Edward's confessor. You are a fine preacher, and one of whom your order expects great things...But we are not blind to the closeness there has always been between that order and Sir Edward; neither is the queen, whose kind heart has approved of your appointment! That closeness is a matter of rejoicing to us, if it be a means to secure eternal life for Sir Edward's soul. It would be a matter of profound concern, however, if it were abused by Sir Edward or any other person as a means even to contemplate securing his liberty! I trust you get my drift, friar." Stephen felt his face reddening, uncertain if or how he should reply.

"Please be aware. Brother Stephen," Sir John intervened, as he now also approached round the other end of the table, "that we have no suspicion of you personally, or indeed of your prior, Brother Walter; but others – perhaps also from within your order – may seek to exploit your closeness to Sir Edward and thus render more difficult our own responsibilities!"

"We have certain requirements, therefore, as to the manner in which you will undertake your duties," said Berkeley, placing a large mailed fist on Stephen's shoulder. "We of course have no wish to pry into any matter of which you shall learn arising purely out of Sir Edward's confessions to you – and we fancy Sir Edward has many long hours of ill-doing to recount!" Berkeley gave an ironic smile first at his brother-in-law, then at Stephen, but then tightened his grip on Stephen's shoulder.

"But should any other person, whether from within the castle or from without, address any word by mouth or in writing to you pertaining to Sir Edward, we require you to notify us – on pain of imprisonment by the Church, every bit as absolute as that of Sir Edward, should you fail us!" After a pause, Lord Berkeley released his grasp, and in silence returned to the opposite side of the table, where he sat down. His grim expression relaxed and was rearranged into a smile.

"Sir John will now explain to you the conditions which will apply whilst you remain confessor to the former king."

Maltravers' voice was quiet, but intent, as he fixed Stephen with his small squinting eyes. From such close quarters, Stephen could not help noticing that Sir John's breath had at first a sweetness to it, as if he had been chewing spices, but that this failed to mask an underlying sourness. He wondered if this indicated some deep-seated symptom of decay, either of the body or soul.

"Lord Berkeley and I have many other duties, apart from that of guarding Sir Edward. Indeed, my brother-in-law will depart on a tour of his outlying estates in only ten days' time. We will therefore take it in turns month by month to be here at the castle. And you will be answerable to whichever of us is resident here for the time being.

"Whilst we do not forbid you to speak to anyone other than Sir Edward and ourselves, we must restrict your intercourse to those who form part of Lord Berkeley's retinue and household. In particular, you shall exchange no words with any visitor to the castle or any other outsider. Neither shall you receive any written materials from beyond the castle walls.

"Brother Walter has requested that you receive manuscripts and books sent to you from the priory, but we have recently refused that request. You may study only those documents that you will find in my lord's library. A key will be supplied to you. There are, you will discover, many miraculous works of learning there, which we are sure will occupy your attention when you are not tending to the spiritual needs of the prisoner or making your own observances."

"But my lords," Stephen managed to interject, "my studies are specific. I am engaged in translations of certain works of the ancients pertinent to the writings of the blessed St Thomas Aquinas, I..."

"You will read and translate such books as we have available, Brother Stephen," said Lord Berkeley, any pretence at good humour now dispelled.

"Of course, my lords," said Stephen. "Of course, my lords. I had no wish to appear impertinent!"

"All is well then, Brother Stephen," said Maltravers, returning to the far side of the table. "Do you have other questions for us, or would you like now to commence your studies?"

Stephen felt that the most obvious questions of all had somehow been overlooked:

"Whilst I would, of course, be most pleased to do so, Sir John, and am most grateful for the opportunity of perusing the contents of your library, Sir Thomas, might I enquire when I am to begin my ministry to Sir Edward? Is he indeed reconciled to the idea that it is I who should be his confessor. He seemed most unhappy when the suggestion was made at our interview last Sunday?"

Lord Berkeley glanced at Sir John with what amounted to a smirk, and said:

"You will find, Brother Stephen, that Sir Edward is a man of many moods and passions, some of them more violent and extreme than, one might say, is fitting for a gentleman! He took against you, it's true, when he heard you had preached before the trial and execution of Despenser. Such foolish irrationality is typical of the man. But, never fear! We shall bring him round! He has had no visitor other than one man-servant since he arrived here, and that servant is under the strictest instructions not to utter a single syllable in the prisoner's presence! Let Sir Edward stew for a few more days. When he can no longer bear his own company, we'll send you to him. Then, no doubt, he'll beg you to recount how Despenser bellowed like a stuck pig when they chopped off his cock!" Both lords sniggered before Berkeley continued:

"Let's say after Easter, Brother Stephen. We'll see if his anger has softened by then...Oh, and when you do begin your ministry to him, Brother Stephen, we will confine your visits to the hour between Nones and supper. – I would suggest the morning, but the man is an incurable sluggard, and so the mid-afternoon seems to us to be most appropriate! Let the evils of Sloth be one of your first homilies to him!" Before Stephen could say anything in reply, Maltravers had intervened again:

"And so, Brother Stephen, you have several more days in which to accustom yourself to life in the castle; that is, before you can begin wrestling with the soul of Sir Edward. You will find it a black soul, friar, for he is not simply a fool and an incompetent, but a murderer too, and a sodomite! I wish you well in your enterprise!"

With that he smiled indicating the door, and Stephen bowed and hurried out, making for his own chamber, where he lay in some discomfort upon the bare rug and bed frame, unable to imagine how now any good could come from his stay at Berkeley.

*

Stephen was grateful in the succeeding days for the duties which Easter itself imposed, for even such an observant monk as he found it difficult to spend every waking hour in private prayer and contemplation. There were periods when, but for the requirements of the great festival, he might have lain in his chamber consumed with worry – over his volatile royal charge, over the impossibility of now achieving anything planned by Brother Walter and Canon Michael, but also over the more general malaise which seemed to afflict him and whereby he sensed a slow leaching away of that holiness with which his life at Blackfriars had been imbued before he first set out for Hereford. As it was, he managed to bury most of these anxieties amongst the prayers and vigils of Good Friday and Easter Day, which he was allowed with others in the household to attend in the Church of St Mary just outside the castle walls.

94

It was from this attendance that Stephen discovered that Lord Berkeley's own religious observance was for the most part confined to this building, which was the parish church of the village, but also the mausoleum of his forebears and the site of his family's chantry. It was the parish priest who served as confessor both to the lord and to his family, and it emerged in consequence that the Berkeleys made scant use of the small chapel of St John in the north-east bastion of the castle keep. There seemed no reason, therefore – and Sir John was to confirm this – that Stephen should not use that chapel for his own purposes: for prayer and for saying mass each day, undisturbed by any of the castle's other occupants. It was, Sir John explained, a chapel also intended for use by Sir Edward, albeit under guard; but never, from the day he arrived at the castle, was Stephen aware that Sir Edward took any advantage of this concession.

Following their meeting, Sir John also assisted Stephen by supplying the key to Lord Berkeley's library, and for a few hours over the two days following Easter Stephen made his first acquaintance with its contents. It indeed held volumes and manuscripts of great interest, though nothing of any direct relevance to the studies he had been undertaking at the priory. There were a number of illuminated gospels, a bestiary, and other works of surprising provenance. He found versions of Ovid and Virgil in Latin, and, with at least a modicum of enthusiasm, resolved to prepare a translation of the latter's Eclogues.

When not studying, praying, or saying mass (which he did daily), or lying on his bed in varying states of perturbation, Stephen also began spending time up on the battlements, both of the inner bailey gate-house and of the eastern range, glad to feel the fresh breezes and mild sun of April on his face. Very soon he familiarised himself with the surrounding landscape: the meadows and marshland to the south and towards the river, Michaelwood beyond (where it appeared Lord Berkeley spent much of his time hunting), and then the lands of the Berkeley Harness stretching from Berkeley itself east to Wootton and the parks and woodlands of the Cotswold Hills (also part of the lord's estates). It was only the nearby village of Berkeley of which he could see little. It was constructed, like the castle, on a slight rise above the Severn plain, but from wherever Stephen stood on the battlements it was concealed behind the castle's bulk and behind dense trees which now began to come into leaf.

As he peered northwards, trying to make out any spires and towers which might belong to Gloucester, flocks of starlings and seagulls from the estuary were his only company. They were the only ones too to see the tears drawn across his cheeks by the buffeting of the wind and by a sudden surge of loneliness.

Chapter 13

When Stephen gazed from the battlements, not outwards to the surrounding landscape, but down into the inner and outer baileys, he saw a world of bustle and activity – a world which intrigued and fascinated him, but of which as yet he felt no part. He was still a visitor from another life.

On the Tuesday after Easter he saw Lord Berkeley, his knights and esquires preparing to ride out to hunt at Michaelwood. From the battlements he watched as they gathered before the castle gate with their coursers and hunting dogs, heard how the walls echoed with the dogs' incessant baying, as if the scent of blood already tingled in their moistening nostrils. He observed too that the huntsmen had birds of prey with them: lanners, sakers, and a peregrine, and that there was a falcon on the wrist of Lord Berkeley himself. Their stillness amidst the turmoil of preparation made these hooded birds seem more menacing than the hounds; and later, when he glimpsed the climax of the chase from afar, he sensed with a shudder the rip of flesh between talons, the clash of beak on bone.

Whenever then or later the huntsmen were in the field, Stephen was surprised to note that perhaps as many as one hundred and fifty of Lord Berkeley's other retainers would remain within the castle, and these to Stephen were of equal interest. He watched as they went about their lord's daily business – dealing with the arrival of produce from the fields, transacting purchases with visitors to the castle, making or mending armour of both plate and mail. From his eyrie they resembled so many insects scuttling here and there about the castle precincts, clad in the red and silver of Lord Berkeley's colours, the edges of their garments embellished with rabbit or with silver stoat fur.

During his early trips to the battlements Stephen also noted that during the daytimes there were no women to be seen amongst the occupants of the castle, other than one washerwoman, whose vast and forbidding form often hauled buckets of water and large laundry baskets in the vicinity of the kitchens. Of Lord Berkeley's wife, Lady Margaret (the daughter of Lord Mortimer), and of their own daughters, he saw nothing, except at services in the nearby church, and in the great hall at suppertime. He imagined that they must spend their daytimes within the state rooms of the castle's west range, where their vanities remained concealed, and they were a danger to none other than themselves. He could not forget how on Easter Sunday their low neck-lines and bared shoulders had been visible beneath their mantles – even whilst they had prayed at the ornate shrine to St Mary herself, oblivious of the holy paradigm before them.

*

It was whilst he was on his way up to the gatehouse battlement the day following the Easter hunt, that Henry de Rockhill, Lord Berkeley's steward, at last brought him word that his presence at Sir Edward's chamber was required, and that he was to attend that very afternoon. The guards had been instructed to admit him one hour before supper on this and all subsequent days. He should take with him his crucifix and any relics which he wished to employ; and he should stay with Sir Edward no longer than the ringing of the supper bell.

Though Lord Berkeley had told him his ministry would begin after Easter, Stephen had assumed he might enjoy at least a few more days' grace before his formal duties began, and this sudden summons caused his guts to churn and his forehead to perspire, despite the cool touch of the breeze. He hurried back to his room, where he prayed for guidance from the Virgin, rocking back and forth as he knelt by his bed, striving to conjure Her beloved image as it appeared in the chancel at Blackfriars. She smiled back at him across the miles, silent and whimsical; but today no more than paint and alabaster.

How was he to counsel – how even address – such a one as Sir Edward, who, from all he had heard and from what little he had seen, was both difficult and arrogant: not a man to take advice, let alone censure, given by a mere priest, even though in the name of God Almighty? As he continued to kneel, he pressed his body hard against the wooden bed-frame, trying to drive away the anxiety which cramped his stomach; but it would not ease, and he soon found himself rushing to the garderobe, snatching away the velvet cushion from the stinking aperture before his bowels spilled their contents down into the gaping void and out into the moat far below, where gulls screeched and wheeled about on the freedom of the breeze.

Later, when his guts were spent and he was back in his room, he slumped upon his bed, devoid of prayer, devoid almost of thought, his mind dulled to all but those sounds of the midday dinner in the great hall and of the other rituals which marked the passage of the castle's day. He could not bring himself to imagine even speaking to his charge – one who was a king in all but name, whom most men still feared despite his fall, and for whom many held a venomous hatred.

When the thin slant of light from his window reached the metal latch on the door, he knew, however, that he could no longer delay departure, for it had now to be mid-afternoon. He hauled his body from the bed, picked up his crucifix, and, almost in a daze, made his way down to the inner bailey and across to the keep. A soldier nodded to him and unlocked the gateway to the narrow staircase which mounted to the first floor.

Having climbed up, he found himself on a small stone platform enclosed by high battlements. Two more soldiers were positioned there, one behind him beside the head of the stairs, the other at the far end of the platform guarding a locked door in the wall of the keep. It was clear they were aware who he was and the nature of his mission, and the second fellow unlocked and then relocked the door behind them after they entered, led him by a short corridor to a larger and mainly empty room, and then on to another door, which had again to be unlocked, and across which three hefty bolts had also to be drawn back.

"This is Sir Edward's cell," said the soldier. "I'll return at the supper bell. If you require me before then, friar, you have only to shout. But shout loudly – the walls are thick!" With that he opened the door, gestured to Stephen to enter, and at once secured the lock and bolts behind him.

The door was low and Stephen ducked his head just as he re-called the need to bow and to kneel on entry to the ex-king's presence. Hesitating, he missed his footing on the three steep steps down to the floor of the chamber, and he found himself sprawling on cold rough flagstones, the more discomfited by the peals of laughter which now filled his ears. As he struggled to his feet, he faced a table, and beside it Sir Edward almost bent double in mirth.

"Oh, friar, what an entry to the royal presence! You looked such a fool!...I thank you, friar, for a moment of joy. They've been scarce of late!" Then he started to laugh again, and could not stop himself till tears trickled down his cheeks, and he had to wipe them away on the sleeve of his tunic of dark blue velvet. Stephen almost felt obliged to laugh too, but he had grazed his shin and stubbed his toe, and was trying to master the pain.

"And so my new confessor arrives!" said Sir Edward, still chuckling and wiping his eyes. "I recall you to be Brother Stephen: the man who preached to the crowd before they butchered Sir Hugh le Despenser..." These words were spoken in a neutral tone, with none of the hostility directed at Stephen ten days before. "Still, come and sit with me at the table...unless, of course, you've any other turns to make me laugh! Do you juggle, perhaps?" He dissolved in chuckles again. "I cannot reward you properly as I did my cook, Maurice. Last Autumn he made the whole court almost die of laughter when he kept falling off his horse!...How long ago that seems now...And what a time it is since I could properly reward anyone!..." By now they were both seated on stools either side of the small rectangular table, which, along with a bed, two stools, a mirror, and a large trunk, provided the only furnishing of the room. Sir Edward was at last calmer, and his laughter subsided, though his face was still wreathed in smiles.

"My lord, it's true, I did indeed preach at Hereford, but..." began Stephen.

"None of that for now," said Sir Edward. "You shall tell me every detail when I command it...and, rest assured, I will do...but I shall bear no grudge. I'm sure you did only as your duty dictated. But tell me firstly of yourself. The confessor shall confess before anything else!"

So smiling and encouraging was Edward's countenance, and so punctured the bladder of Stephen's anxieties after to his tumble, that soon he found himself telling most of his life's history: his birth at the family manor near Tewkesbury and his mother's immediate death, his dim memories of a childhood amongst the ponds and willows of the river valley, his father's passing whilst he was still very young, his enrolment in the Order at the age of seven, and later his years at the Dominicans' hall in Oxford, where he had studied theology, arts and science with the magister, Nicholas Trivet. There was more, of course, that he did not say, but even then his tale took many minutes to unfold. As he talked, Sir Edward paid him every attention and made no interruption – other than to comment that he too had lost his mother when he had been a mere six years old.

The more he spoke, the more Stephen felt himself relaxing, and he became almost surprised at his own garrulity. He was not so immersed in his own story, though, that he failed to register more concerning Edward and his appearance than he had during their previous brief interview. He noticed how the thick fair hair was parted in the middle and fell to the level of the shoulders. It was kept in place by a circlet of pure gold about his brows. There were also rings on Sir Edward's fingers. One bore a ruby – a protection against poison. Others appeared to be encrusted with sapphires, which Stephen knew protected the wearer from madness and illness.

Even seated, Stephen was aware of how much taller Sir Edward was compared with himself, and how strong and sturdy he was in build. It remained a surprise, therefore, when Sir Edward spoke, that his voice was light and seemed much younger than his forty or so years.

"You please me, Brother Stephen…," he now interposed, "which is as well, since it seems you're to be the only person I'm allowed to speak to at any length!...I welcome you, as I have done your predecessors. The Order of Preachers has served me well in the past, Stephen, and all my confessors have been Dominicans...I hope you will not be my last!...But let's not be too dismal!...I will confess to you for my soul's health – and there is much I wish to confess!...

"And let's not talk solely of spiritual matters, but of other things, too. You must tell me of your scholarship, for I love books. I had in my library at King's Langley a history of the English kings written in Latin and a biography of St Edward the Confessor in French, besides many books of romance…And I love music and minstrelsy. I used to have an orchestra of brass with a drummer and a harpist. Could you not sing to me sometimes?…"

Stephen could hardly believe the way in which Sir Edward was addressing him. It was as though they were somehow equals, and this both flattered and alarmed him, for he had heard how mercurial Sir Edward could be, and kept fearing that the radiance of the ex-king's smiles would dissolve into some sudden rage in which he would be accused of being over familiar.

"My lord," began Stephen, "as you know, my purpose here is to hear your confession and to counsel you how best you may atone for your sins in this life, so that you may avoid Hell and may prepare yourself for time in Purgatory." A slight frown interrupted Edward's smiles. "But when time allows, my lord, most surely we may discuss works of learning and of the arts...If I were to sing, though, you would only hear the plain chant of our chapel, which is all the music I know!"

"Then maybe I'll sing for you...and you shall dance..."

"My lord, I..."

"Yes, you shall dance, Brother Stephen. You shall dance. Do you know that once I had Bernard the Fool and fifty-four nude males dance before me at Pontoise?" Stephen could no longer tell if Sir Edward was being serious. His manner had become mischievous, and he began pacing up and down, as he described first one then another of the pastimes he claimed to love, including some which Stephen felt more than a little lewd.

"Are these matters which you wish to confess to me, my lord?" Stephen ventured. "If so, I will gladly take your confession now." Edward stopped pacing, and, as he fixed Stephen with an expressionless stare, his face began to flush red and his lower lip to tremble.

"Oh, if I were to confess, Brother Stephen...if I were to confess!...You'd hear such a tale of sin that the hair round your precious little tonsure would turn grey!...Oh yes, I danced and sang with my friends late into the night. And, yes, we loved dicing and jesters, loved boating, and rowing, even skating when the ponds were frozen!...All this wickedness my enemies accuse me of, I freely confess, my sweet little father!...And, do you know, friar, I also confess that which they – the Mortimers, the Orletons, the Berkeleys and all that crew – despise me for even more: that I was loyal to my friends, that I rewarded those who served me well, made earls of them! What degeneracy, what a betrayal of my nobility!...Oh, and I confess, Stephen...worse and worse!...that once in a while I kept company with the lower orders! – spoke to artisans and journeymen, tried to learn about hedging, ditching and other country pursuits on my estates! Oh, what a revolution was there! What a sacrifice of God's order!...These great great sins I am guilty of, Stephen. This gross depravity, I confess!..."

Sir Edward was now leaning down towards him, almost shouting in his face. Stephen felt himself craning his head backwards.

"My lord, I cannot believe these are matters which have brought you to your present state...or that they are all matters you wish to confess to me. Immodesty is a sin, certainly, dicing and gambling too may indicate...but if you pray for forgiveness, do penance, as I shall command..." But it seemed Sir Edward was no longer listening. He had thrown himself on his bed, and his shoulders shook with sobs, as they had done at Llanthony. Then before Stephen could continue, Edward sprang to his feet and advanced on him again, though this time his words were quiet, almost menacing:

"Tell me, Brother Stephen, do you believe in the holy balm? Do you believe that once consecrated with God's holy oil, a king can ever be other than a king? Can it be washed away by parliaments? Can it be washed away with tears?"

"No, I do not believe it may, my lord...and nor do others in my order...Hence we still acknowledge you as our king...But even a king must confess, and must confess, not to the tittle tattle that others complain of, but to true sins – both venial and grave – matters of substance, those matters for which the great lords and the parliament have sought to depose you..." But again Sir Edward had ceased listening:

"Oh, Stephen, I thank you...you acknowledge me as your king, you say...still!" Edward's tears began to run afresh. "Thank you, Stephen, thank you. God bless the Order of Preachers!...Such words of comfort after so many months!...Stephen, as you are my subject, and shall be my confessor, maybe you will also be my friend...And, as I am your king, I will make a king's confession, which shall be daily, which shall be weighty, and shall be given with all honesty, humility and seriousness as to the circumstances of my life and of my reign..." At that moment there came a sharp rapping on the door, and Stephen heard the sounds of bolts sliding back and the turn of a key.

"It's supper time, Brother Stephen," said the soldier, poking his head under the low arch of the door. "You must leave the prisoner to his prayers now!"

Stephen was unsure whether he felt more relief or more frustration that their interview was being cut short, but he rose to his feet. He was also uncertain quite how he should excuse himself from Sir Edward's presence. In the end he inclined his head a little, then sped past both king and soldier, through the outer room and corridor, out on to the platform and down the stairs, where at the bottom he gave the door a loud and urgent rattle before making his escape into the inner bailey and the cool shadows of late afternoon.

Chapter 14

Stephen had little time to loiter in the bailey pondering the strangeness of his encounter, for his presence was expected at supper. Besides, he had missed dinner earlier in the day, and now felt hungry. As he hurried along the short passage leading to the great hall, he registered, even more, a lightness – almost a sense of joy, which had less to do with the words which had passed between himself and Edward, than with the latter's smile, his welcome, his apparent acceptance of Stephen as his confessor, if not his "friend". He wondered, though, how one could truly be a friend and a confessor at one and the same time.

Once seated for the meal, he was at first enticed by the smell of lampreys served in a rich spiced sauce made of their own blood and liver. But, as he waited for his table to be served, he began to reflect on the bizarre ebb and flow of Edward's moods and emotions. His doubts and uncertainties began to return, and the same queasiness he had felt earlier in the day, swelled and gurgled within him. Would not Edward once more rage and weep, when the tale of Despenser's end could no longer be delayed?

When at last the food was served, Stephen found he could eat little more than a few mouthfuls of bread and a handful of dried fruits, washed down with a flagon of ale. As he nibbled, he rehearsed and re-rehearsed the abrupt chops and changes in Edward's conversation, and pictured that tall muscular form pacing back and forth, at times smiling and enthused, at times tense and angry. So absorbed was he that he paid little attention to the swirl of conversation around him, which for the most part concerned the new campaign against the Scots, but later moved on to the castle and its business, including the works of rebuilding recently commissioned and announced by Sir Thomas. One strident voice became more and more intrusive, until he found himself obliged to listen. Its owner was the now recovered Odo de Bodrugan, who seemed well informed as to the lord's intentions, and – though he struggled with the common speech and spoke no French at all – the Cornishman pressed his opinion as to the disruption the castle would suffer, and in particular how much noise and dust would affect the eastern range, including the kitchens and the great hall – to the detriment of all their stomachs.

Though Stephen had no idea why it was, Odo had taken a dislike to him since their day confined together in Lord Berkeley's wagon, and, whilst Odo knew that Stephen could not join in mealtime banter, he now announced with some glee that those who had chambers near the kitchens could no longer spend hours in worthless study and contemplation – once walls began to tumble, blocks to be smashed, and once the workmen's blasphemies and swearing filled the air!

Later, when Stephen had escaped the boorishness of the table, and had taken the stair to the Chapel of St John, he sought refuge in the peace and certainty of the mass, and in the calming presence of the small wooden Madonna which occupied a niche opposite the altar. When earlier he had tried to summon the Madonna's image as She appeared at Blackfriars, She had graced him with Her face, but not Her voice. Now, as he knelt before this simple icon, rough-hewn as it was, he felt Her presence, as if it lived in the rings and knots of the wood itself, unblemished by the gilt or paint of any artist's hand. He felt too the blessing of Her words – for the words had to be Hers – which now ran through his head telling him to rejoice that the king's enmity had been overcome, and also that Edward had promised he would confess in full, daily and in all seriousness – as befitted a king. What better start could there have been for his ministry? Stephen gave thanks to the Virgin, said three "Hail Marys", and vowed to venerate this small image every day he remained at Berkeley.

Back in his chamber, as he tried to sleep on the unforgiving lumpiness of the tapestry-covered bed-frame, he counted himself doubly blessed: both by the glow of the Virgin's grace, which was now restored to him, and also by the warmth of Edward's favour, which was new and unanticipated.

But then a cool breeze of doubt made him wonder if his reference to the Order's loyalty had been unwise, even though it had led to Edward's promise to confess. Might it not lead their discussions to his own covert mission and the Order's plans for a rescue? – matters which, given the constraints imposed by Berkeley and Maltravers, it might be better never to mention at all.

It was some hours before he lost himself to sleep.

*

When Stephen arrived at Edward's cell the following afternoon, he negotiated the downward steps with greater poise, and was about to commence the formalities of greeting, as explained by Canon Michael, when Edward strode up to him, seized his arm and motioned him once more to sit at the table.

"Come, come, our time together is too short for you to waste it in bowing and scraping, Brother Stephen! Praise be you acknowledge me as your king, but you would do me the greatest service by refraining from such fripperies!" Edward smiled as he said this, and seemed calmer, more composed than at either of their previous meetings. He sat opposite Stephen and now offered him a tumbler of wine from a leather pitcher placed on the table and a piece of chicken from the half-devoured contents of his dinner platter.

"Brother Stephen, I told you I would require you to tell the story of Despenser's death; and that you shall do before long – but only when I sanction it. As it is, I have heard too many falsehoods from those who played a part in it, and were pleased to dip their hands in his precious blood! I need to hear the truth from someone who is less partial – from one who may, I fancy, have shed a tear for his brutal murder!

"But first, Stephen, first, I concede it is so many months since I have been shriven...and of course I know that to be your main purpose here...So many evils have befallen me, so many trials – and I in turn have made so many errors, been guilty of so many sins – that I hardly know which of them is the most grievous and which I must confess to first! All I can do, I think, is to tell you no more nor less than the history of my life from that time a little after St Matthew's Day and a little before last Michaelmas when my calamities began. Will you then hear what I have to confess?"

Edward's tone was measured, his words so unlike any he had uttered previously in Stephen's hearing, that the friar was nonplussed. At once he suspected he was about to hear a speech honed and practised over many weeks of solitude, a speech tailored for just such a day as this. He knew he should distrust any sinner's utterance which seemed to have been rehearsed, for – as the penitentiaries told him – a soul afflicted with evil could hide itself in a polished phrase. If he allowed Edward simply to narrate the story of his life over the past year, there was also the risk that his confession, such as it was, might be fragmented, perhaps devious, and difficult for him either to piece together or to absolve. However, given Edward's promise the previous day to confess in full, he decided for now to accept what was being offered. Perhaps later he might pick over the entrails of its honesty and consider how best to bring Edward to true contrition.

"I will indeed hear your confession, my lord," he replied. "May God bless you and keep you, and cause you fully to open up your heart to His servant here before you."

There was a slight pause, whilst Edward crossed himself and bowed his head. Stephen wondered if he should himself stand, to preserve the formal status between penitent and priest as required by the Church, but before he could do so Edward had already begun to tell of the days before Michaelmas when, for the first time in his long reign, he had dared hope Fortune's Wheel had turned in his favour. With Hugh's help, his enemies had been vanquished, the treasury was full, the Scots had at least been kept at bay, and, with a long warm summer promising a plentiful harvest, there was peace and general happiness in the realm. Yet, in place of a golden autumn of contentment, there had come first portentous storms and tempests, and then, when they had passed, an invasion by sea. His wife, backed by Mortimer and a small army of Hainaulters, had landed in Essex, had gathered support, and had marched toward London.

It struck Stephen that at a later time he would have to challenge Edward over the blissful state he claimed his reign had bestowed on England, for, to his certain knowledge, the latter years had been ones of tyranny and violence, when many had lost their lives and properties, leaving much bitterness and hatred quite unassuaged by the bulging treasury or the balm of summer days. He thought it best, though, for now to allow Edward to continue as he wished, and so did not halt his narrative.

Edward showed more emotion as he told of the rapid ebbing away of his power as Isabella and her army marched westwards, how the support of friends had wavered, how musters had passed unanswered, and appeals to the pope and other potentates had been ignored. His fists tightened as he spoke of London and its sullen rebellious citizens, and how he had been forced to flee the capital with the Despensers (father and son), Baldock, a few clerks of his household, and a troop of archers.

Stephen wondered which elements, if any, of Edward's own conduct during that time amounted to sins in the king's mind, or were indeed sins, bearing in mind the Seven Deadly Sins and the Ten Commandments; but the flow of Edward's tale was such, and indeed became more impassioned as he went on, that Stephen had no opportunity to interrupt, nor to suggest reflection on specific aspects of what Edward had done, nor to question the circumstances which surrounded his acts and decisions.

The tone of Edward's words became more irate still when he spoke of Isabella herself, and Stephen sensed at last a departure from any words Edward had thus far fashioned in his mind:

"My wife, Brother Stephen, my wife has piled disobedience on disobedience. Not content with denying me her own presence and that of my dear son for so many months, not content with raising arms against me, she has poisoned the minds of the commons and barony, and pursued me like a fugitive out of my own lands!...Now, look at this – here, on the table! She sends me capons, wine and delicacies here in my prison, as you see, to salve her guilty conscience; though in truth she's proved the most cancerous of all growths feeding on my kingdom!

"And yet I have been a most dutiful and loyal husband to her...Though for years I refused to believe rumours that she was disloyal to me...Now, when I think back – how blind can I have been?...Her treachery and her jealousy of my friends is the most manifest blight afflicting the whole of my reign! From the very outset after our marriage, when she was little more than a child, she hated and opposed my dearest brother, Gaveston. Later it was poor Hugh who bore the weight of her enmity. Yet, of course, she would always smile and fawn on both of them in my presence, saving her venom till my back was turned!

"Brother Stephen, you would hardly believe the tears she shed when parting from myself and Hugh just two years ago, when she set off on her embassy to France! And all the time, as I now know to my bitterest cost, she planned not to plead my cause over Gascony to King Charles, her brother, as Hugh and I had instructed her, but to make common cause in Paris with the traitor, Mortimer...indeed, to share his bed!...then to kidnap my boy, Edward, my eldest son...and finally return to England at the head of a hostile army, intent on murdering the most loyal of my subjects, butchering poor Hugh, and usurping my power as king!

"Pray God, she was not Mortimer's whore all along. To have mixed...! I tell you, Brother Stephen, if I saw her now I would stab her dead...and, had I no dagger, I would use my own teeth to rip out her throat!"

By now Edward was choking over his words, and Stephen seized the moment both to stand and at last to intervene:

"My lord, let me counsel you, in the name of God's goodness, to be forgiving towards your wife! Christ enjoined us always to turn the other cheek, to pray for those who persecute us, to love our enemies, and to bless those who curse us. So must you do, my lord, for it is God's way. Not only was this revealed to us through the words of his Son, our Redeemer. It also comes to us by way of Reason. For revenge is a base desire, my lord, feeding on itself like a bloated whale, looking always to the way wrongs have arisen in the past, never to the way they may be righted in the future."

As he leaned towards Edward, Stephen could not be sure what degree of attention was being paid, for the king was shaking, his head held in his hands, his eyes staring at his platter of half-eaten food. Having commenced his ministry, though, Stephen could only continue. If he had to repeat his words on later occasions, then there was no vice in that.

"Your Anger at your wife, my lord, your wish for her damnation, will devour your mind – your mind which should have thoughts only for your own soul's salvation. Do not in your confession question your wife's behaviour, for that is a matter for God and her conscience, not for yours. What was it, you must ask yourself, in your own conduct which may have induced such rebellion in her? Look into your heart, my lord, and ask the questions I now shall pose to you – for you must give me answers to them when we meet again tomorrow. First, though a king be paramount on this earth under God Almighty, and though he be great in the eyes of men, may he not fall into the sin of such excessive Pride that it shall poison the affections of those who should love and serve him most? Second, may not a husband conceive such a deep and abiding Anger against his wife, whether provoked or otherwise, that it shall itself become a sin greater than the disobedience which first gave rise to it? And third – and it is a question every wronged husband must ask himself – when a wife rebels against her husband, even to the extent of Lechery, who first fell into this grievous sin, who first stained the sheet of blessed matrimony?"

By now Edward's shaking had ceased, but he continued to gaze downwards, not meeting Stephen's eyes. The silence lengthened, and Edward began to toy with the remnants of his meal. He snapped a chicken bone, hurling both parts over his shoulder towards the window; yet still he refused to look up.

Later Stephen judged it to have been a mistake – and one which undermined some of what he had already said – but he began now to speak again, summoning from his studies passages relating to womankind, which he had found congenial in the past, and which he now felt might be of comfort to Edward:

"My lord, it is fair to say also that you should...before judging your wife, before feeding any Anger which remains within you, and which, if it does, is a mortal sin...you should reflect on woman's weakness, on the greater propensity of womankind for sin. Women cannot be judged by men's standards, for remember always that Eve sinned first in the Garden and was the greater sinner. St Augustine tells us: 'Woman is of feeble nature, tells more lies, is slower in working and in moving than is a man. She is more envious, more given to wilful pleasure, licence and lechery, is more malicious in her soul. And in all ways a man is as superior to a woman as is the soul to the body.' Do not wonder, therefore, my lord, that your wife may have been disobedient, malicious, even depraved in her conduct. Such is woman's nature. So was she created.

"God wills that a wife should be His handmaid, obedient in all things both to the clergy and to her husband: so shall she imitate the true model for all womankind, the Blessed Virgin herself. But if indeed she errs, God wills it that she should be forgiven by her husband, for it is He only who has made her, and He only who will punish her iniquity."

Stephen paused again. This time he made the sign of the cross, and indicated that Edward should kneel and join him in prayer. But Edward's jaws were clenched and he uttered not a word. Suddenly he rose, knocking over his stool, and strode to the small barred window of the room, which looked out over the courtyard within the shell of the keep. There he stood, gripping the bars, his back to Stephen, till he spun round, his eyes blazing, and gesticulated that Stephen should leave.

Stephen's mouth gaped, as he realised that those words, which he had judged both wise and comforting, had only stoked Edward's Anger. Maybe he had erred too in interrupting Edward – though he could not see what else he could have said or done – for was it not the essence of the confessor's role to challenge and to correct?

Not daring to look further in Edward's direction, he bowed and edged towards the door, where he hammered to draw the guard's attention. Bolts flew back at once and he heard the grind of a key in the massive lock. – Had the guard been loitering close, perhaps with his ear clamped to the door to hear what was being said? – It was not this worry, though, which obsessed him as he descended the outer stair and was let out once more into the inner bailey. Rather it was the clear and abject failure of his holy mission at this, its very outset.

Though it was late in the afternoon, he could not contemplate supper, and, if challenged, would have to plead sickness or the need to fast – he cared not which. He turned his steps, therefore, not towards the bustle of the great hall, but towards the small Chapel of St John, where he knew the Virgin waited, ready to hear his words of self-loathing, and his entreaty She should right all he had made wrong. There, whilst daylight lasted, the dull sheen of Her carved face and limbs seemed to do no more than absorb his cries of anguish, to blunt the edge of his desperation. But at dusk, when he had made the offering of six lighted candles, an answer kindled amongst the deep hues and gnarled patterns of Her wooden form – of this, he was sure.

As the cold of the flagstones numbed his knees and the emptiness in his stomach made his head feel light, he heard a voice which seemed to emanate from the Virgin's likeness. It counselled perseverance. Edward's tale might career between events, might be impossible to rein in for that reflection which was mother to true contrition, but the voice urged patience, told him to bide his time till Edward himself paused in his narrative, sought to interpret what had happened to him, himself asked Stephen for justification and reassurance. For these things would happen: when the headlong rush of Edward's words had spent itself, and when his pent up fury had begun to abate. Convinced that it was Mary who had spoken, and still kneeling upright on the uneven slabs of the sandstone floor, Stephen raised his arms high in the air in salutation to the Virgin.

It was then that She vouchsafed him a vision. – Did he swoon? Had the pangs of hunger and exhaustion overtaken him? – He saw Edward prostrate in prayer, his tears bitter, whilst he heard his own voice preach of Hell and of those who did not repent, of souls weighed down under mountainous rocks, of souls thrown from fiery furnaces into a frozen sea, their tongues cut out, their flesh branded, torn and spiked. Then he felt tears on his own face, yet these were tears of joy, for the Virgin now revealed Herself standing beyond Purgatory's final gate, welcoming the souls who had trodden its fiery road, but now emerged into God's Kingdom. They were radiant, bathed in the light of righteousness, and amongst them was Edward himself, clothed all in gold, a jewelled sceptre in his hand. Behind him came Hugh, girt in a spotless loin-cloth, his fair body healed and whole again. Then, it seemed to Stephen, that he beheld himself following on, hand in hand with his beloved, and both were cleansed and lily-white of skin, no longer marked and stained as they had been since their time at Oxford.

In the semi-darkness where he had collapsed, Stephen struggled to his feet once more, and lit two more candles to replace those which were guttering. Then, though his voice seemed weak and tremulous, he raised it in prayer, praising Mary, Mother of God, the Mediatrix, the Second Eve, his own protector; and he thanked Her that he, Stephen, unworthy as he was, would be the instrument by which these miracles would come to pass.

Chapter 15

He slept well that night, and when on waking he recalled his vision, he gave thanks again that his discourse with Edward would from now on be blessed and guided by the Virgin Herself. Feeling free then to devote the morning to study, he went to the library and began work upon the Eclogues. If, from time to time, he paused to think about the afternoon's meeting, he felt muted exultation, rather than mere equanimity, let alone his previous dread and apprehension.

After a substantial dinner he strode along the battlements, and dared to raise his voice in plainsong, casting his joy to the winds. Even when this attracted the keen attention of a servant standing motionless in the shadows of the bailey, he dismissed any fear he was being spied upon; or, even if he was, that any bad report could be made of him to Sir John Maltravers. He was still humming as he mounted the stairs to Edward's chamber some two hours later.

But it was there that he received a rebuff, for during his whole allotted hour Edward would respond to him neither in words, nor with the slightest smile or acknowledgement. When Stephen attempted to reopen discussion of Edward's feelings towards his wife, the king stared towards the window, his breathing slow and deliberate, as though he were striving to calm some anger or contain some bitter words surging within him. When later Stephen invited him to recall further events the previous year, Edward strode to the corner of the room and began feeding morsels from his dinner platter to a large black rat, which Stephen now noted was scuttling back and forth within a large cage placed on a wooden stand. Edward cooed and blew kisses to the creature, until both he and Stephen lapsed into the most awkward silence, broken only when stealthy footsteps approached on the far side of the door, and then could be heard retreating a short while later. When finally a miserable and defeated Stephen descended the stair to the inner bailey, he could not fathom why Edward had not dismissed him upon his arrival, if his presence was now so irksome – unless, of course, Edward's intention was to maximise his confessor's feelings of failure and embarrassment.

The situation repeated itself the following day, and the day after that, so that Stephen's spirits plummeted, and he began to doubt that what had seemed such a portentous vision could have been any more than a dream, or, worse still, a trap baited with Pride and sprung for him by the Devil. He worried too that word would reach Lord Berkeley from the watchers – about whom he was now less sanguine, and whom he suspected round every corner and every half closed door. He imagined being called to explain why his ministry – the sole purpose of his presence in the castle – had foundered when barely under sail.

When next he visited Edward, however, the atmosphere within the cell seemed a little less taut, and, whilst Edward remained morose and again directed his principal attention towards the rat, Stephen felt encouraged to make a further attempt at rekindling their dialogue:

"My lord, if I might mention the account you have given me of your travails this past year, you will know, I'm sure, how vital it is, not only to tell me of the hardships you have encountered since you were last shriven, but to reflect, in doing so, on your own thoughts and deeds, so that you – so that we – may test which of them have perhaps been sinful…and which should now be subject to full confession…"

"I do, indeed, priest," came Edward's dry, but to Stephen welcome, reply.

"And you will know that it is my role here to question and pry into the explanations which you give, to judge the sinfulness of your actions and the circumstances which have surrounded them, and then to bring you to a full understanding of the extent of that sin…So that you shall come to true contrition…"

Edward grunted.

"Then it will be for me, in accordance with my holy office, to grant absolution, but also to prescribe for you what penance shall be required in expiation of those sins…which, given your imprisonment, my lord, can be little other than many many hours of solemn prayer…though, it's true, fasting may also play its part…and if you wished for works of charity to be carried out on your behalf, and were prepared, for instance, to part with a ring or…"

"Priest, you tell me nothing of which I have not been aware for many years!…I am no child to be taught his abacus!…In accordance with your instructions, you may be confident, I will turn my conscience inwards, and will seek out those faults and blemishes which no doubt blacken my soul…As for penitence, priest, be assured my rings are not for sale – for charity or any other purpose!...I will spend my time in prayer as you command, for as Heaven knows, the time to do so is not lacking in this place!"

"My lord, these words are manna to me, for I feared you had taken my words concerning the queen amiss. It was as though Satan had interposed himself between us, and I feared I could be of no further service to you..." At his mention of Isabella, Edward pursed his lips, though he said nothing. He stood and moved again towards the cage, where the rat reached up towards him, its delicate feet clambering on the metalwork, its muzzle quivering in anticipation.

Encouraged, yet still fearful of another lapse into mute anger, Stephen coaxed again:

"My lord, you told me previously of your departure from London. Would you now wish to tell me of the weeks that followed...how and why it was your supporters left you...how you came to be imprisoned...?"

Edward paused whilst he dropped a few bread-crumbs into the cage. For the first time that day he looked Stephen in the eye and then began, hesitantly at first, to describe his flight from London into Gloucestershire, how he had sought, but had not found, supporters with whom to resist Isabella's invasion. He told how from Gloucester his decreasing band of soldiers and courtiers had moved on to Tintern, then to Chepstow, and how in desperation – as Stephen had heard before – they had set sail for Ireland, but had been forced to land and take refuge on the Glamorgan coast. All the while friends, allies, even household servants had melted away from him, vanishing over night, their numbers trickling like sand through an hour-glass.

Stephen dared at this point to press Edward to consider the reasons why his support had proved so fragile, rather than to bemoan the spinelessness of friends and the cheapness of loyalty, as he was wont to do. But there was no reaction, adverse or otherwise to this suggestion, for having again launched on his narrative, Edward seemed oblivious to anything other than his pain at the wrongs he had suffered, and his anger at the blame in others' hearts.

It was when he came to describe the miserable days when he had sought refuge first at Caerphilly, then at Neath, and had been ambushed and taken like a common criminal at Margam, that he first made mention of his servant, Dunsheved. This man had been with

116

him, he said, from London right up until his capture and, by heaven knew what means, had himself escaped and then maintained secret contact with him in the following days. Dunsheved had indeed kept Edward's hopes alive, though had later brought him the news he dreaded most: that of Despenser's journey to trial and likely death at Hereford.

At that recollection Edward's composure left him, and he returned to the table, where he poured himself some wine and sat for a while, his head bowed. Stephen considered allowing time for sad reflection, but, nervous too of any return to the silence of the past few days, seized on Edward's reference to Dunsheved, mentioning his own acquaintance, and the fact he knew of Dunsheved's work as the king's emissary, and of his family and contacts in Warwickshire. Though he went no further, and in no way touched on the Order's plans and Dunsheved's and his own part in them, he saw that Edward's interest was piqued, for he put down his goblet and gazed at Stephen, his eyes narrowing. But the moment passed, and Edward resumed his narrative, engrossing himself with the injustices he had suffered at Monmouth and on his own journey northwards towards Kenilworth.

The early days of his imprisonment, the covetousness of his captors, and especially the treachery of Henry of Lancaster, he described with increasing venom, but his tone changed as he dwelt on his enforced separation from Hugh le Despenser: one who, he said, was his special friend, his best counsellor, his brother even. He harked back again to their last days in each other's company and told Stephen how, when they had seen their capture to be inevitable, they had embraced, had vowed eternal loyalty to each other, and Edward had ordered that Despenser be given as a parting gift one of his dearest books: a precious volume telling the sad history and deaths of Tristan and Isolde. It was as though, Edward said, like the lovers in the story, he and Hugh had drunk a potion which bound them in amity till death itself should part them.

It was then that Edward asked Stephen for his account of Despenser's last day: his trial, his humiliation, his execution. Knowing he must discharge this burden at some point, Stephen was not reluctant to begin recounting all that he had seen that day at Hereford, though he still felt his voice shake and his lip tremble from time to time as he told of the events from Despenser's approach along the Monmouth road to the final quartering of his shattered body within the castle walls.

As he spoke, Edward began to shed tears, then to moan, at last casting himself on his truckle bed. Had Stephen dared, he would have crossed the room, sat down beside Edward, and done anything he could to have comforted him, but he was suspicious of some explosion, whether of anger, grief, or resentment, if he did as much as approach the bed. So he sat in silence at the table, his eyes fixed on Edward, and restrained his own tears for the short time left till it was time for him to go.

*

After supper, as he knelt before the wooden likeness of the Virgin, Stephen reproached himself for his lack of faith, both in the vision She had shown him, and in the power of Her intercession. Again She had granted him extraordinary favour, only for him to doubt its truth and to despair before the working of Her will on earth had become manifest.

Despite his weakness and unworthiness, the gulf between himself and Edward had now been bridged, the fissure healed, and he had cause for jubilation! Even if not one mote of blackness had been removed from Edward's soul that day, he, Stephen, had been granted a fresh chance to pursue what he now perceived must be his life's work: the saving of a king's soul!

Maybe he had allowed Edward too free a rein in his discourse, maybe Edward had failed in any way to compass his own faults; but, for that, time would provide, for so the Virgin had promised; and, as Edward had lamented, time was something which was hardly lacking. He wondered too if he had himself dwelt too much on the horrors he had seen at Hereford, and had thereby caused the king an excess of grief; but, in doing so, at least he had rendered some small service to truth and to the memory of poor Hugh. And in return he had been granted an epiphany: one which his heart now throbbed with tenderness to recall – a king who wept, whose broad shoulders were shaken with sobs – a brother he could comfort by word and touch.

*

The following afternoon when Stephen entered Edward's cell, he found the king composed, and sitting at the table, though he noted at

118

once that the king's right knee quivered with apprehension beneath his gown. The usual flagon of wine was already empty, leaving nothing to be offered him by way of hospitality. He took his seat and paused for a moment to see if Edward would raise whatever topic or events he had upon his mind, but today he sensed a reticence – though not the previous hostile refusal – to begin speaking.

Taking this as a sign for him to guide Edward's confession more than he had before, Stephen again attempted one of his arguments from the previous day, referring first to Edward's narrative, and then suggesting they pray together and address those feelings of Anger which, it was clear, Edward harboured towards those who had imprisoned him. These men, Stephen told him, should now be forgiven, as men merely subject to a higher command. Moreover, Anger itself needed to be admitted, regretted and repented in full.

Before Stephen could expand further on his theme, however, Edward stopped him, raising a hand and addressing, at first in a low tone and with his eyes averted, a topic his confessor had not anticipated:

"Brother Stephen, it is not of Anger that we must talk today...You have seen my tears for Sir Hugh, heard from me of my love for him. I tell you now: had my wife died as he did – even in the years before her evil became clear to me – I would not have mourned her passing one tenth as much as I do his!...Am I wrong in this? Am I sinful?...I know what they say of me, Stephen. I have heard what words Bishop Orleton preached to the court at Hereford and then at Wallingford last Christmas... What do you say, Brother Stephen? What words of rebuke or of comfort can I expect from you?"

"My lord..." Stephen faltered. "What...what is it you wish to confess to me?" A knot of panic had gripped his stomach, and his mind raced as he fought to find words – any words – with which to go on. Yet Edward's look demanded a response. With his thoughts still in flux, Stephen's mouth began speaking before he really knew where it would lead him:

"I would not condemn the noble love felt by one man for another...for his brother, my lord...whether they be brothers by blood...or brothers in arms – knights, who have sworn fealty to each other... or...by those, of course, my lord, who are Brothers in Christ...engaged in God's Holy War..." He swallowed hard, floundering amidst his own evasions, but Edward's silence forced him on: "How indeed could I find fault with a love such as that of Jonathan for David?...David, to whom Jonathan gave his robe, his clothing, even his sword, his bow, and his sash...And, as you know, David lamented: 'I am distressed for thee, my brother Jonathan: very pleasant hast thou been unto me; thy love to me was wonderful, passing the love of woman'."

"So it has been for me, Brother Stephen! So it has been for me. For such a love have I known." Edward seized Stephen's arm across the table. "Such a love, and more, much more...Such were my feelings for Sir Hugh, for others too...You've heard, I do not doubt, of Piers de Gaveston?"

Stephen's heart pounded, and he felt his habit clammy about his limbs. He withdrew his arm and clasped his hands together. "I have, my lord...His body lies in a tomb watched over by my brother Dominicans...at the great priory near your palace of Kings Langley."

"I doubt it was his tomb, Brother Stephen, which brought him to your attention!...Did you not hear first how and why he met so untimely an end? Did they not whisper to you in the cloister that he was the king's lover...that he gave his body up to foul practices?" Edward's face was now flushed, and his hands trembled; yet there was a defiance too in his words: "Do you not know that this was also what they said of Hugh?..."

"I...I...Yes, my lord, I have heard these things," Stephen stammered. Edward now rose and leant over the table, staring Stephen full in the face:

"And how do you, Stephen, respond to 'these things'?"

"I would ask first, my lord,...if these things were true." Edward was silent for a moment, then straightened, approached the window, and stood gazing into the inner courtyard. Then he turned:

"If these things *were* true, Brother Stephen, what would you say then? Would you damn the perpetrators for all eternity? Would you say no remedy exists for their benighted souls...that there is no penance mighty enough to purge the blackness they are guilty of?"

Stephen's wish that day had been to challenge Edward to confront some of his more venial sins, yet now they seemed to have leaped over the venial, to the mortal, and beyond, to the still beating heart of Edward's darkest secret – ripped out and now thrust at Stephen for immediate absolution. A pulse hammered in his temples, and his reason seemed swamped in memories – not Edward's, but his own. In the fifth year of his studies he had loved Brother Aelred; their joy in each other had grown and mastered them both, banishing modesty and restraint. Then one who bore a grudge had betrayed them. They would have been cast out from Blackfriars House had not Stephen first inflicted a drastic penance upon himself, and had not Aelred simply fled – with no word of farewell, let alone explanation.

Stephen all but heaved. The reflux of his memories almost impelled him across the chamber to hammer on the door to gain release from Edward's presence. Yet somehow, somehow, he managed to steady his breathing, and to bow his head in prayer. Somehow too his ghosts began to dissipate, and he fixed his mind on the cup pressed to his lips – the cup he could not now let pass.

Edward had remained standing at the window, grasping the bars as if to still his trembling, his shoulders tensed. Stephen could no longer delay reply to his questions, yet if he was to respond as the Church required he should, he knew he must recite some of its harshest teachings:

"You wish me, my lord, to speak of the sin of Sodomy..." he began. There was no denial or confirmation, and Stephen now felt a tide of words rising within himself demanding to be spoken – words imprinted on his mind, words he had heard again and again when he had confessed his own sins – words he had buried with the iniquity itself in the darkest recesses of his mind:

"Sodomy, of all sins, is of the very gravest, my lord, for it is contrary to Nature and to God's Order in the universe. Union with the body of an animal, or of a Jew, or with those vessels of the female which are not generative are not greater sins than this. For, as the Blessed St Thomas Aquinas has taught us, the final cause of the union of two bodies is progeny. Any union not solely for that purpose, therefore, is against Reason, against Nature, and ultimately against God.

"Furthermore, for a man to play the woman's part is an abomination, as if the anvil should strike the hammer, or as if the seed should prepare the furrow for the ploughshare. It is as if subject should become predicate. St Albert Magnus tells us that its ardour, its odour, its persistence and its virulence are such that there is no alternative but that Sodomy must be rooted out." Stephen paused, overcome both with the rawness of his own recollections, and with a desire somehow to soften the iron logic of this doctrine, for his own as much as for Edward's sake. Cold comfort, however, came to him from his learning:

"It is true, though Sodomy be against Nature herself, that it is still within Nature's ambit, for some are born with this sinful disposition, as though it had leached into their fathers' seed, or as though they had drunk its poison in their mothers' milk. Their sorrow it is to battle with this demon throughout their length of days. Those saints who beat that demon down, doubly shall be blessed. Those in whom he rises up, who yield to him, yet only waste their seed – if they shall confess and do penitence, they too shall purge their souls and find salvation.

"For those whom he conquers utterly, however, know that neither full confession and the severest penance the Church can devise, nor the hottest fires of Purgatory may suffice – even though that penance shall be of the greatest suffering, even though those fires shall be endured till the End of Days. Know rather that for him who gives himself up to this blackest of all the sins, only eternal torment in the deepest reach of Hell may be sufficient for God's justice to be restored."

As Stephen ceased speaking, Edward fell to his knees and, half-praying, half-moaning, began calling on the Lord for forgiveness. His body shook, his hands clasped together in supplication, and his mouth babbled words it was impossible to follow. Stephen knelt by him, and himself began fervent prayer, realising that at another time, if he was to have any hope of leading Edward to salvation, every knot and tangle of the love and lust to which Edward had succumbed would have to be unravelled.

Even now he could taste the gall of his own sins as they had dribbled like bile from his lips years before at Oxford.

Chapter 16

Stephen spent much of the following day in tumult: hoping, believing, convincing himself that he was about to set Edward on the blessed road to his soul's salvation. Yet he could not deny that equally he thirsted for those facts which in confession Edward would now be obliged to reveal. At first he could not explain to himself why this prospect should so obsess him, since contemplation of Edward's sin led him back to the dark hinterland of his own recollections, which for four long years his mind had coffined in the thickest blackest lead. But now that lead had melted, leaving a corpse ready for dissection.

He could not avoid drawing parallels. At Hereford Hugh had been charged with coming between Edward and his wife, whilst in his own case love for Aelred had come between himself and his studies. Aelred and he had lain together in the grain store, when they should have been in class. He pictured Edward lying with Hugh amongst rich hangings and fine sheets, whilst the realm fell into neglect and disharmony all about them. His ears filled with the sound of the Magister's wrath, and he imagined Isabella as she seethed, cursed and tore out the jewels from her hair.

Then he recalled Edward's last meeting with Hugh, when the king made a present of his "Tristan and Isolde". He heard their vows to each other, tasted their tears, felt the warmth of their embrace; then grieved that his own love had fled, with no parting kiss, no words of love, let alone any keepsake, once their secret had become known. More lurid thoughts too possessed him, and though he mouthed prayers to banish them from his mind, his body burned as he imagined Edward's congress with Hugh and with his other lovers, and his heart ached that his own union with Aelred had been so brief.

Then Hugh's butchery and death came into his mind – images of genitals sliced off and cast into the fire, guts ripped out and a heart held aloft. He thanked Mary, Joseph and all the Saints that he, Stephen, had at least confessed his sins, achieved contrition, and, by dint of prayers, fasting, and the chisel's bite, obtained forgiveness.

It must be his dearest wish that Edward could now do likewise.

*

But, when later that afternoon he visited the keep, his hopes proved fruitless. He found Edward not contrite, not ready to confess further and to learn of his penance, but in a skittish mood. On Stephen's entry to the cell, Edward would at first do nothing other than sit before his bronze mirror, intent on his own countenance. Did Stephen see there the face of a king, a god, or merely a fool? Did Stephen not think there were more grey hairs and wrinkles than when first they had met?

Next he demanded Stephen search his scalp for lice and pinch them out, whilst he turned his attention to his teeth, peering at his mouth's reflection, rubbing liquorice into his gums, breathing on the mirror's surface, and sniffing for unwholesome odours, before chewing cardomums and spitting the husks into his chamber pot.

When at last he deigned to pay attention, and Stephen with some tetchiness made reference to the previous day's conversation, there was a swift retort:

"Sodomy, Stephen?... We talked of rumours, yesterday...of black, foul rumours spread by the traitor, Orleton, and his crew...such rumours as are the stock in trade of the unscrupulous...It's a slanderous craft Isabella learned well from the French king, her father, who destroyed the Templars with similar lies, and in the same way robbed good Pope Boniface of his reputation in the world, after he was dead!"

"But my lord, yesterday you told me of your love for Gaveston and for Sir Hugh..."

"And we agreed, did we not, Brother Stephen, how such was the love of David for Jonathan...So, too, you might have mentioned the love of Achilles for Patrochlus, Lancelot for Galahad...It is a noble love, Brother Stephen, 'passing the love of woman'...Did you not say so?...I marvel you didn't mention Christ himself and Saint John, the dear disciple! – or claim David's love for Jonathan to be an allegory of Christ's love for his Church!..."

Stephen felt his skin prickle and a flush upon his cheeks. Struggling to retain an even tone, he said:

"My lord, if this was the nature of your love for Lord Gaveston and Sir Hugh, let me rejoice with you; but I am surprised to learn that we have spent so long in discussion and contemplation of a sin you now say you are not guilty of, but which is the substance only of rumour! Are we priests to absolve sinners not only of their sins, but of the sins others merely *say* they have committed? My lord, such would be a sorry waste of the confessor's time?"

For a moment Edward looked startled, and Stephen realised his tone had been sharper and more critical than any he had used before in their meetings. Then Edward took in a slow deep breath, and his eyes opened wide as if to compass this sudden challenge to his waywardness, but said nothing, and turned to the table where he again took up his mirror and began examining his teeth, ignoring Stephen altogether till they heard the supper bell.

*

From that day onwards Edward displayed a wilful refusal to return to the subject of his feelings for Hugh. Yet Stephen knew that, if rumour, Edward's previous words, and the conviction of his own heart were to be relied on, this was chief amongst the matters with which they both now had to grapple, if his mission was in any way to succeed. He set no store at all by Edward's claim that what had been said before raised nothing other than a conjecture.

More progress was made in addressing the more venial of Edward's sins, for after a few days Edward consented to discuss his dealings with men like Lancaster, even Mortimer himself, and with those who had deserted him on his flight into the West. Pride, Envy, Anger and Avarice were faults he now acknowledged to have been present in his own conduct. Where these had arisen through misunderstanding, or were of trivial importance, Stephen laid his hands on Edward's head granting him absolution, and Edward with due contrition set about his prayers of penitence. However, neither his unbounded Anger against Isabella, nor the unnatural Lechery of which he was accused were matters of which for the present he would endure any further mention.

Those earlier words concerning Hugh and Gaveston continued, nevertheless, to plague Stephen's own thoughts. They returned to him again and again, like a smouldering in the brain, or a simmering in the blood, causing desires he dared not recognise to lick like flames round Edward's limbs as, in his mind's eye, the king either knelt before him in solemn prayer, or in dejection cast himself upon his bed. Try as Stephen might, both with prayer and lamentation, he could not drive these images from his mind. Even when he forced himself to meditate again on Hugh's fate, on his body's mutilation, and on the behaviour of Brother James, which he had himself condemned, even on the very fetor of Barelonde itself, he could not rid himself of feelings at which his reason baulked, but to which his heart opened like a rose in sunlight.

Night after night his hours of prayer and contemplation brought anything but peace, both as he knelt in the chapel before the Virgin, who now seemed to fix him with a uncomprehending frown, and later as the moon's pale finger pried into the secrets of his chamber. During the daylight hours too – those he spent in Lord Berkeley's library – his studies were put to flight, the volume of Virgil's "Eclogues" lying unconsidered before him. Even when he willed himself to focus on the Latin text, and drew blood biting his own hand as punishment for his inattention, he would within moments find himself staring at the grain of the table top, or out through the windows (now unshuttered for the warmer weather), or simply at the painted gryphons on the wall. All the while he rehearsed in his mind conversations he had not yet had with Edward, or which he had had, but regretted, and which nagged at his conscience like a guilty secret; but sometimes he could think of nothing other than of Edward himself, his body's strength, his heart's fragility.

*

Stephen's one relief remained his frequent visits to his eyrie on the battlements. There he was often soothed by the warmth of early summer, by the mild breezes still blowing from the Severn and now laden with the scent of hawthorn blossom and the hum of bees. There, if briefly, he could escape the briar-patch of memory and confused emotion; and, gazing northwards towards Gloucester, he often felt heartened by recollections of the simplicity and blessedness of his existence there, and dared hope that one day he might return.

It was from the battlements early one morning that he caught sight of a young Dominican, whom he recognised as one of Brother Walter's novices, walking through the outer bailey and, it appeared, in search of something, or someone. He dared not shout out, nor wave to draw attention, and before long the man disappeared beneath the bulk of the gatehouse. Nonplussed, Stephen could only continue his usual routine, not sure if anything would happen, but fearful that in some dark passageway hands would fumble to pass a written message to him, or forbidden words would be whispered into his ear, either by the hot breath of the novice or of someone else on his behalf.

A few hours later he received a summons to attend Lord Berkeley – now back from his travels and once more in charge of the royal prisoner. Though Lord Thomas was dressed all in black – news of the death of his brother, the Bishop of Exeter, had only recently arrived – nothing suggested a man crushed by grief, and his manner remained much as before:

"Brother Stephen, you'll recall our conversation when it was impressed upon you that here at the castle, you must have no contact with any person from outside. As we warned you, friar, troublemakers may try to wheedle from you knowledge concerning Sir Edward, or may otherwise seek to compromise your position! Now, I do not say for a moment that you have breached this strict requirement, but I must tell you that one of your fellows from Blackfriars was found earlier today wandering within the precincts with no apparent reason or excuse. He's been despatched back to Gloucester with a message telling Brother Walter that under no circumstances is anyone to seek contact with you again! The man denied having spoken to you, and I trust you'll confirm this to be correct."

"It is, my lord. By my Faith, it is."

"That is well, Brother Stephen. That is well...This remains a dangerous time when we must all be on our guard!...Only lately, I've heard of a further plot to release Sir Edward from Kenilworth at the hands of one Brother John of Stoke – another of your Order, as it happens!...Of course, fortunately, friar, this only shows how well the secret of Sir Edward's whereabouts has been kept, since he was already here in Berkeley when the foolish attempt was made!"

This thought seemed to amuse Sir Thomas, and his tone softened:

"Well then, all is as it should be, Brother Stephen...By the way, how do you find your dealings with Sir Edward, now that you've been striving for his soul for two long weeks?...Believe me, priest, I do not wish to pry into his sins...But how is he now in his disposition towards you personally?"

"As you told me, my lord, he is a man of many moods – none of them easy to deal with!"

Lord Berkeley laughed: "You must have the patience of Job even to try, Brother Stephen! Though I suppose that's your calling!" A malign smile then played round his lips. "I must tell you, priest, of something pertinent! − a cure I've lately learned about for the sin of Sodomy...which you might wish to pass on...should the occasion arise, of course!...It mends the body, not the immortal soul! ...One must take fur from the neck of a filthy, lustful creature called 'hyena', must burn it with pitch, and then grind it to a powder. This is then applied to the offending arsehole...It never fails, they say...though I don't intend myself to experiment with it on my prisoner!...But perhaps you know if it works already, Brother Stephen...After all, you may have heard from others within your Order, who...?"

Stephen knew that had Sir John Maltravers been present, a bout of hearty ribbing would have now ensued, and the two lords would have guffawed and sniggered as each tried to cap the other with his insinuations, but Stephen was not given to banter. Even in his student days, he had never had the inclination, let alone the wit, to think of the gibes and witticisms which seemed so often to fuel conversations among men; and the more he tried to think of such repartee, the more blank his mind would become, and the more embarrassed his appearance. So it was on this occasion, as he stood gaping and blushing before Sir Thomas, who soon lost interest, and sent him on his way.

Back in the library in front of his translation, he found he could no more concentrate than if Virgil had written, not in Latin, but in Welsh. His mind was preoccupied now not only with his recurrent worries about Edward and his mission, but also with what must have been the latest thwarted attempt by Brother Walter to revive their plot for the king's escape. But there was an additional cause for his inattention too, for this was the very day when Lord Berkeley's works of improvement to the adjoining range were due to commence, and soon the noise of demolition and of workmen shattered the peace and quiet which any further study would have demanded. Clouds of dust started to invade the library through the shutters, which he then had to fasten closed, before he surrendered any attempt at further endeavour and retired for several hours to his chamber.

*

When Stephen mounted the stair to the prison cell later that afternoon, he was at a loss to know what topic to address, not daring to predict in what mood he would find Edward that day. Maybe he would be forthcoming, or maybe he would prove hostile and uncooperative, or would be possessed of some new demon Stephen had not so far encountered.

In the event, Edward seemed calm and was polite. He invited Stephen to sit, offered him wine, and enquired if it would be acceptable for him now to relate his experiences at Kenilworth earlier that year; and with this Stephen did not hesitate to concur.

Edward then explained how Henry of Lancaster's regime for his royal prisoner had in fact been quite liberal: Edward had been allowed to keep some of his retinue with him, and to move with comparative liberty round the large grounds in which the castle was situated. He had been treated with respect, and his Christmas had been cheered by the gift of two tons of Rhenish wine from his son. Mid-winter, however, had also brought embassies from Isabella and from the Parliament. An invitation to attend before the Lords and Commons and to abdicate his throne had been delivered by the Bishop of Winchester and by Orleton, the cleric whom Edward despised above all others. This he had rejected in a blaze of anger and curses. A fortnight later, though, the same two bishops had returned.

"At first I thought they came merely to mock me," said Edward, "for the bishops of Winchester and Lincoln entered my chambers with the Earl, and said much as had been said before. But then I was told that in the great hall of Kenilworth some thirty officials and worthies were waiting for me, that my misdemeanours would be read out to me, and that if, before that gathering, I did not agree to abdicate in favour of my son, Edward, then another house would supplant the Plantagenets!

"I know you'd not credit such a threat, Brother Stephen, and I could not myself believe that they were serious, but my shock at their words was of course very great...Before I could frame any sort of response, I was led to the great hall itself, where, as they had said, a gathering of lords, churchmen, knights of the shire and officials was arrayed, all glaring as though I were a Turk or a Mahometan!...I tell you, Stephen, seeing God's order standing on its head before me, the earth beneath seemed to tremble, and I fell in a dead faint at their feet!

"Winchester and Lancaster raised me, splashed water on my face, and made me listen whilst Orleton with bare effrontery read out from a parchment that I was found guilty of many crimes...In my befuddled state I could barely comprehend, let alone remember what was said...but I believe I was declared incompetent, incapable of taking good advice, responsible for the imprisonment, death, and exile of many lords and of damage to the Church, and further that I and others had governed solely for our own profit...I confess I wept when I heard these cruel and unjust words.

"Then again they put me to the choice, which was like a dagger at my throat: I must either abdicate in favour of my son, or be supplanted by one, not of royal blood, but well used to government – by which they could have meant none other than Mortimer...What was I to say? There was no one there to plead my case, no one to refute these lies...It came to me then that I was now a king in name only, and that that name, which once had the power to summon armies, had dwindled to a mere puff of air...I gave way, agreed to their demand: said my son should rule in my place... sloughed off what little remained of my kingship...said how grieved I was that my rule had been so hateful to my people...

"Trussel then stood before me to withdraw homage on behalf of the lords. He was a rebel – one of Mortimer's gang from the start – and I expected nothing better from him. But my heart bled when next Sir Thomas le Blount, steward of my household till he fled from me at Chepstow, stepped forward, broke his staff of office – as if I were already in my coffin – and so signalled that household to be at an end."

Edward sat before Stephen, his eyes downcast, the misery of his experience once more contorting his broad fair features, and Stephen had not the heart to draw morals from his words, could not bring himself to speak of Hell, Purgatory and the need to repent. Rather he chose to place his hands over Edward's, to bow his own head, and to give comfort by prayer and thought, by the touch of fingers, and by the slightest murmur of pulse against pulse.

Chapter 17

Spring had begun to yield to early Summer, and Stephen had passed from a general apprehension at the task ahead of him to a state of occasional ecstasy at the blessed burden Providence had imposed upon him. Its occurrence depended from day to day on how cooperative he found Edward to be, on how much attention Edward was prepared to afford to him rather than to the pet rat.

The brief period of Stephen's visits to the keep had already been sufficient for Edward – in dribs and drabs – to give a full account of the events since he had last confessed. In the course of that narration some progress had been made by Stephen in bringing him to an acceptance of his own wrong-doing, at least in respect of lesser sins. When Edward seemed in a receptive mood, Stephen would linger over events from the king's tale of disaster and desertion and would try to tease out their true context. He would seek to understand what had been in the king's mind when he had made his many ill-fated decisions, to ponder what in those very circumstances God might have required of one who was indeed his substitute on earth, and, in the light of that, then measure the true weight of Edward's sinfulness.

Even with regard to venial matters, this was a hazardous process: it involved prodding the boil of the king's conscience, at times opening wounds that had festered. Sometimes faults would be acknowledged, and Stephen would prescribe penances which, it seemed, Edward observed with due contrition. When on other occasions Stephen probed too far – maybe touched on more mortal matters: those intertwined with his relations both with Isabella and Lord Hugh, Edward would explode in rage, and would rebuke and curse him, or would rant at the memory of some cruelty or ingratitude he felt others had shown him. This in turn might lead to one of his sulks and to the excruciation of his resentful silence, which could endure for days; and then Stephen would become desperate to know what he might do to crack once more the carapace of the king's hostility.

*

Such an instance occurred one day when Stephen was so bold as to suggest that Edward's affection for Hugh had deprived Hugh's wife and Isabella of their husbands, was a betrayal of the marriage bond, was a kind of Avarice, and had, as things stood, deprived Christ of four souls! Edward had become quite incoherent in his fury, had thrown himself upon his truckle bed, and had begun to tear at his sheets with his teeth. Stephen had been obliged to call for the guard, partly out of fear for his own safety, partly from fear that Edward would harm himself. For a week afterwards Edward had refused to utter one syllable till Stephen, unable to conceive of any other approach which might breach the new barricade between them, at last ventured a confession of his own. He approached Edward and, fretful there might be listeners at the door, kept his voice low:

"My lord, please believe me when I say that, far from seeking to offend or cause unnecessary pain, I have truly striven with every fibre of my being to serve as your confessor these past few weeks. In doing so I have sought to play a part vital to the salvation of your eternal soul, as sanctioned by God and my order. But if in this, my lord, I have failed so miserably, then I must tell you something which till now I had thought it best to conceal: I come here not only as your confessor, my lord, but also for another secret purpose." Stephen felt Edward's look transfix him, and he now lowered his voice still more to little more than a whisper:

"When we first met at Llanthony, my lord, it was Brother Walter's idea, in order to advance certain plots for your rescue and escape which were then under discussion with Thomas Dunsheved, that I should be placed in your company to act, not only as your confessor, but also as the means by which you, my lord, could be kept informed if, when and how any attempt at your liberation could be made. Brother Walter's plan then was that information would be provided under cover of documents sent to me from Gloucester.

"I'm sorry to say, my lord, that in the event Lord Berkeley has been far too vigilant, and since my arrival I've been denied all contact and correspondence with the outside world. Hence, no word have I had from Brother Walter, nor he from me. I can only wait, as must you, my lord, to see what, if anything, the cunning of Dunsheved and others in the Order can engineer."

A smile spread across Edward's face. He at once leapt from his stool and gestured that Stephen should kneel and kiss one of the rings on his right hand. Before Stephen could rise again, Edward leant forward and kissed him on the forehead, his glowering mood dispelled.

"Brother Stephen, I do so thank you for this news. It has cheered me more than anything else these past twelve months! May God bless you, priest – my spiritual deliverer and my temporal!...Forgive the harsh words I have uttered. Please excuse my Anger against you, which most truly I now repent. Continue your ministry to me, Stephen, do. And in all things from now on, please believe me, I will endeavour to be like you, Brother Stephen, my spiritual guide, and to lead the holy and apostolic life!...Then surely, surely I shall be worthy of rescue, and God will grant a way. What do you say, Stephen, what do you say?..."

*

When Edward was neither raging, nor sulking, yet was weary or bored with the toil of examining his own conscience, he would sometimes try to thwart Stephen's purpose out of pure perversity, or so it seemed to Stephen. Then he would avoid any reference to his own conduct, but might try to engage Stephen in debate on religious or philosophical matters, such as the efficacy of holy oil in the royal coronation, or the need for men to wear sackcloth and pour embers over their heads on St Mark's Day which, he explained, was of great importance to him, since it was his own birthday. Or he might interrogate Stephen over his own history – over his memories of the manor house and demesne where he was raised, over his studies, or over his reverence for Brother Walter, and, it seemed to Stephen, sometimes would to excess prod and pry concerning the few comments Stephen had made regarding his days at the University.

Then again Edward might refuse to focus on anything other than the mundane, or even the comical, though Stephen would then still consider it his first duty to draw out a parable, a precept or a parallel needful for salvation. Convinced as he was of the Virgin's blessing for his ministry to Edward, he felt sure that whatever banality or nonsense seized the king's attention, it must contain somewhere a kernel of holy truth worthy of exploitation.

It was on the first truly warm day of Summer that Stephen found Edward in just such a distracted mood. He was sitting at his table wearing nothing but his braies, whilst before him steamed three brass basins, each filled with water, each exuding a variety of strong aromas.

"Good day to you, Brother Stephen," said Edward looking up with an inscrutable smile. "You find me about my toilet, for it's two whole months since my hair was washed and perfumed. Sir John Maltravers has provided me with cumin, cinnamon and liquorice, which I've placed in these bowls. I was going to plunge my head into each in turn, but now you've arrived you can rinse my hair by using this goblet."

Stephen was by now well used to Edward's uninhibited, but apparently guileless requests that from time to time he should perform various intimate tasks for him – whether it was to scratch his back, or attempt the removal of an eyelash from his eye with the corner of a napkin, or something else, and he set about this latest task without demur. As he gathered up the fragrant liquors in the goblet and poured them over the back of Edward's scalp, he at first hesitated to support his free hand on the muscular shoulders which were flexed before him, but when he did so, Edward neither complained, nor flinched, though Stephen felt his own stomach knotted with anxiety.

"Might I ask, my lord, why you would wish the inconvenience of washing your hair so frequently?" he ventured. "It's surely unnecessary to perform this task so often…And don't the spices weaken the hair's strength?…Like any form of toilet, other than the most basic and necessary, all it does is to provide a diversion for one's thoughts, which might be better focused elsewhere. When carried to excess, any preening of the body may prove a vice, my lord. Indeed it may be an outward expression of the sin of Pride."

"Do you priests not wash your hair, then?" spluttered Edward, as liquorice water entered his eyes and mouth.

"Most certainly we do, my lord, but no more than twice a year…and then only with unseasoned water… But our hair, of course, is shorter generally than amongst lay people, and therefore harbours fewer lice. The tonsure is another matter. I shave my head myself with a sharp blade every fortnight at this time of year, and every three weeks during winter. That cannot be a vice, for it is a practice sanctioned by our Mother Church since olden times!"

"But as for me, Stephen, don't you think I should try to look the part of a king? All else is taken from me. Should I not at least maintain my appearance?"

"You should question in your heart, my lord, what part it is you do play, and what part it is you should play; and you must frame your thoughts and your behaviours accordingly…Which, I ask you, is more pertinent to the role you should be playing now: the kingdom of men or the Kingdom of God?"

"Brother Stephen, that's a bitter lesson to draw from the washing of my hair!" exclaimed Edward, jerking his head backwards so that water trickled from his bedraggled beard onto his chest and made pale rivulets through the thick golden hairs sprouting above his nipples. "Do you not think I shall be king again? Or do you think I shall end my days in this prison, or one like it?" Edward was now standing, and had knocked over his stool.

"I advise only, my lord, that you consider whether there may be vanity – which is a breed of Pride – in what are no more than the trappings of kingship... whether you rule again or not..." But Edward was not listening, and his countenance had changed to one of defiance. Whether he had himself drawn a parallel between the washing of his hair and his anointment as king, Stephen could not tell, but Edward now seized the nearest basin and poured its whole contents over his head:

"Can they wash the consecrating oils away," he bellowed, then hurled the basin against the wall with an almighty clatter. His body now was drenched, his soaking braies clinging to his flesh. As quickly as it had come, though, his rage dissipated, and to Stephen's surprise he began to laugh. "Take these off me!…and help me dry myself, Brother Stephen," he chuckled.

Stephen hesitated, then began to fumble with the waist-band round Edward's middle, at last managing to drag the sodden linen down over the full firm buttocks and thighs. Edward then seized a great linen towel and began rubbing himself dry and, oblivious to his confessor's blushing, motioned to Stephen to assist.

"I'll tell you what, priest: I will not wash my hair again – not with these womanish spices – at least, not till I'm free again!…Will that satisfy your preachifying?…I said I would seek to be more like you, Stephen, and I shall – I shall put away such vanities!…What, man! Are you bashful? Rub harder – I don't want to catch my death of cold."

When he was dry, Edward dropped his towel upon the floor and sauntered over to the cage where the rat snuffled and squeaked in anticipation of some tid-bit. As he bent down to drop some crumbs inside he noticed Stephen averting his gaze and staring out of the window. He chuckled again:

"Oh, come, Brother Stephen, have you never seen your monarch naked?...I suppose you have not! So gaze your fill, my dear little priest!" And with that, he began capering about the cell, so that Stephen could not avoid observing him, and in particular the half roused manhood which swayed and bobbed as Edward moved, transfixing not only Stephen's eye, but his heart and soul.

"You'll see that we are but as other men – our bodies just as hairy, our limbs formed the same, our flesh as liable to wounding. If kingship lies not in our outward form, where does it dwell? Where?...It's almost like a riddle, Stephen!...Where?"

"In the blood, my lord" stammered Stephen. "In the royal blood...in God's choice, of course...and in the oil, you mentioned just a moment ago."

Edward halted his capers and drew closer to Stephen.

"You are a good little priest, Stephen," he confided. "And a true subject...perhaps now my only one!" He placed his hands on Stephen's shoulders and, smiling, brushed each cheek with a gentle kiss.

Stephen could no longer speak. He struggled to breathe, and the whole core of his body felt riven with an uncontrollable trembling. (How would his sinful eyes dare even to glance on the wooden Virgin later that evening?) But Edward pulled away, appearing quite unconscious of his priest's discomfort, and began donning first a fresh pair of braies, then his outer clothing.

"Now, Stephen," he said, "let's sit together at the table and finish the pitcher of Gascon wine they left with me at lunch time. Till they ring the supper bell, you may comb out my hair, while I sing you a lay of Arthur I learned from Gaveston many many years ago! I trust that won't displease you?"

Chapter 18

On the eve of Whitsunday Stephen kept vigil in the Chapel of St John. He pondered and prayed all night long concerning the nature of his feelings for Edward, but by dawn no words either of comfort or explanation had been delivered to him. Edward was now the lodestar, almost the sole burden of his prayers and meditations, indeed of most of his waking thoughts. At times he could persuade himself that this was needful for his holy task – that it was to be expected, when a priest had confessed one penitent alone for weeks on end, that he should eat, drink, breathe, dream that one man's sinfulness. Yet Stephen knew, when he examined the precepts of his religion, that his obsession had no heavenly origin. It was rooted on earth, or more likely in the regions below, for at its heart was a corruption of the Devil's making. When he listened to his heart, rather than to his reason, however, he sensed a sea of desires dammed up since his days at Oxford, which threatened to overwhelm him – as it had done James, as it had done Edward, whose drowning soul he was now charged with saving.

"Can a drowning man save a drowning man?" he wondered.

In his daily ministry Stephen still played the role of polite, but firm admonisher of the wayward monarch, though at times he felt their roles reversed. The more he came to know Edward's flawed and shattered majesty, the more in awe he felt, the more he craved Edward's protection against the world's flux. He also strove to overcome a perversity gnawing at his very core: that his affection for Edward derived as much from his faults as from his qualities. Sympathy and understanding for a sinner's weakness – trusted weapons in the confessor's armoury – were indeed as mines beneath his citadel, when they implied a wish the sinner remain unchanged!

If Edward was aware of the turbulence he had produced in his priest's heart and soul, Stephen saw no indication of it. Any change in his demeanour, Stephen guessed, was more a result of his new appreciation of Stephen's role in his hoped for liberation than of anything else. It was true, though, he now became less likely to let his temper blaze, or to let his conversation career from one topic to another. His manner seemed more reflective, and he appeared genuine in treating Stephen as a friend, as well as confessor and sole remaining subject.

As for Edward's avowed intention of earning his liberty by amending his ways, following Stephen's example, and adopting a more holy and apostolic way of life, Stephen again saw little evidence as the weeks went by; and in any case he doubted the holiness of its motivation. It was true Edward did not again allow matters of his toilet to obtrude on their meetings, though Stephen saw little diminution of the lustrous quality and perfumed aura of his hair; and from what he could tell from the dirty cups and dishes sometimes piled high on his table after dinner, no request had yet gone out to Berkeley and Maltravers for a more limited diet, nor yet any declaration that Edward wished to abjure meats with the richest sauces, and chose henceforth to abstain from strong liquor!

Occasionally, though, Edward would seem reminded of what he had promised, and would question Stephen upon the manner in which he passed his time, the efficacy of hair-shirts, and the diet of the monks at Gloucester. He took Stephen's counsel too upon the prayers he should address to the Virgin Mary, and sought guidance concerning the ecstasy to be experienced by Her grace. It was here, though, that Stephen felt himself most fraudulent, for he now realised that the joy he had felt in the early weeks of Edward's confession derived not from the manifest workings of Mary's grace, but from the promptings of his own nature.

The joy of Her favour in fact remained withheld from him even when, naked before Her wooden image, he scourged his back with bundles of the stinging nettles he found growing amongst the builders' rubble. Neither grace nor relief was granted, and this mortification in no way quelled the madness of his love for Edward, or the baser urgings of the Devil, which beset him more and more in the twilit loneliness of his chamber.

*

It was during those weeks up to and beyond Whitsuntide that the noise and disruption of the building works caused even more disruption to the conditions of Stephen's life. The kitchen and great hall of the castle were largely untouched, but the buildings beyond, where the flank wall dog-legged from south to west, were now in process of demolition. So too were those buildings – a broad passageway and several large storerooms – situated between the great hall and the kitchen itself. This meant that food from the kitchen had to be brought out into the open air and into the dirt and disorder of a builders' yard before it could be served, much to the annoyance, albeit muted, of the lord's retainers, as they devoured lukewarm meals flecked with grime.

Whereas at first Stephen had found the comfort of his quarters and his access to the library an unanticipated, almost an embarrassing luxury, both were now blighted by dust and racket, so that quiet contemplation was no longer possible, at least in the daytime. Odo de Bodrugan had been right. Nor could Stephen any longer obtain access to the battlements of the eastern range. Confined to those of the inner gatehouse, his view was limited, encompassing only the west and south. He could no longer gaze in the direction of Gloucester, though he still wondered how his fellow friars were faring, and longed to be with them once again.

From the gatehouse he was, however, able to watch the progress of the works themselves. By this time, if he looked down towards the eastern range, he could see many changes, including mounds of rubble, a huge but neat stack of fresh cut stone, and a large hole which had been opened up in the outer wall, though this was partly obscured from his view behind a mesh of scaffolding supporting the masonry above. This provided ready access for both men and materials, though at night it was barred by a stout barricade.

A little after Whitsuntide, and some three weeks before Mid-Summer's Eve, when the bright sunny weather of early Summer was turning warmer, more humid, and more uncomfortable, the castle's routines suffered further dislocation, when Sir John Maltravers, who was then in charge, received an urgent summons to join Lord Berkeley and many of his retainers at the royal muster. The latest campaign against the Scots, it seemed, trumped the responsibilities imposed jointly on the two lords regarding Edward, and so the castle and its royal prisoner were left under the control of a deputy, Sir William Wauton.

From the battlements Stephen observed how the absence of the lords and their retainers diminished the bustle of men and wagons, beasts and provender within both baileys, and this lack of activity made him feel even more alone, more deserted by the world, more dependent on his daily meetings with Edward to give purpose to his existence.

*

One morning when he was venturing a closer inspection of the works of demolition, and at the same time searching for more nettles, a workman came and squatted beside him and, though Stephen stood up for fear he would be seen speaking to an outsider, the message was quickly uttered and lodged like an arrow in his brain:

"Your brother says that between the Baptist and the Apostle Paul comes Salvation. Prayers shall be answered before Vespers."

The workman then scuttled away and was soon lost in the mêlée of masons, scaffolders and carpenters milling about the bailey.

It did not take Stephen long to reason what the message implied: between Mid-Summer's Eve (which was the Feast of St John) and the Feast of St Paul the Apostle (six days later) an attempt was to be made to release Edward, and this would occur in the early evening. He fled immediately to his own room, where he lay trembling on his bed. When, however, a few hours later, he whispered to Edward the words which had been spoken and the meaning they must have, a smile spread across Edward's face and he enfolded Stephen in the warmest embrace:

"Our prayers have indeed been answered, Stephen!" he whispered. "By your ministry and my penitence, I've regained my Saviour's favour!...Come, Stephen, come. Let's kneel. Join me in joyful prayer...but not too loudly, for we must always be discreet!"

The two weeks which followed, however, were far from joyful where Stephen was concerned. He did not know what was expected of him by Brother Walter and the other conspirators. He did not know if, when the raid was made, he would be taken away in flight with Edward, or would be expected to remain where he was; and, in either case, what would happen to him. He did not know if Edward's rescuers would be aware where in the castle the king was kept, and whether he, Stephen, would have to show them; though he very much hoped that the workman-spy who had spoken to him would have relayed such information back to those who had sent him.

Meanwhile the humid weather continued. Little was seen of the sun, but instead a thick film of cloud enclosed the valley day after day, stretching unbroken from the Forest hills to the Cotswolds, and from the estuary to the Malverns away to the north. Even in the mornings when it felt cooler, sweat would trickle beneath Stephen's tunic. It would drip from his brow and nose on to the translations at which he worked spasmodically, causing ink to run and smudge. It would trickle down his back and between his buttocks making his undergarments stick to his loins.

By the middle of each day, the workmen themselves would be stripped all but naked. Even then Stephen could not imagine how in such humidity they managed to scale the scaffolding with apparent ease, whilst for him the ascent of any staircase made him pant and often pause for breath. In the evenings, clouds of gnats would hover in the stale air of the inner bailey, whilst bigger insects from the marshes, whose name he did not know, but whose high drone he learned to dread, would feast on his exposed face and legs. They fed on the rest of him as well, when it occurred to him to remove all of his clothing so that their bites might assist his body's mortification – a suffering so needful, it seemed to him, as to outweigh the Order's requirement he sleep fully clothed. After all, he reasoned, modesty was no longer an issue when now he slept alone.

This was weather too to make men short of temper, for the heavy sky oppressed the spirits, whilst the thick air seemed to clog the lungs, draining effort, forcing lethargy. Squabbles and brawls often broke out amongst the workmen. In Edward's cell too it brought disharmony, for Stephen's worries seemed to fester in its moist warmth. The more Edward paced up and down, excited at the prospect of what the following weeks might bring, the more Stephen fretted over the difficulties and dangers that might be involved. He became more taciturn, less able to engage with Edward in debate, to remonstrate over the perils afflicting his soul, or to argue him down from the pinnacles of unreason where his fancy often led him.

One afternoon when Edward's hopes for his release had so inflamed his imagination that he had begun speculating on a triumphant re-entry into London, and all the while Stephen had been sitting, his hands clasped, his legs knotted together with anxiety, Edward suddenly seized the rat's cage and brandished it at Stephen. As its occupant screeched and snapped at Edward's fingers, he bellowed his frustration in Stephen's face:

"Where's your heart, priest? Has it shrivelled away? Have you no blood in your veins? Why don't you rejoice with me at the good fortune that beckons us?" Glancing quickly at the door, he then lowered his voice:

"This pitiful rat, Stephen, is dearer to me than you are when you are in this mood, what with your worries and your nay-saying, and your reasons why not! If only, when the fellow spoke to you, you'd detained him longer and sought more details, we'd have far more certainty about Walter's plans. What were you thinking of? And why at the very least did you not send him back with more details about our situation?"

"But my lord," Stephen attempted, "the fellow was here, and then he was gone. It was all so unexpected. No sooner had he spoken, than he vanished, and I've seen neither hide nor hair of him since. If anyone had seen us speaking, we'd both have been in danger – even more so if I'd tried to detain him. You know the rules their lordships have laid down!"

It was a conversation they had rehearsed many times since the day of the spy's appearance, and, despite Stephen's protestations, it would be repeated again in the days which followed.

It was in vain, too, that Stephen prayed and prostrated himself before the Virgin, used ever more painful means to punish his flesh, and begged relief from the sharpness of Edward's rebukes. She would in no way assist him. He knew then that his suffering was a just and proper punishment both for his failure as a confessor and for his sinfulness as a man.

*

When Midsummer's Eve at last arrived it brought with it a welcome change in the weather: the skies cleared, the sun shone hot and bright, and there was a freshness in the air which spoke of the sea, of hulks and cogs bobbing in the Channel beyond Bristol, of journeys, and of escape.

Nevertheless, Stephen's anxiety mounted as the day progressed. After an hour spent with Edward in the most desultory of conversations, he had no stomach for supper, and he thought he would die of apprehension, as he then waited till well after Vespers for something, anything, to happen. When at last it became clear that this was not the evening chosen for the king's liberation, he felt almost dazed with relief, absurdly happy that Destiny – whatever it might involve – had been delayed a short while longer.

The next day also dawned warm and clear, and again Stephen was first stretched on the rack of expectation, only to be released later into an ecstasy of disappointment.

Not so the day that followed. For that evening after supper, as he knelt at prayer in his room, there came the most thunderous knocking at the main gate to the inner bailey. His stomach lurched as he scrambled to a narrow window along the corridor. From there, stretching forward, he could just glimpse the inner gatehouse to which several retainers were now running. There were shouts. There was more hammering. Then there were voices raised from beyond the gate, but no words which he could understand. More retainers, Sir William Wauton amongst them, rushed from the direction of the great hall and joined their fellows, whilst a loud altercation rose on both sides of the gate.

At last, those within were persuaded to admit those without. The great bolts were drawn back, and, as the gate swung open, five armed horsemen cantered under the arch of the gatehouse. They seemed on the point of dismounting and surrendering weapons when the sound of a trumpet blared out from the far end of the bailey. Stephen guessed it came from beyond the castle wall, perhaps from the barricade made by the builders Almost immediately there was a resounding crash, as if a great weight of wood and masonry had collapsed to the ground. Some fifteen horsemen then galloped into view and charged the throng of retainers from the rear. On foot and taken by surprise, these now found themselves assaulted from both sides, as the first five riders joined in the fray. Soon the cobblestones before the gatehouse were strewn with corpses and severed limbs, and the victorious attackers turned their attention to the rest of the household cowering in the castle buildings.

Stephen was terrified for his own safety. In the growing dusk screams rang out from all quarters, and he could see fires had been started at the bottom of several staircases. Some of the raiders were storming the steps leading up to Edward's cell, and there was more yelling as the guards were overcome. From the sound of steady crashing, Stephen guessed an attempt was being made to break down the doors into the keep and the prison itself.

Afraid the intruders might not know of his own role in their plot, Stephen hurried to the Chapel of St John, only to find the kitchen staff already there in sanctuary. If he joined them and later they saw him speak to any of the attackers, as well he might have to, his duplicity would be revealed. He doubled back towards his own room, holding his crucifix before him, and was about to cross its threshold when a slight cough from the garderobe made the sweat freeze on his brow.

"God give you good evening, Brother Stephen," a voice whispered, as a hand took his shoulder and pushed him into his own room. "I hope I did not startle you." The hand now pulled back the man's hood to reveal the face of Brother Thomas Dunsheved.

"And I hope you will not mind if I now tie you up! Please, lie face down upon the bed. We must make it look as though you were in no way involved with this dastardly raid!" Stephen's hands shook behind his back as he proffered them to Dunsheved.

"Then I am to stay here, and not accompany you and the king," he said, his words muffled by the tapestry on the bed-frame.

"Yes, you will be safer here, always provided you come under no suspicion! Hence these precautions! Besides, we must make every haste in our escape, and cannot be encumbered by a Dominican who refuses to mount a horse! You don't mind being referred to as an encumbrance, Brother Stephen?" Dunsheved chuckled to himself as he tied Stephen's wrists and then his ankles together with strong thick twine.

"Stay on the bed...and if I smear some of this blood from my dagger on your habit and on your hands...oh, and if I just nick you... so...it will look as if you put up a fight!" As Dunsheved pulled Stephen's head back, he felt the sting of steel upon his face, and, as he gasped, he felt a slight warmth begin to run over his chin and drip upon the tapestry. Another voice rang out in the corridor:

"Come, Thomas, we have the king, and must be gone! Sir Rhys and Sir Edmund have found the stables, so we'll have horses for booty too!" A second man had entered the chamber, and, as Stephen strained round to see who it might be, he saw a man strongly resembling Dunsheved, though a little older.

"Brother Stephen," said Dunsheved, "we must always meet and part in such haste! Pray for our mission, and for the king's safety. For my part, I pray that you may soon resume your studies at Gloucester!"

With that the two were gone, leaving Stephen, his chin unpleasantly moist, his eyes beginning to smart as thick smoke wafted up from the lower corridor.

PART FOUR: TO CORFE

Chapter 19

"Then I may not return to my priory in Gloucester?" Stephen tried to conceal his feelings, as he stood before Berkeley and Maltravers in the gatehouse tower. The two lords had returned immediately news of Edward's escape had reached Mortimer and the queen, and they had now been released from any further part in the Scottish War.

"I'm afraid that will not be possible, at least for the present," said Lord Thomas. "As I say, our investigations reveal no suspicion against your own conduct, Brother Stephen – quite the reverse – but your presence here remains a necessity. Sir Edward will be recaptured – you can rest assured of that! Sir John and I have been appointed special commissioners to scour the West Country for trouble-makers, and this we intend to do till we hunt down the kidnappers and have Sir Edward back in our custody…He will then have need of his confessor once again!"

"Also, if you assume," said Sir John, "that it is known generally that the former king is at large, then that is not the case! And so it must remain…Not, of course, that you would speak loosely, if you were to return to Gloucester, Brother Stephen. We know that!" Sir John's smile was sour. "But the very fact of your leaving Berkeley would set tongues wagging. So, I'm afraid that here you must stay."

"My fate seems bound up with that of Sir Edward…" began Stephen.

"So too is ours. You may believe it," said Berkeley, a certain grimness in his own tone. "But we shall not be dragged down by his treachery…Furthermore, we take exception to the way our hospitality has been spurned; and once we have him back, he'll learn how a guest should behave…No doubt you will help us instil in him a proper respect for the legitimate authorities under God, Brother Stephen!"

Stephen did not intend to bandy words, or to prolong the interview any more than was necessary, so he mumbled his non-committal assent, and was soon relieved to find Sir John ushering him towards the door. But Sir John had not quite finished with him:

"As will be obvious, Brother Stephen, it's vital appearances be maintained. You will attend the great hall at least once every day, without exception, and will work in the library as before. Most importantly, you should also attend the cell within the keep every afternoon...Whilst many of our own people are aware of what has happened, and have been sworn to secrecy on pain of severe chastisement, any visitor to the castle – dare one say, any spy – must see and believe that Sir Edward remains where he has been since before Easter, and continues to receive the benefit of your ministry!...And, you will appreciate, it is more necessary than ever, Brother Stephen, that you should refrain from speech with such a person!"

*

Since most of the retainers had returned from the North with their master, life in the castle now returned very much to what it had been in the early Summer – save, from Stephen's standpoint, for the eviscerating absence of Edward himself. Without Edward and their daily meetings in the keep, his life's purpose seemed to have fallen away, and those other pursuits, even those of the chapel and the library, even his attempts at communion with the Blessed Virgin, all of which had meant so much to him when he had first arrived at the castle, now lacked any but the slightest savour. Likewise, when he tried to comfort himself by recalling times, places, people whom in the past had been dear to him, all now seemed dull as pewter or tarnished brass, whilst Edward's memory glowed with the lustre of an illuminated manuscript, or the sparkling radiance of a many faceted jewel.

The worst time each day for Stephen was the empty hour he had to spend in Edward's cell, pretending that he was about his priestly business. The only business he could transact was in fact to try feeding the caged rat from the plates of food still brought in for Edward, and then later carried away by one of Berkeley's most trusted servants. However, the rat's appetite seemed lacking. Perhaps it too was pining. He fell to talking to it as if it were a lost soul, though in truth it was he that was lost, deprived as he was of his freedom, his mission, and his heart's focus. Berkeley had become *his* prison, for within its walls he had no joy, company, nor means of escape.

At times it was as though he was Edward's substitute, locked away from the world in expiation for the monarch's years of misrule. Yet he could not become Edward – even if deep down some part of him wished that he could. Neither was he the lamb by whose sacrifice Edward's wrong-doings might be forgiven. His was an imprisonment without purpose, redemptive or otherwise. At times he smiled as he imagined himself the most pitiful king in Christendom, one whose realm comprised his room, the cell, the chapel, and the library. It was a land where his will was sovereign, but where no subjects dwelt – other than the rat – and freedom to act was a delusion.

Stephen knew that it was now that he should have spent more time upon his studies, taking full advantage of the treasures to be found in Lord Berkeley's library. But somehow he could not do so. Indeed, he now abandoned any attempt at translating Virgil's "Eclogues". It was better somehow to be seduced by the fabulous images of a bestiary, or to ponder learned texts from Cicero and Aristotle on Friendship's meaning and on Friendship as an ideal, or to sit gazing towards the keep through the library's open shutters, reflecting on those many hours of discourse he had had with Edward, even those which had been difficult and vexatious, but were now hallowed through absence and time's passage.

*

St Swithin's Day brought the briefest respite from his loneliness when, as he was entering the library, Sir John surprised him with the request that he follow him to the great hall where a visitor awaited. As they entered together, Stephen was at first startled, then alarmed to see none other than Brother James seated at one of the servants' tables. James leaped to his feet and ran to greet Stephen, kissing him on both cheeks, and beaming through his gums and gaps.

It was clear that any diffidence at what had passed between them was vanquished, at least where James was concerned. But Stephen found himself torn between the warmth of the smile which at once rose to his own lips and Barelonde's cool breeze still blowing through his memory. He knew too, though, that whatever resentment might still lurk in his breast, all must appear normal, if Sir John was to remain with them, as Stephen imagined he would. It was in fact Sir John who first spoke:

"Since I'm sure Brother James need not detain you long, I trust this corner of the great hall will serve for your discussion, and I of course will be pleased to keep you company! Please go ahead, Brother James. I'm sure we'd both welcome the latest news from Gloucester." Brother James looked more than a little discomfited.

"I do indeed bring greetings from Brother Walter, who is currently in Paris at the meeting of the Chapter, and from the other monks," he began. "But as to news, there's little to report from the priory itself. Life continues much as normal…though I had many sicknesses to deal with in the months after you left, Brother Stephen…No, it is news of *you* that in fact I, or rather we, seek…It's so many months since we've heard a word from you, Stephen. We were afraid you might have suffered a recurrence of your illness of the winter months."

"I am well. I am well – as you can see," said Stephen. "And I thank you and all my brothers for their greetings and their concern. As for my failure to write, I…"

"Feel no need to apologise, Brother Stephen," said Sir John. "I'm surprised your brothers do not realise the importance of your great mission here, your need to devote yourself to Sir Edward, and not to waste your time in idle correspondence."

"But of course, of course," said Brother James. "Far be it for us to…to… But, then again, what of your studies, Brother Stephen? Brother Drogo was most eager to know…Surely…"

"My studies…"

"Oh, have no fear on that account, Brother James," said Sir John. "Brother Stephen has spent many hours perusing the fine volumes kept here in Lord Berkeley's library. No doubt, in due course you and your fellows at the priory will enjoy the fruits of those labours. But for now I must emphasise Brother Stephen's main purpose here is to wrestle with the soul of Sir Edward, and indeed he will shortly be needed at the prisoner's room to begin his efforts once more!"

"Yes, but not for another hour," Stephen blurted out, desperate not to see the meeting terminated almost before it had begun. "Of course, Sir Edward occupies very much of my time, Brother James, but I'm truly sorry if my brothers think I have neglected either them or my other duties. Believe me, it was far from my intention."

"Ah, am I mistaken as to the time?" said Sir John, with an innocent smile. "If there really is another hour before you see Sir Edward, perhaps you'd like to enlighten Brother James on the progress you've made with the soul of our former monarch. And I would certainly be more than fascinated to hear of this myself!" Here Stephen felt himself on firmer ground:

"As you know, Sir John, for me to disclose anything Sir Edward has said to me would be to breach the secrecy of the confession,

152

which I am not permitted even to contemplate." Now he needed to seize the initiative in a way Sir John could not then sabotage:

"Brother James, you must tell me of the sicknesses you've treated this spring. Are all of our brethren still in good health? – I pray none have passed away... And are there any new members of our fraternity? Do you yet have a new novice to help with your work in the infirmary...and perhaps in your care for the beggars of the Barelonde?"

He was not sure why he mentioned this, but in his nervousness to divert discussion away from Edward somehow it had tumbled from his lips. Now he had placed Brother James in difficult territory:

"A novice?...Yes...there is Brother Felix, with whom...but I am sure, you...Yes, he helps me about the infirmary...But you asked about the illnesses I have encountered?..." With that, James embarked on a detailed account of his ministrations to each and every of his patients, and there, amongst the humours – black, yellow, blood and phlegm – the planetary influences, and the endless variegations of urine, he and Stephen were at least able to communicate uninterrupted by Sir John, though in a way which pleased neither of them, for nothing was said which enlightened James as to the matters weighing on Stephen's mind, and Stephen himself learned nothing of value concerning the world beyond the castle walls.

When at last the topic of medicine had been exhausted, James looked with expectation at Stephen, and there was a silence, whilst Maltravers smirked.

"Well, Brother," said James at last, "do you have any message I can relay to Brother Drogo and, when he returns, to our father prior?"

"Only my heartfelt love, and my wish that before long we may all meet again," responded Stephen, fearing there was nothing more he could say. Then in desperation he added: "And by the Baptist and the Apostle, you may say that all is well with me," and wished at once he had not done so, for James looked surprised at such an unusual oath, whilst Sir John's eyes narrowed as he fixed Stephen with a keen gaze.

They passed out into the inner bailey, where the walls beyond the kitchens were now in the process of being rebuilt. All around there was a banging and a chiselling, as workmen fashioned piles of rough boulders into building blocks for the new extension to the range, others wheeled great barrows to and fro, and yet others mixed lime into a mortar. Sir John summoned a servant who was sent to accompany James to the outer gate, and so the two friars could do no more than embrace once again and bid farewell to each other, unsaid words hovering like the dust in the air about them.

As they walked in the direction of the keep, Stephen was relieved when Sir John made no comment on his invocation of Saints John and Paul, or on any other aspect of their interview. He seemed more concerned to hasten about his other duties, and soon Stephen was able – albeit with his now usual reluctance – to take the stair to the first floor of the keep, where no one but a disconsolate rat awaited him. In the long lacuna before the supper bell, his thoughts reverted to James, no doubt now toiling on foot towards the highway, and he wondered at the way the old James seemed to have returned, no longer hostile, no longer resentful, and, it seemed, no longer possessed of the demon that had shown itself at Barelonde. He wondered what feat of the confessor's skill Brother Walter or Brother Drogo had performed to release James from its tutelage. Or perhaps it was simply that, without realising it, he had himself forgiven James, as Brother Walter had been most insistent that he should; or maybe in the maelstrom of his own recent emotions a magnanimity had been bred, which, despite its origin, he must accept as God's blessing.

Once the supper bell had rung, and Stephen emerged from the staircase to the inner bailey, still absorbed with James and their discussion, he had the slight suspicion that, as he approached the great hall, and later, when he left after supper and mounted to the Chapel of St John, he was again being followed. He was unsure at first if it was his imagination, but the feeling continued that evening and during the weeks which followed. If he drew to a sudden halt and turned round, he would never see anyone who beyond doubt was stalking him, yet he became convinced that since James' visit he had come under closer surveillance than he had been before. Perhaps the very fact of the visit had alerted Maltravers' suspicions rather more than he had supposed.

From then on, even when both Sir John and Lord Berkeley were away from the castle at the same time – something which now occurred often, due to their new duties as special commissioners – Stephen rarely found that he could pass an hour undisturbed in the library, or even in the Chapel of St John, without one or other of Lord Berkeley's servants finding an excuse to enter, to check on something which they would not then specify, or merely, they claimed, to pass the time of day.

Chapter 20

During the four weeks which followed Edward's escape, there were many days when the sun blazed down upon the small hillock on which Berkeley sat amongst the marshes and fields of grain. Predictions were made of a fine harvest. Stephen hoped and prayed that the weather augured well for the Dunsheveds and their raiding party, and that in such conditions they might have made speedy progress towards the sea. If they had headed for the Bristol Channel coast, they might well already have set sail for Ireland, or perhaps even for Brittany, or distant Gascony. If instead they were making for the South Coast, their journey would, he imagined, have been longer and much more arduous, though he knew little about the terrain beyond the Avon and the Mendip Hills, his own travels never having taken him further south than Bristol.

He craved news of their progress, but none came, nor was likely, given Lord Berkeley's embargo on any mention within the castle of the ex-king's absence or of his possible whereabouts. Stephen implored the Virgin for a sign that Dunsheved had succeeded and that, even as he uttered his prayers, Edward was aboard ship and bound for safety. But the veil of silence which had fallen between himself and the Holy Mother remained intact. On this, as on all else, She remained mute, impassive, unmoved by tears or self-chastisement.

The days became more and more a torture to him, as his observance of the religious hours, his attendance at meals, his desultory study in the library – all filled but a fraction of the time between dawn and dusk, or so it seemed to him; and nothing he did seemed to help him understand and prepare for whatever future lay ahead. If Edward had reached Ireland or the continent, Stephen worried that this would mean closer scrutiny of the escape and his own part in it. If, instead, Edward had been captured and was imprisoned at the Tower or elsewhere, would he, Stephen, be required to join the king? Or would he remain at Berkeley, or perhaps even be allowed to return to his priory? The world felt more uncertain and unsafe than it had ever been, and this when the joy of Edward's company and his belief in his own ministry had been snatched away from him.

He fell to vain repetition of every prayer he knew, every text he could recall, and to telling the rosary beads a fantastical number of times daily – partly as a penance, partly to fill the empty hours, partly to annihilate the doubts which beset him as to the very point of his existence. When he did not fill his mind with prayer or the semblance of prayer, he would fall to worrying about his own health: would sense a residue of the winter's illness within him; would fear that his night-sweats owed more to a malady deep within his body than to the summer heat; would eventually persuade himself that the discomfort in his belly was the gnawing of some evil worm such as were contained in the Bestiary, stirred from dormancy by the rich fare served in the great hall, or, worse still, nourished and bloating on his own life's blood.

At Lammastide the weather broke, and for days squalls blew in from the Estuary, flattening the barley, driving workmen from the fields, making the inner walls of the castle moist and slimy. In places rivulets of rain-water would trickle and drip from ceilings and mantelpieces, rousing to activity the pale whiskery insects and crustaceans normally concealed deep within the castle's blocks and mortar. Stephen found himself more than ever confined to his small desolate kingdom, due to the weather itself, but also to his own resolve to take only one meal a day in the great hall, for otherwise the worm might grow and grow, and might eventually burrow from his stomach to his other organs, spreading poison and putrefaction as it went. But when challenged on his absences, he pleaded his need to fast in readiness for the Feast of the Assumption.

One evening as the sun made its sole appearance of the day, struggling to gleam briefly at the edge of clouds shrouding the Forest hills, Stephen was leaving the great hall after his one meal, when he witnessed the arrival of a troop of horsemen beneath the arch of the inner gatehouse. All seemed bedraggled. Their pennants sagged against their spears, and their colours were barely visible beneath a thick coating of mud, but Stephen recognised at least the voice giving orders. It was that of Sir John Maltravers, who had been absent from the castle now for many days. Stephen turned away, and was about to enter the stairs to his own chamber, when the sound of another voice made him halt and turn round. It was lighter than Sir John's, and was cursing those who were pulling its owner from his horse, the man's hands being bound. Stephen felt a stab of fear and disbelief. There was a scuffle as the man was hauled to his feet, and then dragged still shouting oaths into the gatehouse tower. Stephen could not bring himself to move, neither to approach Sir John, nor to retreat within the building, for tears were welling in his eyes – whether for grief or exhilaration, he could not say.

*

It was several days before Stephen was allowed to resume his ministry to Edward, though in the interim he was still required to visit Edward's empty cell each afternoon, and he could only assume that during this period Edward himself was being kept elsewhere by way of punishment – perhaps in one of the many dank dungeons Lord Thomas had at his disposal. When they were at last permitted to meet, it was on the Feast of the Virgin's Assumption – a festival in the past dear to Stephen's heart, and one on which at other times he would have spent many hours in a state approaching spiritual ecstasy. On this occasion, though, the Virgin's diffidence, his apprehension at what Edward would have to tell him, and his general feelings of unease and illness, robbed him of any such sentiment, and he mounted the narrow staircase to the keep more full of ruefulness than of rap-

ew locks and hinges had been fixed to the door of the cell dur-
he preceding few days, and it took the guard longer than usual to
rd Stephen access. As he entered down the short flight of steps, he
ild see Edward lying motionless on his bed, his back to the room,
id it was not until the guard had once more closed and locked the
oor behind him that Edward turned his head to face his visitor.

At once Stephen observed how Edward had suffered for the sake of his six weeks' liberty – whether through the privations of his journey, or more recent ill-treatment at the hands of his captors, he would soon discover. Edward's face was thinner, more drawn, he thought; and there was none of the usual lustre about his beard and his hair, which hung in lank skeins about his head. His body too seemed thinner. But from Edward's demeanour it was clear at once that it was the inner man which had suffered most: his countenance was grim and there was little sparkle, either of joy or of anger, about his eyes. He eased himself up and swung his legs round till he was facing Stephen.

"Brother priest, I am happy to see *you*, if nothing else in this loathsome place! But you...you do not look well, Brother Stephen...if I may say so...Pray, don't tell me you are ill as well, for I had hoped *you* might cure *me* of the sickness of body and of soul I've fallen into these last few weeks."

Stephen felt his cheeks burn as tears spilled upon them, and he fell to his knees before Edward, clasping his hands, kissing them repeatedly:

"Oh my lord...yes, it's true I have not been in the best of health, but it does me such good now to see you again...even if I'm sure we both wish you were many miles from here! Believe me, my lord, I'd rather have been bound for weeks in a dungeon myself, than to see you imprisoned again here in this cell!" Stephen found himself sobbing, unable to say any more for the moment, and to his surprise Edward wrapped his arms round his shoulders, kissing him on the lips and cheeks, as if to calm him.

"May God bless you for your love and loyalty to me, Brother Stephen! – My friend and best subject!...What a sorry couple we make..." But emotion stifled further speech, and they remained clasped together in silence for a long while until their grief was spent. When at last their grip on each other relaxed and they moved apart, Edward motioned to Stephen to sit beside him on the bed, and there they remained their arms just touching by way of comfort, their mouths still mute, till it was time for Stephen to leave.

From then on their daily meetings became less a confessional, less a litany of events and self-justifications on Edward's part, but more a communion between two fractured souls – the one, loathed and rejected by almost all whom he had once ruled; the other, racked by fears for the future and cast adrift from the certainties that had governed so much of his life till then. Though in time Edward's bodily strength began to return with the regular nourishment once more provided by his captors, his spirit, it seemed to Stephen, remained broken, lacking much of the energy and wilfulness which had made him so tantalisingly perverse, so difficult to reason with, and so needful of Stephen's patient ministry. At the same time, Stephen felt himself less inclined when they met to censure Edward's words or actions, or to enter into disputation with him. Their discourse therefore became gentler in its tone, more spasmodic and diffuse in its nature, and this betokened, Stephen told himself, the withering of Edward's Pride and Anger, and the beating within his breast of a now contrite heart.

Stephen knew now that, despite his own wilful blindness to the Virgin's ineffable goodness, and despite Her apparent indifference to his pleadings, She had on Her Assumption Day entered his life once more, had instilled in his mind a ministry which complemented that which he had employed to date – a new ministry both of love and moreover empathy, a ministry that smoothed sin away through the touch of a hand, through the warmth of a smile, and often through a paucity, rather than an effusion of words. He told himself that She had been caring for him as She always had, that once again he had been blinded by his own error, by his own focus on the wrong worries, the wrong questions. It was indeed a miracle beyond understanding that the Virgin could overlook such waywardness on his part, and persist in Her beneficence towards him.

His own ailments began to recede. He no longer worried so much over the worm gnawing at his guts, and resumed attendance at the great hall both for dinner and supper. His self-confidence too began to recover, with his life grounded once again on Edward – the rod and staff, almost the pillar of his purpose and existence. Their meetings became a sacrament, no less necessary for his own soul's health, than for Edward's. And if sometimes, when they embraced, their lips or maybe their tongues touched, and if within Stephen there burned a molten ember of desire they might uncover one another's nakedness, he would clothe his conscience, fill his mind with words spoken by Edward many weeks before. So he would praise God that David was beloved of Jonathan, and that John was the Saviour's beloved disciple. He would tell himself also that God dwelt in Friendship, and that loving a friend meant also loving God.

Only in the shadow on the stair, or in the darkness beyond the flicker of a candle – and beyond his mind's fickle compass – dwelt any horror such as he had felt at Barelonde, or any guilt such as had racked him at Oxford, or any admission that he was now in mortal error for which punishment must ensue.

*

The day following their renewed and almost silent encounter, Edward strove to tell the story of his failed attempt at liberty, as they sat either side of the plain wooden table, their hands clasped together across its width. From time to time Edward paused in his narrative, as if his own words had the taste of bile:

160

"As we galloped from the castle, my friend, you would not believe how thrilled I was at the rush of air about me – the pounding of hooves, the fresh smell of heathland – as we approached Michaelwood…I could not care my enemies might pursue me – though in fact we had stolen or turned loose all of their horses. I rode for sheer exhilaration of being free, and could have gone on, and on, and on, if we'd not needed in the end to rest and water the horses, and take cover ourselves during the hours of daylight.

"By that first dawn we had passed though Michaelwood, and also through much of the Kingswood Chase, despite being hampered by the endless tangle of brambles and the furze which grows there…We lay low near the banks of the Avon till nightfall, then made our way to the old bridge at Keynsham, and so on into Somerset.

"It was Dunsheved's intention that not all of the raiding party would accompany us once we had passed the river. We hoped to draw less attention to ourselves, if our numbers were small, though for my own safety's sake it was agreed that at least six swordsmen should stay with me as we skirted the vast marshlands of the Levels and passed on into the Mendip wastelands…We avoided villages. We did not even raid the most outlying dwellings for supplies – preferring to go hungry till we could eat and rest at those priories along the way – mostly Augustinian – whom the Dunsheveds had warned to expect our arrival.

"Our progress became slower and slower as we moved southwards. Dunsheved's plan was that we should reach the coast of Dorset within a week, but we passed too far to the east and lost our way in the forests of Selwood. Thomas and his brother had by this time left us, which was perhaps the biggest mistake made, for those who remained were for the most part ruffians of less ability and cunning. It was obvious they had no clear idea of the direction in which we should have been heading! We learned too, at the few friaries where we were able to take shelter, that by now Berkeley's agents were searching the countryside for 'certain brigands and escaped malefactors', as it was said, though there seemed to be no rumours as to our true identity!

"Twice by the time we crossed into Dorset we had encountered small groups of horsemen who challenged us to explain who we were. Then of course we had no alternative but to attack and butcher them, which in turn only led to our whereabouts and the route we were following becoming more and more apparent to Berkeley and his henchmen, who were in pursuit.

"We became weakened by lack of food, and at night we suffered from heat and from clouds of midges. – These were of course the weeks of summer before the weather broke! – Our situation became desperate, and in the end we were surprised and I was taken prisoner near Shaftesbury. It was an all too familiar experience for me...and it made me think time and again of poor Hugh.

"I don't know what became of my companions at the end, though I'm sure they will have been slaughtered...I heard later on – in fact, the swine, Maltravers, took considerable delight in telling me – that the Dunsheveds had also been taken, as had other members of the gang. All our efforts therefore had come to nothing.

"I was then held prisoner at the huge castle which overlooks the sea at Corfe. – It's a castle where Maltravers himself is governor. – My God, it was a miserable time! Not least because of the taunts and cruelty I had to endure when Maltravers, and in due course Berkeley, came to gloat...How vastly relieved they must have been no longer to have to answer to Mortimer for my escape!

"What else can I tell you, Stephen!...I received some show of kindness from the castle's constable, but he was the only one...For the rest it was as if I were no more than a chained bear or dog to be baited and abused...How they loved telling me of the Great Mortimer and his *successful* escape from the Tower! How they enjoyed reminding me that another King Edward had been murdered at Corfe in olden times!...But in the end they did not have the mercy to kill *me*! Instead I was bound up like a common thief, and forced to ride with Maltravers and his men for days through rain, mud, and hailstones, till we returned here to Berkeley just five days ago, where – were it not for your love and kindness, Stephen – I'd hang myself, or starve myself, or beat my brains out against the walls of this prison cell."

Edward could say no more, but took up his goblet, which he drained of wine, then refilled and drained again. Neither could Stephen think of words which would offer anything approaching solace, though he stood and moved to Edward's side of the table, where he placed his hands upon his shoulders, letting Edward rest his head against his breast. It was in fact Edward who then began reciting from the Book of Job:

"Why did I not die from the womb? Why did I not give up the ghost when I came out of my mother's belly?...Man that is born of woman is of few days, and is full of troubles. He comes forth like a flower and is cut down: he flees also like a shadow, and does not continue..."

Chapter 21

His hopes thwarted, Edward became more taciturn, more prone to listen, rather than to rail, even when Stephen spoke of guilt and penance. Yet yellow bile still seemed to course through his body at the mention of certain individuals. He became bitter towards the Dunsheveds, the more he meditated on the woeful decisions they had taken, and his temper could still flare at the very mention of his wife and Mortimer. It was, however, Sir John Maltravers who bore the brunt of his hostility.

During the weeks at Corfe and on the hard road north again it was clear Edward had come to know Sir John for the first time. (Previously he seemed to have been aware of him only as a kinsman of Lord Berkeley). His embittered view of him was, of course, due to the privations and indignities meted out to him under Sir John's command, but, as Stephen knew all too well, there was also a cruelty in Sir John's words as much as in his actions, and a sneering insincerity in his manner, which made him all the more loathsome, and of this Edward was now cognisant. If ever Fortune's Wheel turned the world once more on its head, a fate worse than Lord Hugh's would be reserved for Sir John, and afterwards his quartered body would adorn the gates of Corfe, Berkeley, Kenilworth, and London – or so Edward vowed.

When Edward spoke in this way, Stephen often tried to counsel him against thoughts of personal revenge, and urged on him the virtue of endurance, though he himself felt more than a flicker of sympathy for Edward's attitude, for from the moment of their first meeting at Hereford, Stephen had disliked the snide insinuations and serpentine temperament of a man who appeared the more malign alongside his staid, less imaginative brother-in-law.

It was with no enthusiasm, therefore, that Stephen found himself obliged to answer a summons from Sir John one Monday morning, just as summer began to turn to autumn – that season when in other years Stephen's thoughts would have been full of rejoicing at the Feast of the Virgin's Birth, rather than of the manifold worries and responsibilities now afflicting him at Berkeley. As before, he was required to report to the inner gatehouse, where he found Sir John alone. To his surprise Sir John at once asked him to be seated and invited him to share the remains of a breakfast of eel meat and ale.

"I trust, Brother Stephen, you now see how important it was that you remained here, whilst we were hunting down Sir Edward and his kidnappers. I knew it would not be long before we had him back under our control...And be assured, Brother Stephen, that I thank our Saviour, both that we were able to rescue him from people who intended him harm, and that you were here on his return and able so swiftly to resume your ministry...Might I enquire how you find him, now that it is several weeks since he became our guest again?"

"In health, my lord, he was certainly weak when he first returned, but his strength is recovering now. His spirit is somewhat crushed, though...I need hardly say, Sir John, that he finds it a calamity to have been recaptured, and is by no means reconciled to the thought he must remain your prisoner here at Berkeley for an indefinite period."

"It's as I feared, then. He remains deluded as to his true interests. Does he not realise that the men who secured his release only wished to use him? They were little better than brigands who'd have ransomed him to the highest bidder. Surely that's obvious!...You, Brother Stephen, would have no knowledge of these matters, of course, but the gang was notorious, gathered round a renegade priest called Dunsheved – a man once employed by Sir Edward himself, but apparently later condemned for the gross irregularities of his life! God be praised, though – not only the rabble which were taken with Sir Edward, but the ring-leaders too have been captured and currently await a bitter punishment.

"Is Sir Edward still so blind that he does not realize he is safest here under our protection, and that – though we must appear to him in the role of gaolers – it is Lord Thomas and myself who have his best interests at heart?" Stephen could not bring himself to respond, but waited expectantly while Sir John paused, and then helped himself to more ale.

"But it was not the kidnappers I wished to discuss with you," he resumed. "Nor indeed the humble efforts we have made to date on Sir Edward's behalf...The fact is, Brother Stephen, that Sir Edward's life is now more in jeopardy than it ever was. Not only from adventurers like Dunsheved, but from others: some of considerably higher rank, some indeed of the court, who would like to be rid of a person they see both as an embarrassment and a threat to those who wield power...Though I speak to you in confidence – even my brother-in-law is not aware of our discussion – neither he nor I are of that persuasion, and we will do all we can to preserve Sir Edward's life and comfort...It would be well, Brother Stephen, if Sir Edward were made aware of this..." Stephen almost gasped, but managed to reply:

"But, my lord – I may speak freely? – Sir Edward was condemned, found guilty of many crimes, stripped of his crown at Kenilworth, and later was committed by Mortimer to the custody of yourself and of Lord Berkeley. How should he consider you other than as gaolers and oppressors? What cause would he have to think of you as allies? And besides, he smarts still from the indignities he tells me he suffered after his recapture..."

"The times are fluid, Brother Stephen. The times are fluid. And in such times a man must often play outwardly a role which pains him inwardly. Neither you nor Sir Edward should assume anything...or anyone... is quite as they seem!...

"Now, let me reassure you, Brother Stephen, I have spoken with your prior, Brother Walter. We are agreed that certain measures must now be taken which may preserve and benefit Sir Edward...But for the time being it's necessary only that Sir Edward be aware and accept that it is we, that is Lord Thomas and myself, who are his true friends...In that respect, I was hoping that you, Brother Stephen, might use your best endeavours to persuade him...?"

Stephen felt perspiration on his brow, and a dizziness, as if the castle was no longer moored to its foundations. Could it be true Brother Walter was in correspondence with Sir John Maltravers? Could they really be in league? He could not think so. It must surely be that for some dark objective Stephen could not yet fathom, Sir John now needed to reverse Edward's antipathy, and, to secure that end, sought to use his confessor as intermediary and to lie over Walter's involvement.

"I will tell him what you say, my lord," was the only response he could muster. But Sir John had not finished:

"You must realise, Brother Stephen, how highly I and my brother-in-law value the role you've played over the last few months here. Rest assured, I've said so in my discussions with Brother Walter, and would be only too pleased to say as much again and more to others in your order. I'm sure you get my drift..."

*

When Stephen discussed all that Sir John had said with Edward, they agreed on the utmost caution. Neither could believe Brother Walter to be involved in any plot hatched by Sir John, so they could only suppose some kind of trap, either for Walter, or more likely for Edward himself. Maltravers' intention might be to spawn further evidence of treason, which could then be used by Mortimer in any trial against him, and Edward cursed Sir John more than ever, likening him to Samson's tormentors when he was bound and powerless, to Satan and Beelzebub and then, as his fancy took wing, to a would-be Judas, and he vowed vengeance, even if he had to rip out Maltravers' lying tongue with his own teeth.

Stephen had to be more than circumspect the following day when he left Edward only to find Sir John on the stairs down to the courtyard. He seemed eager to accompany Stephen on his way to the great hall, and most keen to have whispered to him any news of Edward's favour. Stephen's neutral response was not intended to give Maltravers hope that any work of ingratiation was under way, but when on the next day he spied Sir John emerging from the same staircase shortly before his own appointed hour, he feared that he might nevertheless have seemed too encouraging. From a distance he could not tell whether Maltravers was in good humour or seethed with anger – though the latter seemed more likely – and as Stephen hastened across the bailey and himself gained admission to the keep, his heart pounded at the thought that Edward might already have spurned, denigrated, even assaulted his gaoler, and that at that very moment some vengeful punishment or humiliation for Edward was being devised in the gatehouse.

When he gained access to the cell, however, trepidation turned at once to astonishment when he found Edward wreathed in smiles. Edward seized his arm, guided him quickly to the table, and sat opposite him, an excited gleam in his eyes:

"We've judged Maltravers too harshly!" he said. "He was here just a few moments ago and, though at first we snarled at each other like two angry lions, at last I let him have his say and he's convinced me to trust him, for he has made plans to secure my liberty within the month!

"It seems," continued Edward, as Stephen could only gape, "that Sir John and many like him already groan with the burdens heaped on them by my wife and Mortimer. Apparently there are rumours too of disaster in the war against the Scots. So Fortune's Wheel *is* turning once again, and certain lords wish therefore to have me spirited away – out of the usurpers' control – so that when the time is right, I can return. It's thought my son will then willingly give up the crown to its rightful wearer, and so God's order will be restored."

"This cannot be, my lord!" exclaimed Stephen. Almost sick at the error he saw Edward falling into, he could not hold back: "When has Maltravers intended anything but ill towards you, my lord? You yourself told me how he brought you back a prisoner from Corfe, humiliated you, and showed you not the slightest regard or kindness...And this after many months when he has been a stern and cruel gaoler, and has in my own hearing often scorned and traduced you...Why should he now change so completely? Tell me what great event has made a friend of your enemy?...And what of Lord Berkeley? Is he involved with this plot? And are they not both still in league with Mortimer, seeking nothing but your destruction?"

"Enough, Stephen. Enough! Do you think I am no judge of men? Do you think I couldn't smell out such falsehood if it confronted me?...As for Berkeley, since you presume to ask, he is party to everything Maltravers has told me, but at present he is sick with the cholic. That's why Maltravers currently has charge of the castle!...I am surprised, Stephen, surprised and deeply disappointed, that you prove so contrary to..."

"My lord, you are deceived. Please believe me..." Stephen had fallen to his knees, but before he could continue, a blow from Edward's fist sent him sprawling on the floor, so that his head smashed into the table leg. As he lay dazed, Edward was on him again, seizing his tunic, thrusting forward his face, florid with rage:

"Why do you seek to oppose me, priest? Who is it you really serve? Who was it that sent me a catamite for my confessor?" Edward's features seemed to melt before him, then solidify, then melt again. Stephen gasped for breath, as tears sprang to his eyes at the fierce pain now pounding in his forehead. Edward spat and cursed, letting him slump to the ground, once more striking his head against the table.

The fierce commotion had by now roused the guards, and a frenetic rattling of locks and keys heralded their bursting into the room, both to restrain Edward and to seize the almost comatose Stephen and drag him down the stairs to the inner bailey, where they left him in a heap upon the ground.

When the warm afternoon air at last revived him, in utter wretchedness he crawled then staggered his way back to his own chamber. There the throb of injury made his stomach nauseous, but his mind suffered even more – from dread, not only that Edward was about to commit one of his gravest follies yet, but that his own few words, blurted out for the best of motives, seemed to have cleft their hearts asunder.

*

Three days of anguish followed during which, as Stephen had feared, Edward refused to see him, and he felt more bereft than at any time, even during Edward's absence from the castle. But the nightmare came to an abrupt and unlooked for end when he was informed that in fact Edward desired his presence again, and at the accustomed time. He hurried to the keep, pulling his hood close around his face to conceal the purplish bruising on his cheek and forehead.

Immediately on his entry to the cell he threw himself at Edward's feet:

"Oh, my lord, if my zeal for your safety has caused me unwittingly to give offence, please believe me, that it was very far from my intention. I sought only to warn against trusting those whom till now have been your sworn enemies."

There was a long silence. Then Edward, into whose eyes he had dared not look, raised him to his feet, pushed back his hood, and touched the ugly wound with the lightest brush of his fingers, and then his lips.

"Forgive *me*, Stephen. Forgive *my* words and *my* violence towards you. It was undeserved on your part." Their eyes met, and for a moment a beam of warmth and light pierced the mist of Stephen's fears. But then Edward turned away and when he spoke again, there was a coolness in his tone:

169

"I would not wish our difference over Sir John to force a rift between us, Stephen. I know you spoke out of honest, if misguided, fears, and I forgive you tenfold. I treasure your loyalty and friendship too highly, Stephen, to cast them aside so lightly – even more so, when it seems we are soon to part...Do not speak, Stephen – only listen, listen to what I have to say!...

"I have discussed matters further with Sir John, and he warns that an attempt is to be made on my life – perhaps before Michaelmas – you may guess by whom. He will do all in his power to spirit me away from the castle before Mortimer's henchmen arrive. And, Stephen, if that were not sufficient proof of his good intentions, he will then go with me into exile till it is safe for both of us to return!" Seeing Stephen's look of disbelief, Edward once more smiled and took hold of both his shoulders:

"Now, in this, Stephen, you must help us, and once I am free it is vital you be very discreet. My escape must seem to have nothing to do with Lord Thomas, who will claim to be sick in bed, or to be away visiting his other manors when the escape takes place. He must be free from suspicion, so that he may remain in England to defend Sir John's and his own estates, and to act as our contact whilst we are away...Sir John's own involvement must also be kept secret – at least till we're abroad. In fact, it's already been given out that he has left Berkeley and is on his way once more to Corfe...

"There is danger in this, Stephen. That is certain!...for the assassins may arrive soon, and there's much for Sir John to arrange...but he has sworn a solemn oath to me that as soon as plans are in place for our passage abroad – or at the very latest, when he has knowledge of the assassins' approach – he will ensure that I am stowed in safety elsewhere!"

Stephen bowed his head and struggled against the urge once more to contradict what had just been said, but he knew Edward would be obdurate. Besides, he could not deny the need to procure Edward's safety, if indeed Mortimer had taken measures once and for all to destroy him. Yet how could they be sure such a plot was anything but a deception on Sir John's part, perhaps at Mortimer's behest?

"Do not seek to persuade me otherwise, Stephen. My mind's made up... Now, let's sit together as we've done so often... today and for so many days as are left to us. Let us pray together, let us comfort

170

each other, for the way ahead remains perilous for me...perhaps for you also, for who can guess where suspicion will lodge when my escape becomes known?...Let's sit, let's pray...

"Teach me a little more of your philosophy, Stephen, dear brother and friend...You may hardly believe it, but over the months your words have often brought me knowledge and comfort: knowledge of my own weaknesses, comfort that, with your help and my own repentance, my own sorry soul may not go to Hell or writhe unendingly in Purgatory's fires before the final trumpet! You are my model, Stephen: one I would follow, for my soul's sake, not simply to save my flesh!"

Despite a dull ache of apprehension at the pit of his stomach, Stephen did as Edward asked, and they sat in prayer for what remained of their hour together. If for nothing else, his heart swelled a little to think that Edward was now able to forgive those who crossed him, and to accept that the thoughts of others might differ from his own, even if the possibility that he was himself in error was something which as yet he could not countenance. It was a small comfort before the glowering certainty that their lives were about to be sundered again, perhaps forever.

Chapter 22

Although the worm had begun burrowing once again within his guts, Stephen had promised Edward that he would continue attending the great hall – for the sake of any rumours he might pick up, rather than for his nourishment. On the Feast of St Matthew, a week or so after their reconciliation, he was present, therefore, when a new guest took his seat at the lord's high table. Eating little himself, just sipping at his ale, Stephen listened to the gossip which rippled up and down the tables concerning this newcomer.

It appeared his name was Sir William Beaukaire, and he was one of the royal sergeants-at-arms. Yet it was whispered that he had been amongst the former king's most loyal supporters – even at the end, during those bleak grey days the previous autumn, when he had assisted Edward evade capture and had continued defending Caerphilly Castle till there could be no further doubt his master's cause was lost. A strange story also ran that he had then received pardon at Mortimer's hand, and over the months since had become close to the new court. Here was indeed an enigma.

No one seemed to know the actual purpose of Beaukaire's visit, and Stephen could tell little from the man's appearance. He had a powerful frame, and was clearly a warrior, but his facial expression was bland, almost peaceful. Throughout dinner he exchanged few words with those about him, and for the most part concentrated only upon his food.

When that afternoon Stephen discussed Beaukaire's presence with Edward, they could not decide whether to be alarmed or merely curious. Edward was adamant that Beaukaire had been a man of integrity, a true friend to himself and to the Despensers: hardly someone whom now he should fear as an assassin; and yet his rumoured adherence to Mortimer was troubling, and must presumably be true, for otherwise he would not have been welcomed in public as Lord Berkeley's guest. Edward begged Stephen not only to attend supper that evening, but to do all he could to find out more.

Later in the great hall, waiting for the meal to begin, Stephen noted that the impassive Beaukaire was again seated at the high table along with Lord Berkeley's wife and daughters, and his eldest son, who sat at the head of the table, in the absence of his ailing father.

Again the sergeant-at-arms seemed intent on drawing the least possible attention to himself.

More disquieting news, however, quickly emerged from the babble of conversation all around Stephen: Beaukaire was not the castle's only visitor that day. Three others had arrived, though where they were at present was uncertain. One was called Thomas Gurney – someone already known to Stephen: one of Berkeley's retainers from Inglescombe in his Somerset estates. Indeed, he had been amongst those accompanying Edward and Stephen on the journey from Llanthony to Berkeley nearly six months before. The names of his two companions, however, meant nothing to Stephen, and he strained to catch the words of Henry de Rockhill, the steward, who sat two places away from him, and was describing what he knew to Odo de Bodrugan at a neighbouring table:

"One is a foul-tempered fellow called Simon Beresford. He's one of Mortimer's henchmen, but what his business is here, I don't yet know. Every question I ask of him and every politeness I attempt is met with an oath! He seems a most uncouth lout! I'm only grateful her ladyship isn't suffering his company at table!

"As for the other, I can tell you a little more. He is William de Ockley, an esquire in the new royal household. He used to be part of Lady Mortimer's retinue, whilst she was imprisoned, but now, believe it or not, he's a loyal servant of her adulterous husband!"

As the servants began to load the tables with trenchers of meats, Stephen struggled to suppress his alarm. Gurney, Ockley and Beresford sounded much more likely murderers than Beaukaire. Where could they be at that moment, and also where was Sir John, given his vow to protect Edward? When a large platter of brawn and mustard was placed near his left elbow and began assailing his nostrils with a sickly-sweet odour, he felt ready to heave. He felt no better as he viewed a large bladder stuffed with pork, eggs and dates, in a sauce of blood and alkanet, which the steward began slicing with his dagger. Stephen took a draught of ale and nibbled at a little wastel bread. He hoped it would settle his stomach, but his nerves felt so ragged that it was impossible for him to swallow anything else.

The conversation round him had by now switched to the illness of Lord Berkeley, who, it appeared, was confined to his chamber with a fever and a cramping of the guts. The steward complained that, on the physician's insistence, he had had to send to Winchester for pomegranates, which had cost no less than three shillings each!

Stephen's own guts began to calm a little, and he wrestled with what he should do. He could not leave the table early without attracting attention. Yet delay might cost Edward's life, if the three newcomers were already inside the keep! Even if they were not and there was still time, what could he do on his own? How could he even gain access to the cell to warn Edward what might be afoot? The guards would not let him in, for he had already paid his one visit of the day. And what guard would believe him, if he claimed three of the lord's guests were about to commit murder? If only he knew where Sir John was. If only he could believe Sir John really meant to protect Edward.

Stephen closed his eyes, and implored the Virgin for help. Sinner, failed acolyte though he knew himself to be, and despite all his faults, surely in this extremity She would not stay silent. Surely on Virtue's scales his years' devotion counted far more than his recent waywardness. Surely She would answer his prayers, and quickly!

As he bowed his head, screwing up his eyes in supplication, the wave of chatter engulfing the hall suddenly ebbed back on itself. He raised his eyelids in surprise, and saw the cause of it: two strangers together with Gurney were now being shown to the high table. Servants were laying out extra places, and presentations were being made by Beaukaire to members of Lord Berkeley's family.

Such late-comings were unusual, and indeed unmannerly, but Stephen's heart almost hymned his thanks to the Virgin that the three were at least there in the great hall under his very eyes, not wreaking havoc somewhere else. As the tide of gossip flowed back, he comforted himself that if the worst had already occurred, the three would have left in haste, or would have concealed themselves away from the throng. Even men like these would not have sauntered up to the lord's high table, and gorged themselves on the richest fare after committing a cold-blooded murder!

His panic began to subside, and he found himself wondering if his fears had been misplaced. It was difficult not to imagine the worst of men such as Gurney, Ockley and Beresford, who even now, as he perceived, remained grim faced and taciturn as they sat cramming

174

their mouths with great handfuls of food, still dressed in their mud-spattered travelling clothes, despite their presence before ladies.

After fruits and sweetmeats, the main dishes of the second course were brought out on to the tables: coneys and woodcock, partridge and roasted kid. There was also a delicacy of beaver meat in jelly, and since beaver was a creature of the water and therefore technically a fish, Stephen felt free to sample it, relief at the latest turn of events making him realise his hunger.

As he was chewing on the slightly oily flesh, Odo de Bodrugan, from whom the steward had now turned, shouted over to him from his own table. With no other victim to harangue, Odo abandoned his usual hostility, and set about describing in tedious detail the delicacies of sea and land which were to be found in his native Cornwall; and Stephen felt obliged to listen, though his occasional nod of agreement, or slight indulgent smile were the only responses he felt permitted by the Order's Rule to make.

As Odo leaned towards him, Stephen lost his view of the high table, and it was only when Odo leaned back again to allow the servants to lay out fresh platters of plums, damsons and skewered starlings, that Stephen realised he had so far missed the fact that Gurney, Beresford and Ockley were already rising from their places and were excusing themselves, leaving Beaukaire to mollify Lady Berkeley and her family for this second seeming impertinence. The three men were edging behind the dining tables towards the main doorway giving on to the screens passage, their departure prompting another swell of chatter and speculation.

Stephen felt his heart pounding again, and, despite his previous doubts, thought in panic how he might now himself take his leave and somehow warn Edward, or perhaps the guards to his chamber, indeed anyone who might be prepared to listen to him. Unable to think of any other pretext, he first snatched at a skewer and started to gnaw at a starling's bony breast, and then feigned a fit of choking. Gesticulating that a bone was stuck in his throat, he began moving towards the exit, though he had to struggle away from the steward, who had leapt to his assistance and had began thumping him on the back. Spluttering apologies and thanks, Stephen staggered from the hall, still hawking and coughing for maximum effect.

There were long shadows in the inner bailey, and it was a few moments before he made out a group of four men huddled right outside the stairway to the keep. Sickened, he realised three were the men who had just left the great hall. He scurried back into the deeper shadows of the screens passage, and peered out again, trying to discern whom the fourth man might be. This man was dressed in the livery of the castle, and so could be a servant; yet it seemed to be he who was giving the instructions, the one lecturing the other three. His words were whispered, but something in his manner struck Stephen as familiar and now he grasped, almost to his disbelief, that the man in livery was Sir John Maltravers.

Before he could decide anything, the men's conversation ceased, and there was a brief moment when wrists were clasped, and shoulders slapped. The three visitors then hastened off towards the inner gatehouse, whilst Sir John unlocked the gate and began ascending the stair to Edward's room. He had with him a large bundle. It was then Stephen noticed that no guard was on duty – something he had never known to be the case before.

Supper was continuing, and no one else had yet emerged from the hall. Gurney, Ockley and Beresford were also now out of sight, and so Stephen seized his chance and followed Sir John. At the first level, as at the ground floor, he found none of the guards present, so Edward's chamber was neither defended from attack, nor barred to prevent escape! He felt himself shaking, his knees weak beneath him, as he stumbled along the corridor through half-open doorways towards Edward's cell.

As he pushed back the final heavy door, and in his haste almost tottered down the steps again, Sir John was before him, helping Edward into a change of clothes, which must have been contained within the bundle.

"Brother Stephen, it's as I told you. Sir John's been as be good as his word," said Edward. "He tells me Mortimer's agents are at this moment within the castle and are intent on my death! Quick, quick, help us with this clothing of his – we're to escape in disguise…But, Stephen, why do you …?"

"My lord, I beg you: don't listen to Sir John. He's deceiving you…" Stephen advanced towards them, but before he had taken three paces Sir John had leaped forward and grabbed his throat:

"This is the traitor, who would foil our plans, my liege. I've suspected him all along. You can see now he wants to delay us till Mortimer's men arrive."

"Believe me, my lord," said Stephen almost choking, "it's Sir John who's in league with them. I..."

"Silence, priest." It was Edward who interrupted him. "Silence your doubts, and help us...or else it will...!"

"I will not, my lord. Sir John's leading you into a trap. I'm sure of it..." But Edward would have none of it:

"I'm tired of your whinging, Stephen, and of your hate-filled attitude towards Sir John! He's the one, not you, who's helping me escape. Fool! Don't you see that? What, apart from fawning attentions, have I ever been able to expect from you?"

Sir John still had hold of Stephen's throat, and was all but throttling him. Suddenly he produced a dagger and placed the blade at Stephen's neck:

"We must make haste. One more word, priest, and I'll stick you like a pig." Stephen gasped for breath, then made a last desperate attempt, jerking his head free:

"My lord, I've seen Sir John talking with the ruffians..."

But with that Sir John clapped his hand over Stephen's mouth and in an instant plunged his dagger deep into his chest, piercing the flesh just below the left shoulder. Stephen staggered backwards, then fell to the ground. There was no pain, only shock; no anger, only disbelief. There was no word from Edward.

Time seemed to judder to a halt, pinioning him to that instant. All about him there was motion and activity, but as if in another world. Sir John was slashing strips from the short cloak he had himself been wearing, whilst Edward was completing his disguise. They both moved more and more quickly, whilst Stephen's heart-beat slowed. They were leaving him behind, or so it seemed.

Sir John now used the strips he had slashed swiftly to bind Stephen's hands and feet, leaving him slumped on the floor; then he wrapped up Edward's discarded clothes in a fresh bundle. All the while Stephen's only sense was of the chill of flagstones striking up into his body, whilst a warm moistness spread down across his chest. A confusion of legs passed to and fro faster and faster before his eyes, then headed for the doorway, leaping up the steps, and disappearing into the corridor. There had been four. Now there were none.

He remained motionless, trying to make himself think what it was he could or should do, but his thoughts seemed frozen. Time ceased, and the enormity of pain took its place. The sound of Hugh's wailing seemed to fill the room, but it was a sound coming from his own lips. He began to shiver and then to convulse. His upper habit was now sodden, and at that thought, which brought with it the sudden and certain knowledge he would bleed to death, his head began to swim and faintness overcame him.

He should be praying. He knew he should confess his sins, beg for the Virgin's intercession. But suddenly there were other footsteps tugging his mind back to wakefulness: footsteps climbing the stair, pounding along the corridor toward the chamber itself. The world had shrunk. When he tried to see what was happening, his eyes seemed to have sunk back into his head, or the room about him seemed to have withdrawn into the distance. There, framed in the greying margins of his consciousness, three figures were entering the room in a flicker of torch-light, halting in front of him: Gurney, Beresford, Ockley.

"What have we here?" Was the voice Gurney's? Hands seized him. (He must pray to the Virgin; implore her forgiveness. The stars swimming in the firmament about Her head almost dazzled him with their beauty...) He was being raised to his feet. (Hail Mary, full of grace...Had he confessed everything...anything ...lately? Was he contrite?) All about him blurred, his bound legs buckled, and he remembered no more till the iciness of flagstones and the jaggedness of broken teeth against his lip brought awareness again. He was opening his eyes, wondering if he would see angels, but there was redness all around him. Beyond, three figures were moving, scuttling about the chamber like giant cockroaches, gathering, it seemed to him, the king's possessions: books, icons, jewellery...

"The queen will thank us," a voice said far away.

"But she'll not thank us, if this priest lives to tell his story," said another.

"You know it's to be spread about Sir Edward's dead, that he died in his sleep, or by accident," said the voice. Was it Ockley's? "No one must know where he is! No one must say he's alive."

"Then there's nothing for it. We must finish this one off," said a third voice, and it seemed then to Stephen that someone was moving toward him, and had seized him again, though he had no feeling any longer in his body. He sensed only the motion of again being hauled upwards. (His rosary beads. Where were his rosary beads? And his crucifix? Hail Mary, full of grace...) All about him began to swim again, but he could now see Beresford's face very close to his own:

"This shall be my pleasure," said a voice, but the lips were at odds with the words, and seemed to snarl and curl like those of a dog. "I've always longed to kill a priest!"

There were blows against his chest, and it seemed something entered his body repeatedly. Was this pain or was it ecstasy? Then all was red again. A gurgling in his throat made Stephen know he was no longer breathing. His lungs no longer heaved and strained for air, and his body seemed to slip away towards the floor. A burden had been removed.

Gradually the room became clear again. He was looking from on high down through a strange translucence, which was not air, though neither was it mist, nor water, neither fire, nor smoke. Night had fallen, but there were no shadows and no darkness, and everything in the room was visible to him. He could see the bloodstained body of a priest slumped against a table, and the three men, who had by now wrapped the king's belongings in sacking and were again debating with each other:

"Let's use him for the corpse," said Gurney. "It'll be the best way to conceal him, if he plays the king in death!...Better that than use the porter's body. If the porter's body's found in the gatehouse, it'll be taken as no more than common murder. If they find a priest's body full of stab-wounds, there'll be hell to pay."

He watched as they wrapped the body in more sacking, brought buckets of water, and scrubbed at the blood which had splashed upon the table and was oozing between the flagstones.

Then it was as though an eye had closed, and remained tight shut. Stephen's spirit floated in darkness.

PART FIVE: BEYOND

Chapter 23

For a long while Stephen was aware only of darkness, till he realised the very fact of his awareness – not being part of the darkness itself – meant that he existed, that he was conscious, if nothing else. And when, as if on emerging from sleep, memory began a counterpoint to this consciousness, it came to him that he was Stephen de Birstin, a Dominican friar; but also that he was dead. That being so, his mind, his consciousness, was the mind and consciousness of spirit only. His body was no more; or rather, though it still existed – for he had seen it slumped in Edward's cell – from now till Judgement Day it was no longer the temple his soul inhabited, but a thing of dust and putrefaction to be committed to the earth. Even as spirit, though, he had no sense of incorruptibility, nor that he was immortal – even if that remained an encouraging conjecture – nor, for that matter, that he was without gender – as his new form was supposed to be; for though he had left his body, Stephen was still Stephen, son, brother, monk, as he had always been.

When he tried to turn his mind outwards once again to the darkness in which, it seemed, it floated – and which, of itself, was not an entirely objectionable element – he felt a certain disappointment for the lack of those signs he had believed would show him where on Salvation's road through Purgatory death had deposited him. For he had always understood that, whilst saints went straight to Heaven, those who had confessed and were contrite, but who had not expiated their sins in full, would spend some time in Purgatory – time which might be short, but would seem of immense duration. Then came the enervating realisation that he had in fact died *un*shriven, that he had *not* confessed, nor even admitted to himself fully those sins of mind and body to which of late he had been subject. Therefore, he would be destined for a place far worse than Purgatory, where fire was not the fire of purification, but of eternal punishment.

Yet wherever it was that he now found himself, it was manifest that it was not Hell. Was he adrift, not in Purgatory, nor in "Abraham's Bosom", nor even in "Limbo" – for there dwelt only infants who were not baptised and the Patriarchs of old – but somewhere else, which was neither Heaven nor Hell, but some gradation of afterlife between those two extremes? To think so, he knew, was heresy, but in this strange state of being and unbeing, for which nothing in his studies had prepared him, such blasphemy seemed quite congenial.

And what, he pondered, of the Virgin Mary? After all that She had been to him, at least till lately, after all the blessings given to him by Her grace, notwithstanding Her recent diffidence, it must be that She would appear, that She would at last make clear to him all that was, or had been, or was yet to be. Or had the time for that already passed? The more he thought about the Virgin and sought to turn his mind to prayer, the more he found that faith no longer dwelt within him: faith that She was any more than man's fashioning in wood or stone, that She could guide him or explain, or that his prayers to Her were more than worthless puffs of air. For he had died, and was alone, floating weightless in the blackness of a void.

Perhaps he should wait, drift, wander in the dark, which had an undoubted peacefulness, till the faculty of sight, which had blinked shut a moment (or maybe centuries) ago, once more returned, and he could gaze again on Edward's chamber, or on the flat meads stretching away towards the Severn, or on his priory at Gloucester, or Blackfriars Hall at Oxford, or on a small manor house near Tewkesbury, where the two great rivers met and his brief sad story had begun. Maybe the fate of those who died was merely to visit and revisit all those places they had known, like a beam for ever reflected from the glassy surface of death itself.

*

Sight returned. Again an eye which had been closed opened, not gently as on wakening, but abruptly as if willed, yet not by Stephen. He saw once more the room where he had died: empty now of bodies, dead or living; devoid also of any sign that once it had been Edward's. The flagstones had been scrubbed clean, and bore no witness to what had happened, though there remained the slightest blush about the mortar here and there; and on all sides of the room the castle walls rose silent, massive, impenetrable, guarding now in their inmost depths a reverberation of his own cries, his own death. How was it that he knew this?

*

The eye closed again – whose will dictated it? – then opened upon a panelled chamber, where Brother Walter knelt, prayed, wept,

184

begged news of Edward, news of Stephen, cursed himself for the failure of his plans; made no mention of Sir John Maltravers. As Stephen watched from far above, every word muttered under Walter's breath, every lamentation which sobbed or dribbled from his mouth was audible, as if spoken from Stephen's own lips or whispered in his ear. The stale air of the chamber and the warmth emanating from a solitary candle were also more noticeable – far more striking – than ever they would have been to him whilst he lived.

How could this be? He had been taught that the soul outwith the body was unable to enjoy the slightest stimulus of sense. Yet now he enjoyed senses far excelling that of his earthly body. If somehow he had found himself, not hovering above, but kneeling right next to Walter, perhaps he could even have touched the man's skin, felt each hair and pore on the surface of his arm, sensed the rush of blood within in his veins and arteries.

The sound of a latch grated on his hearing, as Brother Drogo entered from the inner room, placed his hand on the prior's shoulder, then kissed his cheek.

*

Darkness again – but when the eye opened this time, it was upon a small cell which Stephen thought he recognised as again within the priory: a room which, as far as he could recall, had in general been unused – perhaps a storeroom, perhaps the one beneath the library. At one end there now stood a crucifix on what appeared to be a crude altar made of wooden boxes. Opposite knelt Brother James, who like Walter was weeping, though his tears were of anger and of loathing; and his words were not mumbled, but tumbled out in a frenzy of cackling vituperation towards God and all the saints for the death of hope and the loss of his dearest friend.

James stood, spat towards the crucifix, bared his buttocks, and snarled a prayer, which to Stephen lacked all meaning, till "caelis in es qui, noster Pater" gave the lie to Christ and to the faith they had once shared.

*

These visions flared, then guttered. Stephen had no time to feel melancholy or grief for those who had once been dear to him, but on whom he now felt himself to be prying. He could only wonder at their purpose, or whether everything he saw, or was shown, was random.

Then before him was the broad chase stretching from Berkeley to Michaelwood. It was night-time and the moon was hidden, yet every feature of the landscape, every tree, every blade of grass had a strange luminosity making it visible, even though once more Stephen seemed to view everything from far above. There were Edward and Maltravers, disguised as he had seen them in the keep, but now spattered with blood. Around them was gathered a small posse of men, of whom one was Beaukaire, though the others Stephen could not identify.

He could hear Sir John recounting the tale of his and Edward's escape – how, by his own cunning and in the nick of time, they had evaded those who would have killed or kidnapped Sir Edward, and how they had crept from the castle unobserved. It seemed, further, that Edward, in the exhilaration of escape, had slain the sleeping porter as they passed through the outer gatehouse. There was no mention, though, of any second death – of Stephen's own sorry role in the night's proceedings. Embraces were exchanged, hands clasped, and the party divided, Beaukaire making his way back toward the castle, the others hastening southwards to the forest's eaves.

Stephen's soul then soared above the Vale, and Time itself took wing upon a gale which blew faster than reckoning. He glimpsed the posse's progress toward Dorset and the coast, sensed Edward's joy as he retraced steps which only lately had been doleful to him. But then the vision faded, and once more Stephen was at Berkeley.

There, in a chamber hung with thick German tapestries, before a desk inlaid with gem stones – it must have belonged to Lord Thomas – sat Beaukaire, quill in hand, the slightest smile playing about his otherwise impassive features. Stephen needed no confession, nor explanation, nor indeed to read the letter which Beaukaire was writing. For, whether from a momentary gleam of insight, or a radiant perception with which his soul was now charged for all eternity, he could penetrate to the heart of things, could pierce the murk of the darkest shadows; and at this instant he grasped the very essence of Beaukaire's thoughts, his secret correspondence, the scheming with his master, Mortimer, and the great deceit which together they were perpetrating.

Edward would be thought dead. He would be spirited away, not to the freedom promised by Maltravers, but to a prison, more secure, more impregnable, more utterly dismal than either Kenilworth or

Berkeley. There his survival would be concealed: a secret, but also a weapon in Mortimer's hands, should Isabella tire of his bed, or her son rail against his bullying and manipulation. For her existence and his throne would hang by a thread: that of Edward's living death.

*

In little time the images blurred, divided, disintegrated into a jumble, which became ever darker, till he sensed no difference from the black void he had first encountered in death's aftermath. Indeed, he felt once more divorced from all reality, afloat with nothing but his awareness of himself; or so he thought at first, till a sense of motion impressed itself upon him, a motion forwards, towards some goal... towards some future?

Stars appeared: above, below, around him. They were not still, or rather it was he who was not still, for he seemed to move past them, and at increasing pace, which made their tiny lights smear and smudge into each other till they lost distinctness and were once more absorbed into blackness. But at last there came an utter stillness, both of sound and motion, as one by one, through a narrow window to his left, the stars rekindled.

First the window, then other features of the room it served gained murky resolution. The room was circular, lofty, as in the tower of a castle or a monastery, but it was in no way familiar to Stephen. Apart from the faint glimmer of starlight, it was illuminated only by two reed lamps, in the light of which a monk such as himself, though far older, laboured at a manuscript. His eyes were strained, the lids swollen, and as sour tears vented cross his cheeks, he wrote a chronicle, which Stephen could read, as if gazing over his shoulder.

As he pictured the events of which it told, Stephen beheld Edward once more imprisoned within his cell, yet set upon by Ockley, Beresford and Gurney, and by others too who were quite unknown to him. They stripped him of his raiment, forced him on his back across the truckle bed, where two of them pinioned him, pressing down upon his chest with the small table. Now, as Edward fought for breath, the others splayed his legs back and apart, forcing a large horn deep into his rectum. This was the funnel through which a burning plumber's iron was next plunged into his innermost parts, which scorched and burned, making the greatest stench throughout the chamber; and all this while the king screamed out in such agony and with such terrible force that no one who dwelled nearby could fail to have been awakened by it – or so it was woven by the monk into his narrative.

Stephen was vexed, but little moved, by what he read, for it was to him no more than lurid fantasy. He had cause to know what had and had not happened in the keep at Berkeley, so he felt no pity, still less any liking for the monk, whose gruesome imaginings, no doubt nurtured by the lies and bile of others, he guessed these to be.

Then his crystalline perception observed as strands of mucous began floating cross the monk's eyes, so that he rubbed them to prevent letters in the manuscript elongating and blurring before him. With a sigh he ceased writing, put aside his quill, snuffed out his candles, and prepared to sleep in the chair where he sat.

In the darkness Stephen found himself grieving for Edward, James, even his former self, and for all whose very being, because not commonplace, prompted such vileness and vengeance in the minds and at the hands of others.

Chapter 24

Stephen became used to perception's sudden shifts of time and place, and to the sense that time itself no longer obeyed any rule or rationale he could identify. Yet, he still welcomed those periods when his attention was not engaged at all: those periods of deep all-enveloping darkness which seemed no mere backdrop or frame to his epiphanies, but a necessary balm when they were extinguished – almost a cocoon of stasis and reflection.

Reflection itself, though, could nurture perplexity. It occurred to him that every scene which was revealed related not to times before his death, but to times since, or to the future – if there could be any "future", any more than any "present", in the realm he now inhabited. Surely, it was his past life, his past deeds which demanded judgement in the after-life. It was for them that he should atone on the rough road through Purgatory to Heaven's crystal gate; if, of course, such realms existed; if, indeed, they held any place for him.

After one such bout of worrying speculation, it was a relief to find himself, neither adrift in nothingness, nor cast upon some unfamiliar shore, but beholding what could not have been more familiar, nor more welcome, for he was once again at the entrance to Edward's cell. If put to justification of himself, he could render good account of his efforts there, of the months when he had striven to save the soul of the former king – of all, indeed, that he had attempted to do, and which had become his life's main work. If his soul needed to be pleaded for, if he had to cite actions with weight enough to cancel out his failings, it was here in Edward's cell that a memory of them dwelt, here that he could best advocate his cause.

The room, though, had altered. Through the door he could see none of King Edward's possessions. The truckle bed had been up-turned. Its bare mattress sagged against the far wall by the grate, where a brushwood fire had been kindled and now roared and crackled, whilst smoke billowed back into the room on the down-draught. The table too was not in its usual position. As his perception raked the room, the mournful reason became clear: the table had been drawn over to the inner wall where it was serving as a catafalque for a body lying naked, dead, a gaping stab-wound between the heart and shoulder; others, smaller, patterned across the chest.

A tall well-built man now entered the room. It was Sir William Beaukaire. He was followed by an elderly woman dressed all in black, carrying a bucket of what must have been hot water in which herbs had been steeped, for a powerful, but pleasant odour now permeated the atmosphere. Stephen thought of Edward's thick hair dripping wet, rivulets of perfumed water running across his breast.

Around her midriff the woman wore a belt which held several implements of metal: a small saw, an array of knives of various lengths and widths, and a large pair of what looked to be pliers. Beaukaire moved a stool to the window which gave on to the keep's inner courtyard, and sat looking outwards, averting his gaze from the business the woman was now about. From time to time he dabbed at his nose with a scented handkerchief, or swotted at the flies, which began to swarm and buzz their way into the room.

It was, of course, Stephen's own body which lay upon the table – his own body to which the woman would now apply her weaponry, and the mystery of her craft. Stephen had often pictured Hell's bitterest torments, or the writhing of souls skewered on Purgatory's roasting spits – sometimes in his reading and in his studies, frequently in his more fevered imaginings, like those which had spewed from his lips in the market place at Hereford. Nothing, however, had prepared him for the horror he was about to witness. Nothing had ever suggested that as a spectator he would now endure the butchery of his own body.

What could he do? – There was no remedy in prayer, the Virgin's image having cracked and crumbled, the paint upon her lips and eye having chipped or flaked away. If only he could will perception's eye to close, to blink, if but for a second. If only by thinking he could thrust his soul deep into the darkest darkness of the void! But this was all to no avail. As the woman began her work, he seemed to hover over what lay dead and prone upon the table, as if he had become its invisible reflection. He felt crucified to the struts and timbers of the roof, his gaze locked on the corpse, the woman and her actions.

She began with care to wash the wounds, which must already have been wiped of any excess gore, but which she now cleansed both in and out, before sewing together the severed flaps of skin over punctured flesh and shattered bone. The body thus made whole, she now unbraced it afresh, slicing open the abdomen from sternum to pubis, and then crossways in the sign of the cross. As a putrid stench filled the room, making Beaukaire choke and then retch through the window, she threw herbs upon the fire and fetched further bowls of scented water, which Stephen was to discover she would use both to purify the air and to sluice out the eviscerated corpse. She herself seemed quite oblivious to the odour of putrescence.

The folds of flesh about the abdomen were now pinned back, whilst she slit the many sinews and tendons, detaching the heart and then each of the other vital organs and the intestines themselves from one another and from all muscle and bone surrounding them. (How her skill excelled that of Hugh le Despenser's executioner!) With a practised hand she lifted each organ into a large metal bowl, where she sprinkled them with salts and spices, as if preparing a delicacy for a lord's table, but then sealed them within a large silver chalice, which she had brought into the room, and which was now placed on the window ledge at Beaukaire's elbow.

Her attention then returned to the gaping void beneath the thorax, which she cleansed as best she could with perfumed water from her bowls and buckets till, satisfied at last with her handiwork, she fetched an assortment of pots, bags and boxes, which till then had remained outside the room, and from which she took bunched flowers and herbs, aromatic grasses and many bags of spice, and with these lined and stuffed the cavity, till it was filled and she was ready once more to take up her needle and thread.

Her work took several hours, for each aspect was carried out both with solemn reverence and great attention, lest for instance any organ should become punctured and should then leak viscous fluids on to surfaces, which would then require to be scrubbed clean. To Stephen, obliged to watch, whether he would or no, it was as though he suffered many days of torture. Though he felt no physical pain as his cadaver was gutted and carved, a barely endurable sense of grief and loss, but also of horror at what he beheld, filled his mind, the room, and his universe.

Towards the middle of the day the woman removed most of the containers she had brought into the room, only to replace them with other pots and bowls. Then she sat upon a stool next to the grate and devoured cocket bread and cheese, washed down with a jug of ale, whilst Beaukaire ate nothing, though several times he disappeared to the garderobe.

Once replete, the woman began to mix herbs and other substances from her pots in the various bowls. Camphor, coloquiath, vinegar, honey, rosewater, frankincense, myrrh, aloe, and resins were added to mercury and salt in several different compounds, making the air dense, aromatic, yet at the same time fetid and stifling too. She now smeared her palms from one of the bowls and began rubbing a thick brown paste into the limbs of the corpse. A greyish liquid she rubbed into the face and neck, whilst the grease with which she larded the trunk was more reddish in colour. She sprinkled a chalk-white dust over the private parts and pressed a pig's bladder containing herbs into the anus. These last refinements themselves grieved Stephen less than the fact they were performed by a woman.

*

An evening and night must have passed outside his consciousness, for the light in the room seemed to have shifted to that of early morning again. The air had thinned and become less oppressive. Stephen became aware also that the corpse was now in process of being wrapped by the woman in layers of wax impregnated linen. Slowly the skin (which had been his skin) disappeared from view, as layer followed layer. Slowly the contours of the body (his body), even the indentations caused by the wounds and evisceration, became all but indistinguishable. Even the face (his face) was concealed as ribbons of cerecloth were wound and wound about the head, till Stephen's whole body became a thing of memory only, and utter sadness and loss overwhelmed him.

*

Darkness again intervened, enveloping him with its curative calm, so that his strong disposition to wail and gnash his teeth at all he had seen melted away, and he slipped into forgetfulness. If, as consciousness dissolved, it engaged with anything it knew, or thought it knew, it was with Lethe, the river of the ancients, not with Heaven, nor with Hell, nor with the strait or gaping gate of either.

*

Once more he was gazing down upon his corpse, but this time no longer within Edward's chamber. Instead it lay inside a plain wooden coffin on a stand before an altar, wrapped in its cerecloth, but also sewn into undergarments and a tunic far richer than any Stephen had ever worn. He recognised the altar as that of his beloved Chapel of St John, where memories of prayer-filled nights, unanswered questions and desires burdened the perfumed air. To the left of the corpse's head stood Sir William Beaukaire, ever watchful, ever vigilant, ever his master's eyes. With him three men unknown to Stephen stood at each of the other corners of the coffin, whilst a pale sun cast vague shadows within the room, a wind sighed through the narrow vents of two loop holes, and the crackle of dry leaves outside confirmed autumn's advance.

From time to time others came to the doorway of the chapel: notables of the locality, retainers of the castle whom Stephen recognised; at one point Lord Berkeley himself arrived, accompanied by the ladies of his household; but none ventured within the room, for a rope suspended across the doorway prevented access, and afforded but a passing glimpse of the coffin's contents. Visitors would kneel outside, cross themselves, utter groans and cries.

"Oh, Sovereign, Lord Edward, our late lamented king," they murmured, their faces creased in tears, before turning, descending the stair, and yielding their places to others who, like them, would now mourn for him they previously reviled.

It seemed to Stephen that he lingered long hours within this room, almost intoxicated by the resinous aromas rising from the corpse, calmed by the quiet respectfulness of those watching over it, though which of them knew whom it was in fact that they watched, he could not guess. Others replaced the four men whom he had first seen, though later they returned, and a rota of attendance was maintained both by day or night.

Scenes within the chapel were interspersed with others which imposed themselves on his consciousness, in no way bidden by him, disparate, melding one into another. The chapel altar with its crucifix and his viscera housed in their gleaming silver vessel for a while gave way to the chancel altar of his priory at Gloucester, and, as he listened, he heard Brother Walter in hushed anguished tones telling his brethren of King Edward's sudden death and of the strange disappearance – might St Anthony of Padua protect him – of their own dear fellow monk, who had been his confessor.

The chancel altar itself then seemed to shrink before him into no more than a few boxes on which, leaning against the wall of the storeroom he had been shown before, stood an inverted cross. Before this Brother James wept bitter tears, rent his clothes, and bellowed to Beelzebub.

Back at Berkeley and at night-time within the Chapel of St John, a strong gale from the south extinguished candles, however many times Beaukaire sought to relight them, and on that wind Stephen heard Edward's breath, his words too, but coming from afar. Then he saw his master kneeling at a different altar within a cell at Corfe, where he was imprisoned once more, and where he too prayed and cursed, but in his case against the treachery of Maltravers.

*

From the russet and gold of the trees round Berkeley Castle Stephen could see that autumn had indeed advanced several weeks, perhaps a month from the point at which life had been taken from him, yet from the surprising warmth of the wan sun and the balminess of the air, he guessed it might be the time known to him from his youth as St Luke's Little Summer, when dry sunny weather often followed on from the saint's festival.

At first he found himself gazing out across meadows and fields, as he had so many times from the battlements above the inner gatehouse. But, whatever force or caprice it was that determined what it was he saw, it then turned his attention inwards to the bailey itself. There, at the foot of the stairway leading up to the chapel, he saw a large open chariot to which four large black sumpter horses were harnessed. The chariot was swathed all in black canvass; the cords and trappings of the horses were of black, too; and upon the side of the chariot he could see the arms of the Abbey of St Peter's at Gloucester. Indeed, he then saw Abbot Thokay himself standing beyond the horses in conversation with Lord Berkeley and Sir John Maltravers, both of them clothed as if for a funeral mass.

The sound of footsteps could be heard from the stairway, and Beaukaire emerged, followed by several of the men with whom he had kept watch in the chapel. After another short pause, during which the sound of boots clattering on stone and other slippings and scrapings came from the stairwell, two further men, whom Stephen had learned were two of the new king's chaplains, backed their way out of

194

the entrance and into the bailey. They were struggling under the weight of a large wooden coffin, the rear of which at last appeared supported by two sergeants-at-arms. Again with considerable effort, six men were then required to lift the coffin on to the chariot. Stephen guessed that within was not only his own stuffed, trussed, and swaddled corpse, but a second coffin too, perhaps made of lead.

Those who had watched over the body now took up their places in two rows of six behind the chariot, with Berkeley and Maltravers joining on at the rear. All bowed their heads as Abbot Thokay, assisted by two monks, anointed the hearse and coffin with holy water and offered prayers for the soul of the late departed king. Flanked by the two monks, who had taken up blackened crosses, and by a third, who had charge of the horses, Abbot Thokay then led what was now a procession out of the courtyard and through the gatehouse to the outer bailey, where the way was lined by the retainers and servants of the castle, and by Berkeley's own family, all of whom knelt with their heads bowed as the hearse trundled by.

The route which Stephen had taken when he arrived at the castle six months before was retraced, through the outer gatehouse, down the track to the road which led to Berkeley village, and from there east towards the old Roman road, which ran from Bristol north to Gloucester. In the clear autumn air Thokay's prayers and lamentations, and from time to time those of the other mourners, rang out across the fields, where villeins paused from their labours and crossed themselves, or fell to their knees wailing for their own salvation.

And all the while, as Stephen watched – it seemed now from a great height – his sense of sadness grew: not on his own account (unfairly dead, though he was), but for Edward (alive, though reckoned dead), and for his country, across whose bosom the procession was advancing, maggot-like in its blackness, engorged of a monstrous lie.

*

That evening at Standish, they set the coffin down before the altar of the small parish church, and again took turns to watch over it, whilst outside, as a frost formed on the ground and in the clear night air, locals stood till dawn watching with reverence over their church and its holy contents, and whilst Stephen watched them all from above, from a clear sky sprinkled with frozen tears.

It was then that Stephen first noticed that a music pervaded the Heavens, almost inaudible at first, but ever present amongst the subtle motions of the stars and planets.

Chapter 25

The stars began to fade and the moon slipped below the hunched shoulders of the Forest hills, and all reverted to blackness. Then a tolling bell summoned him back – maybe the tower bell of Standish church, or maybe the dead-bell which Thokay carried as he headed the solemn procession.

Where the moon had been but a short time before, however, the sun now dipped westward, its weak rays conjuring gold from the stones of Gloucester's South Gate, kindling warmth in the ancient timbers of its mighty drawbridge.

A day had passed, or so Stephen concluded, and it was St Owen's Church bells – whose mellow voice he knew so well – which were ringing a sad welcome, as the funeral cortege approached from the south. Soon other towers and spires about the town began their own refrain, and from as far away as Llanthony, and all the way from St Nicholas to St John, a mournful clangour filled the air.

A throng of townsfolk had gathered in front of the gate, at their head the mayor and aldermen. In the crowd Stephen spied Brothers Walter, Drogo, and James, and many others of his order. Moans and sighs mounted as the procession drew nearer, and indeed gave way to an even greater outpouring of grief, as some within the crowd broke into loud wailing, or tore at their clothes, or threw themselves on the ground, where they licked at the dust, their faces anguished.

As the cortege reached the lane leading from the highway to St Owen's itself, Abbot Thokay signalled that those accompanying him should halt, whilst the mayor and aldermen approached and delivered solemn greetings. Many of the townsfolk also shuffled forward to join them, and, whilst prayers were said, they knelt in silence, then stood and led the way back to and over the drawbridge. Their fellows who had remained in front of the South Gate parted to allow them passage, then joined on behind.

The horse-drawn chariot, now in the midst of a very large throng, was thus led at a slow pace into and through the streets of the town towards St Peter's Abbey, where, Stephen guessed, its burden was to lie in state. As it passed, more and more inhabitants joined from side streets and alleys, and from the fish stalls and pavements of Southgatestrete, so that when at the High Cross the procession turned left down Ebbruggestrete and on through the narrow passageways either side of St Mary de Grace, there was a great crush of bodies just as evening turned to dusk and darkness began to fall.

Amidst the press and jostling the chariot passed before the King's Board, where the butter and cheese counters were all shuttered up, and Ironmongers' Row – the first entry towards the abbey. When it arrived at Lich Lane, in front of the Lich Gate in the abbey's high perimeter wall, the mayor and burgesses once more stepped aside and made way for Abbot Thokay, who pronounced acceptance of King Edward's remains on behalf of the Benedictine Order. As a thick fog began to gather, the crowd dispersed, and only those few who had accompanied the chariot all the way from Berkeley kept pace with it as it disappeared into the shadows beneath the gate's vast archway.

*

It was only when those shadows deepened, thickened, and seemed to swallow all that had just entered them that Stephen grasped that he had once more become absorbed into the darkness of his own spiritual void, and was again drifting quite beyond the curtilege of abbey, town, indeed of time and apprehension. As so often before, his mind could think, reason, above all was aware of itself, but his senses were again bereft of any matter with which they might engage. In the abstraction which remained, the darkness once more soothed and healed, smoothed away any grief, mourning, loss, even the distaste which he had felt at the grim deception paraded through the countryside from Berkeley to Gloucester. His wounds, his evisceration, the indignity and subterfuge to which his body had been subjected, all were now cleansed of agony. Instead, they were mere aspects of a life which was past and done with. Maybe it was pain, rather than sin, which was purged in life's aftermath.

*

Darkness yielded – at least a little. Had sight returned to him? If it had, then night must be at its darkest hour, for he could discern before him nothing more than the curves of a great archway: black against the lesser murkiness of whatever space it enclosed or led to. Either that, or those senses which in death's slipstream had been so raw and keen were now dulled and blunted, for he could make out nothing else.

Then hoarfrost began gnawing at his toes and fingers, and he smelled the stale dankness of a thick fog. He thought for a moment of the tow-path beneath the Wye Bridge, where in a different, distant winter his troubles had begun; but here there was a distinctive mustiness – less foul, more familiar, almost welcome. Then he recalled the bridges of Ebbruggestrete and knew he must be somewhere in their vicinity – perhaps beneath the Lich Gate itself, through which Thokay and the funeral procession had passed just a moment before his latest interlude of oblivion.

As sight accustomed itself to the gloom, he could indeed make out the vast bulk of St Peter's Abbey, the faintest glimmer of a brazier barely gilding the ornate carvings and pillars about its southern portal. Through this, perception now passed – into the bowels of the abbey itself, where, in the empty cavern of the nave, torches flickering on the vastnesses of the rounded pillars hardly penetrated the sea of darkness all around. At the eastern end of the abbey, however, there seemed to be an orb of light, which, as Stephen watched, took on a warmer glow, which then grew and grew and drew him in, like a moth to a flame.

Of a sudden, all was brightness. All was fire. He seemed to stand before the high altar, the blaze of its magnificence filling his vision. It was aglow with gold, silver, jewels, and with the lustre of rich colours larded upon icons and on its many carvings both of wood and stone. Light reflected from each of its myriad surfaces, making them gleam and glitter, as if the brightest moonbeams were striking down from the clerestory windows high above, and Stephen realised that a great source of light must in fact be coming from behind his vantage point, from the body of the presbytery, where the muttering of prayers and snatches of plainsong suggested Matins was being celebrated.

Then that vista too was granted him, and he beheld so many banks of candles on great wooden stands blazing forth before him, that at first he was more mesmerized by the flames themselves than by the awesome tableau which they illuminated.

Adjusting to their brilliance, he first made out four men whose backs were turned towards him. They were motionless, their heads bowed, and candle-light played on their buckles and the hilts of their sword. One of them, for sure, was Beaukaire. Then he became riveted by the spectacle which lay beyond them. There stood an enormous hearse, quite unlike that which had travelled from Berkeley – twice as large, and in the form of a great black barque. In place of wheels, its structure rested on four carved and gilded lions, each with a mantle bearing the royal coat of arms, each with its great maned head facing down towards the nave. Beyond them and standing apart were two leopards, again carved and gilded, but with their spots crafted out of ebony. Along either side of the hearse were painted images of angels with pillar-like containers wafting incense, whilst way above, and over the coffin itself, was a thick cloth canopy on which a golden leopard had been embroidered. At the point where each of the canopy's supporting struts was attached to the hearse itself, there was a painted image of a seated evangelist.

More striking still, on top of the coffin there was now a wooden effigy: life-sized, and of King Edward, the head crowned, the body wrapped about in coronation robes, and clothed beneath in cloth-of-gold. Neither its dimensions, though, nor its lurid majesty chilled Stephen's soul so much as the thought that beneath, within coffins of wood and lead lay a body which was not Edward's at all, but was his own. And for the briefest moment, to him – if to no one else – the scent of camphor and coloquiath overwhelmed that of incense.

*

Stephen's gaze returned to the four men who kept vigil, but time seemed to have folded over upon itself, and it became apparent to him that another day, or even days, had passed. Now, not only four, but all of those who at Berkeley Castle had shared in watching over the corpse were present: seven stood hooded, four before, three behind the hearse; one, whom Stephen knew to be Andrew, Edward's candelarius, tended the multitude of candles which surrounded it. Meanwhile, a cleric, who from his garb was both a bishop and a Dominican, first sprinkled holy water about the coffin, then joined other priests in readings from holy texts. Beyond in the nave – itself much more illuminated than previously – there was now gathered a huge congregation of paupers and many others, all, it appeared, of low estate. Those at the front were pressed hard against new oaken barriers, which must have been erected to protect the hearse. Then Stephen realised that this must be the eve of Edward's funeral, indeed the night before his own remains would be consigned to earth for all time.

Once Matins and Lauds had been said, the greyest light of the greyest dawn of Christmas week gave shape and form to the windows at either end of the nave, and the congregation of the poor made their slow exit, leaving the Benedictines to sweep and air the abbey in readiness for the main funeral service. Bells tolled in the tower above, and from other parts of the town, where once he had lived, and Prime was celebrated with a mass for the Virgin Mary, whom once he had served with the entirety of his being.

After breakfast-time the nave filled again, this time with merchants and yeomen of the county, but also with dignitaries and men of account, many from much further afield. Then the court, the barons, the earls, and finally the royal family itself all came to stand not behind, but in front of the wooden barriers in the space facing the gilded leopards and the first of the gilded lions. Stephen watched as the new young king together with his mother approached the hearse and then knelt for a while in silent prayer. Both wore golden circlets about their brows and robes of the blackest satin. As they returned to front the host of mourners, Stephen noticed a small table to Isabella's right on which was placed a silver vessel. It must contain his own offal, by now no doubt festering, despite its generous seasoning and the chill touch of mid-winter.

Behind and to Isabella's left stood Mortimer, resplendent in a new sable cloak and tunic. He had turned his eyes without expression towards the hearse, and Stephen wondered if, at that moment, within the wood and leaden caskets, beneath the swathes of cerecloth, and despite the craft lavished by the wise woman of Berkeley, his own wounds had begun to bleed afresh.

When at last the great rituals of the Church began, though this was his own requiem – the only one of any type he would receive – Stephen's mind could not dwell upon the holy prayers for Redemption and Salvation, which he himself had uttered so many times before. The words were empty to him now – now that he knew the Fathers of the Church to have been in error, now that the walls of Heaven, Hell and Purgatory were as the rubble around Jericho.

And when the bishop preached his sermon, it was all of worms and of decay, of the pitiful meanness of the grave's dwelling, and of the unutterable loneliness of the body after death. This meant little to him, too, for, if the body – his body – would not be raised on Judgement Day, despite the ceremony which now attended it, despite whatever penance he had or had not performed, then it was a mere flint for the soul's flame, or so much chaff to be discarded, so much dung to feed the soil, and he felt no claim nor further interest in it.

Besides, that corpse within the coffin was no longer his, but Edward's. At last they were as one, as if on the truckle-bed in Edward's cell they had indeed become one flesh: an image no longer causing him shock or guilt, no longer making him fear hell-fire. Instead, it pleased him by its naturalness, amused him with its inconsequence: its lack of bearing on the true frame of things, as now he knew it to be.

As the Requiem went on, his thoughts ranged further, and he fell to musing what would happen when this corpse which was no longer his was buried after the ceremony – no doubt in a tomb of utmost luxury, whose very opulence would appear to attest the identity of its occupant. Pilgrims would walk weary miles to Gloucester, would weep contrite tears, place grieving lips on cold stones, and give alms for remembrance, and thus the body would remain Edward's for all time.

The emptiness of all he observed bore in upon him, and it felt to Stephen as if his soul mingled with the incense which rose around the hearse, as if his perception wreathed up towards the vaulted roof of the abbey. From there he looked down on the vast congregation, where there were many faces from a year before at the market place in Hereford, amongst them Lancaster, Wake and Trussel, but also Kent and Norfolk, so like their brother in appearance. He glimpsed too his own family, who had arrived from Tewkesbury, quite unaware how much cause they had to mourn. And he saw Brother Walter, and others from his priory, though Brother James, for whom he searched and searched, he did not find.

The smell of incense faded. The sound of choirs wavered, and seemed to lose definition, before merging in time with the music of the spheres.

Chapter 26

That planetary music had become more and more familiar to him since its first resonance over Standish. The harmony was absolute, the sound so ceaseless, that at times it enthralled his consciousness. Yet at others, through its very euphony, lacking dissonance, it could recede to the edge of his awareness, leaving his mind free to wander where it would.

It was because other sounds now intruded on this aural hinterland, creating discords, unsettling modes, muddying harmonies, that he realised a new epiphany was upon him, for there had been no visual prompting: no diminution in the profound darkness he inhabited; no star-shine, nor moonbeam to elicit interest. Rather it was the sound of prayer and plainsong from all about him, the toll of hand-bells to his left, then away to his right what might be the sliding of paving stones across an aperture which snared his attention. Yet these sounds were muffled, as though the utter blackness all around had spawned a thickness to impede their clarity.

When he heard the grating of paving stones again, this time more faintly still, but without question from way above him, it occurred to him that a burial had taken place, that he had been its witness from within the very coffin, and that the entombment had been his own – even if only as Edward's proxy. He found it strange that he could smell no camphor, nor coloquiath, nor any more noxious odour he would have anticipated in the grave; and this puzzled him during the long black nothingness which followed the obsequies in which he had played such a central, but anonymous part.

From this point on he found that, whenever his consciousness slipped or was drawn back within the mortal coil – which occurred less frequently than it had before – his perception seemed faulty, his senses dulled or only half engaged. Smells were missing, sights blurred, and sounds often fractured. Whatever he experienced became more dream-like, more a series of mere glimpses of reality seen through a veil or prism of uncertainty. And whenever he drifted in the void, in the darkness which was no mere darkness of the tomb, but had become his favoured element, it seemed the more profound, the more absolute, the more restful even than before.

He pondered whether burial had marked a "station" on his own dolorous way towards Heaven, God, Oblivion, or whatever else awaited him. Perhaps it marked his passage to a different state of un-being: a turn in his perception, in his involvement with the life Beyond.

*

He had glimpses – or were they dreams? – of Edward, once more imprisoned, once more at Corfe, where Maltravers held him hidden from the world. Stephen no longer heard any words which Edward spoke or were spoken to him, but he could read derision and delight in the prison warders' faces, and guessed that they taunted Edward, not only with his fall, but with his nothingness, and with the fact that the nation believed him dead and buried. At that, Stephen grieved for a king who had lost not only his crown and his sacrality, but his family too, and now his very name. Yet, through the cracked glass of his per-ception, he also noted how Edward, despite his woes, seemed not to despair, that he bore his indignities, spent hours in prayer to a statue of the Blessed Virgin, fasted, wore a shirt of hair which crawled with lice, and that from time to time he told the beads of his rosary in the manner of the Dominicans.

Interspersed amongst these tableaux of Edward, there were others of less certain meaning to Stephen. They centred on another man: a man much like Edward, though younger, and one whom in time he remembered to be Edward's brother, Edmund, Earl of Kent, whom he had seen at Hereford, then latterly amid the sea of mourners in St Pe-ter's Abbey. Apart from his likeness to Edward, nothing else about the earl was clearer to Stephen than a sense of suspiciousness, of re-sentment, and of growing disbelief which emanated from him.

At first, when the earl appeared to Stephen, he would do so alone, devoid of context, setting, scene: a malcontent divorced from any-thing which would explain the darkness of his mood, or indeed his bearing on Stephen's own after-life. In time, though, he came before Stephen's consciousness in company with others. Who those others were surprised Stephen, for he saw him converse firstly with Brother Walter at the priory, then – stranger still – with Brother James amidst the trash heaps and fetor of Barelonde. When the scene shifted to the sumptuous apartments of a palace unknown to Stephen, he was in fact less perplexed to see the earl meet with Mortimer and the queen.

204

However, on that occasion, though no words were audible to Stephen, he perceived a haze of anger and dispute swirling about all three of them: a mist which was flecked with blood and fire.

Though he had loved Edward – and loved him still – he could care little for this brother, who had both betrayed the king, and joined others in condemning Hugh to death at Hereford. If the meaning of the dispute he had just witnessed was that Edmund now saw through Mortimer's deceptions, plotted against the regime, perhaps planned Edward's restoration, what relevance could such matters have for Stephen himself? Why should they trouble any further the tranquillity of the void?

As he debated this, the red mist seemed to thicken, then ceased its motion and faded into a grey fog, which he found welcome. He let it invade his mind, smother thought, obliterate perception, till it extinguished any curiosity he had concerning these latest visions. In time its dense vapours merged into the true and blessed darkness, where any thought or recollection of Edmund, Earl of Kent, seemed otiose.

There in the blackness, no pain, no sense of sin, no guilt remained. He was in blissful stasis, his mind subsumed in the smooth reverberations of the planets, his soul at peace both with itself and with the universe. This, he mused, must be the state to which all souls aspired: a state ultimate and desirable in itself – no mere prelude to the Judgement Day. And if that was so, what purpose could there be in onward pilgrimage by his soul, what spiritual profit in further congress with the world?

*

But then there came a tear in time, a breach in the order of what should and should not have been. Stephen felt himself called, conjured, cajoled back into the living world. Wrenched like a tooth from its roots – seized, twisted, dragged from one element and thrust into another – he found himself writhing like a landed fish, tortured by the very act of being, agonising in the plenitude of his senses, which no longer waned, but waxed both strong and raw.

A voice summoned him, calling him by name, demanding that he show himself. It was a familiar voice – one he had known and loved – yet now it was harsh, vulgar and repellent. It all but bellowed at him, and mingled his name with sacred words, again familiar, but for their disjointed order and the black invocations which accompanied them.

Now he found his sentient self to be close – far too close – to a fire, over which a cauldron bubbled and steamed foulness. Bones and body parts, powders and herbs were being thrown into it, though some fell into the flames themselves, making them smoke purple, green and ochre. It was as though he inhabited that fire, that steam, that cloud of exhalations, and in panic it came to him that he had at last arrived in Purgatory, perhaps in Hell, and that the teachings of Mother Church had indeed been truthful after all. What he thought to have learned since death had been error, perhaps trickery to make retribution the more painful and unbearable, when at last it came upon him. Maybe his faith had been put to trial, and, if so, its failure had been total.

In the midst of a terrible scorching and burning, to searing pain was added yet more confusion, as he perceived the voice he had heard to be that of James, that it was James who had invoked his name, uttered prayers to Beelzebub, and even now stood before the fire and cauldron adding new ingredients to the noxious brew within. The smoke and steam from the cauldron began to shift and mould themselves into the form of a man. Stupefied, he saw that it resembled his own earthly body, and, as James uttered new oaths and clapped his hands three times, Stephen felt himself subsumed within it – once more part of the material world, albeit nebulous and insubstantial.

Through the intense shimmering of heat, and despite the pain that wracked every element of his being, he struggled to see through the eyes of the phantasm to what place it was he had been summoned, and to what purpose this could be. Shadows cast by the fire cavorted on low whitewashed walls or lost themselves in the thicket of black thatch overhead. He must be in some mean hovel, its hearth venting to a crude chimney at the roof's apex.

To one side was a doorway, and near that he now spied a second man. This fellow was standing, his arms folded, his expression intense, as he watched what James was doing. Then he began to gaze upwards, as if trying to decipher the spectral form which Stephen had assumed. Light from the flames fell full on his horrified face, and it was that of the Earl of Kent. Just at that moment the earl himself appeared to see Stephen, or at least to perceive some spirit writhing in agony in the cloud above the cauldron.

Whilst James repeated at ever greater volume his words of power and incantation, and trembled now and wept at the strength of his own emotions, Kent bounded forward, questions tumbling from his lips: What was the truth of Edward's death? Was he indeed alive, and where was he now? Whose body lay in the sepulchre at Gloucester?

Stephen's torture intensified. Each of his senses now had that same keenness first bestowed after death, and this compounded his suffering. Such was his pain and desire to escape that in wild desperation he began to spew the tale of Edward and his confessor out into the room, obscenities and curses larding the truths which had been concealed by Mortimer. Words stumbled one over another as he vomited them forth, fought to void his conscience and to discharge whatever duty had brought him here to be staked and skewered in agony.

Even when all his words were spent, his ordeal continued, for Kent leaped almost into the fire itself in his eagerness to ply more questions, and Stephen could do no more than wail and babble in misery, till at last James cried out an oath, threw sandalwood into the flames, and clapped his hands twice more. At this, a great draught blew from the doorway, causing the flames to lick high round the cauldron, the smoke to billow, and Stephen's ghostly form to wreathe away and upwards. He felt himself rising, borne up by a great heat, up into the summit of the thatch, and out through the smoke hole into the night sky.

The firmament was at first bejewelled with stars, but they dimmed the higher he ascended, till at last all light had been extinguished, all pain had drained away, and he felt himself absorbed into the blackness again. This time, however, respite was withheld, for he found the darkness peopled with doubts and fears. What sufferings would he face, if the black arts were again used – by James, or indeed anyone else – to drag him back, to break the order of things, to conjure him as servant to their Evil? What pain would be his, even if he did no more than witness events pertinent to himself as he had before, now his senses were once more sharp as a scimitar, thanks to James' witchcraft?

*

With trepidation, Stephen grasped that the next thinning of the blackness was upon him, though this time no voice summoned him, and no fire crackled out a perilous greeting. Vague forms became concrete about him, and he beheld a high castle wall, and before it a scaffold. He feared for a moment he was condemned to watch the execution of Despenser once again. The wall, though, was of different stone, the scaffold smaller, and, in place of two lofty gibbets, a solitary block stood at its centre with a basket and straw to one side. A large crowd was standing before the scaffold, but bathed in the brittle light of a bright spring morning, rather than the dregs of a winter afternoon. Its mood seemed sullen: one of resentment, rather than of lust for slaughter; and, though he could have retched at its stench, a slight breeze brought relief with a scent of daffodil and primrose, and the astringent tang of fresh sawn pinewood.

When a tall man in shirt-sleeves was led by soldiers from a doorway in the castle wall towards the scaffold, Stephen saw that it was Kent who now faced death. Whatever plots and intrigues – let alone spells and incantations – the earl had become involved in, in order to release and restore his brother, all must have come to nothing, for it was clear Edmund was now but the latest victim of Mortimer and Isabella. Stephen felt dread, knowing how unbearable it had been to watch Despenser's end. How much worse would it now be with his heightened senses to listen to Kent's final whimperings, to smell the rankness of his sweat as he laid his head upon the block, and on the fresh spring air to taste the zest of his spurting blood.

Stephen's fears remained only speculative – at least for many hours – for though the charge was read out, and Kent's condemnation proclaimed to the crowd – for seeking the restoration of "that worshipful knight, Sir Edward, sometime King of England", and though Kent himself mounted the scaffold and prayed with a Dominican priest, no one then came forward to carry out the sentence of decapitation. Stephen's acute hearing gleaned the rumour running through the assembly that the castle's executioner had fled, unwilling to despatch a man who was the king's uncle and the brother of a king, despite Mortimer's wishes and the order of his tribunal. He overheard too the whispered disputation amongst the soldiers, as first one and then another refused their commander's request for a volunteer to fetch an axe and bring the proceedings to a close. The sun rose higher until midday had passed, starlings flew to and fro eager for eyes to peck at, and the grumbles of the crowd at times rumbled like a distant storm, before subsiding into mutinous silence. The earl himself paced and prayed, paced and prayed.

Many in the crowd had in fact begun the lunches they had brought with them – cheeses, sausages, pitchers of ale – when in seeming desperation the earl strode to the front of the scaffold and begged, if any loved him and wished to end his suffering, that they should take up an axe and release his troubled soul; but not one dared. Stephen felt the earl's anguish, heard the relentless pounding of his heart, watched the rivulets of perspiration which, despite the cool breeze, began to drench his shirt, even to soak his hose already be-fouled and moist with urine.

Later, as heavy clouds blew in from the west, Stephen heard the desperate order of the troops' commander that a prisoner from the dungeon be sought, who, for the price of a pardon, should wield the axe. Just as rain began to fall, a wretch was indeed hauled forth, whom rumour held be a cleaner of latrines sentenced to death for stealing a pyx. An axe was placed in his trembling hands, and the earl, till then slumped on the scaffold in despair, struggled to his feet, and with dignity approached the block.

The end, when it came, was swift – less harrowing to view than Stephen had feared. Kent himself had no more prayers to offer, and though, after he had laid his head on the block and the axe fell, Ste-phen endured the sound of the variegated severing of flesh, bone and artery, the stench of Edmund's fear, and the smell of blood lingering on the breeze after the head had dropped, the cold purgation of the rain somehow soothed Stephen's senses, cleansed horror from the moment, and wept with him for the young earl's sacrifice.

He now felt sympathy for Edmund, for, whatever his weakness, sins and treachery, his death, like Stephen's own and Hugh's before, was an abomination suffered on account of Edward, which bound them together in mournful trinity.

*

It was Edward himself whom Stephen next observed, or rather came to realise he was observing. Under the thin light of a crescent moon a man was hurrying down the short rutted track from the castle to the village of Corfe. He was dressed as a Dominican. Were it not for the location, the man's gait and posture, and the golden beard which protruded slightly from beneath his hood, even Stephen's pene-trating sight might not have recognised him as his lord and friend. Edward was not alone, but was accompanied by another man, who was similarly clad, but whom Stephen did not know. Their manner was furtive: they did not speak, and Edward often looked back over his shoulder towards the castle. Yet no hue and cry was raised, no pursuers followed, and no blaze of lights shone out from the castle keep.

Stephen's perception then seemed to be borne up into the heavens, and the higher it soared, the faster time raced by on the earth beneath. The grains could not have run through an hourglass before he had seen Edward sail by cog into the west, and wander many leagues through a land of rain and low green hills, till at last he and his companion found refuge at the hall of a local chieftain. There, for a while at least, the harp's sound beguiled him, though Edward no longer danced nor sang, and spent much time instead in prayer and fasting.

That Edward had not been pursued, and that he was now free to wander where he would, seemed at first curious to Stephen, and it made him wonder whether Edward had in fact escaped, or had not rather been allowed to depart. Maybe the times were again in turmoil, or Edward's enemies had fallen, or maybe Edward himself was so changed – or judged so deranged – that he was no longer considered a danger to anyone but himself.

But as far as Stephen could discern, Edward was neither dangerous nor deranged. If now he dressed always as a Dominican, it seemed not only for the purpose of disguise, but to express something of the inner man. And when Stephen listened to Edward's whispered prayers, he learned how often they were uttered in memory of a confessor, who had caused a revolution in Edward's life, and whose soul he now sought to speed its way through Purgatory. When Edward confessed, it was also clear that he no longer sought to be king, had renounced all riches and power, and wished only to follow the apostolic life, as his confessor had done.

Stephen reflected that, whilst he unwillingly had taken Edward's place, so now Edward willingly had taken his. Despite the vagaries of time, of place and of station, Edward now led a life he might have lived himself, and their two fates had once more cleaved together, like a husband to his wife.

*

Since James had wrought his mischief, not only had Stephen's senses returned to their previous painful acuity, but the frequent dark lacunae in which till then he had found increasing respite, had all but been denied to him. It made him fear that the epiphanies would never cease, and that at no point could he ever expect peace, judgement, let alone explanation.

The briefest sojourn in the darkness now gave way to two further glimpses of Edward's later life, though both were fleeting. In one the two companions followed a road beside a great river flowing south through a land of vines and olive trees till they came to a city at whose centre was a vast palace of many towers and arches. There Stephen saw Edward gain admittance by showing his emerald signet ring, and with pleasure saw him entertained, in manner befitting a sovereign, by the Church's greatest prince.

In the second, in a large unfinished cathedral beside another great river – this time flowing north – the companions knelt from dawn till dusk before a shrine of gold and silver shaped like a basilica, yet comprising three sarcophagi. There Edward did homage, beat his breast, prayed to the Magi for forgiveness. To what avail this might be, Stephen could not say, for his own faith in miracles, indeed in saintly intercession, had long since withered. Besides, he now knew bones within shrines were not always what they seemed.

The vision faded, and he was relieved to find that a slightly longer period of repose came upon him. As he melded into its music, let his consciousness dissipate, he pondered on Edward's pilgrimage, wondered where and in what land it might culminate, and whether, when it did, his own soul's shacklement to the world might come to an end.

*

When after a time the darkness receded and a further vision interposed itself, it was again of a land he had never seen: a land where range upon range of mighty snow-capped mountains to the north guarded a vast and fertile plain studded with cities of wealth and power. To the south lofty hills rose towards yet more mountains, beyond which was a gulf on the inland sea, where a great port perched between mighty precipices and the deep.

It was neither to the cities, though, for all their wealth and magnificence, nor to the mountains, for all their majesty, that Stephen was drawn. By the unfathomable logic which governed his visions, it was instead to the gentler landscape of the hill-country, with its deep valleys and steep escarpments, softened, clothed, made beautiful by thick groves of chestnut trees, sometimes of beech – an upland region from which many streams flowed down to a third great river meandering eastwards across the plain. Within those valleys, amongst those dense groves, men had raised buildings in praise of God, sometimes small and plain, but often in the form of large abbeys decorated with frescoes of saints and sinners, patrons and princes, but which also spoke almost in passing of cloth and wine, and of the wealth to be made from them. In such buildings there was peace for those who would pray and contemplate, those who would turn from the world and its vicissitudes, or from their own lives and troubled pasts, or for those whom simply the world had left behind.

Such an abbey Stephen now beheld. It was high on a promontory, itself flanked on three sides by hills which were loftier still. Some force hurried his perception through its precincts, past an imposing bell-tower to the left, through a nave with an array of altars, but then out into a smaller chapel, which ran parallel to the nave, and where Stephen observed the tomb of a saint. Though he read from an inscription that the bones interred there were those of Saint Albert of Butrio, he had no time to linger, to ponder on these bones' provenance, or even to wonder why this building rather than any other should be shown to him. Instead he was impelled onwards to steps which led down to a short cloister, which itself gave on to an orderly and well-tended garden of many herbs, flowers and vegetables. Beyond, through a gap in the hills, the garden commanded views out over the valleys and villages of the locality, and in the distance out over the great river plain itself.

It was then that the vision's purpose became manifest, for towards the far side of the garden Stephen saw a tall, but rather stooped man, who wore a monk's habit, and who looked not at the wondrous vista, but only down to his rosary or from time to time back towards the cloister. Golden locks no longer graced either his head or cheek, and what grey stubble there was upon his pate had been shaved to form a tonsure. His limbs were wasted now, so that when he raised his voice in prayer, its lightness sorted better with his frame. There was a milkiness about the eyes, which no longer flashed in anger or in passion, but seemed benign and tranquil. The only fire came from a signet ring, which from time to time gleamed in the southern sun as his fingers told the beads.

Though the sun itself was warm, drawing scents from herbs and flowers to infuse the air, there was a cool breeze too from the peaks above. It sighed its way through grove and coppice, set flocks of birds wheeling, and caused the folds of the man's habit to sway, whilst he himself remained motionless. An insistent hum of bees was also carried on the wind, as they busied themselves in the fields and about the many hives along the abbey's boundary; and, as the sun tempted gnats to hang in clouds about the cloister where the breeze did not penetrate, greedy swifts darted back and forth making sport and harvest.

Yet it seemed Edward's mind noted none of this, for its focus was beyond the plain's horizon, quite beyond any kingdom this Eden could provide. Either that, or now with age his senses faded; and indeed his body seemed to wither, even as Stephen watched, even as Stephen gave thanks his friend had weathered life's trials, and been born again, long after the world had thought him dead; even as Stephen realised that his life's mission had been accomplished.

Now Stephen's own senses began once more to falter, for the song of birds, the wind's sigh in the chestnut groves, the drowsy hum of bees, all seemed to dissolve one into the other, till there was nothing but one long exhalation of awe and valediction. The sun dimmed even before it had kissed the valley's edge, and the hills yielded their definition. If in the air the scent of marjoram and thyme still hung, it was now less distinct, became tinged with other fragrances: those of camphor, coloquiath, and other funerary spices familiar to Stephen, but of which he had never known the names.

*

There was a sound of tapping, hammering, of prizing apart. Stone slid against stone, and there was a creak of wooden and then leaden lids being opened. A greyer shade of darkness appeared above him, before lighted candles, dropping hot wax, were thrust into the aperture, and faces, on which shadows danced, peered into the darkness – his darkness – below.

He barely noticed as a body wrapped in cerecloth, smelling of frankincense and myrrh, was lowered into the grave till it rested on his own remains. Neither did he pay much heed to the sounds of closing, sliding, hammering and tapping, which marked once more the sealing of the tomb.

If he felt anything over the centuries of mould and putrefaction which followed, it was a sense of rightness and satisfaction as their bones eroded into dust and their detritus merged.

Bibliography

Ailes, M J – "The Medieval Male Couple and the Language of Homosociality" in Hadley, DM – "Masculinity in Medieval Europe", pp 214-37 – ISBN 978-0582316454

Biller, Peter and Minnis, A.J.(eds) – "Handling Sin: Confession in the Middle Ages" – ISBN 978-1903153482

Bossy, John – "Christianity in the West 1400-1700" – ISBN 978-0192891624

Boswell, John – "Christianity, Social Tolerance and Homosexuality" – ISBN 978-0226067117

Boyd, David -"Seeking Goddes Pryvetee: Sodomy, Quitting, and Desire in the Miller's Tale" – in Baker, Peter and Howe, Nicholas (eds) – "Words and Works – Studies in Medieval English Language and Literature in Honour of Fred C Robinson", pp243-60 – ISBN 978-0802041531

Brooke, Rosalind and Christopher – "Popular Religion in the Middle Ages – Western Europe 1000-1300" – ISBN 978-0500273814

Burden, Joel – "Re-writing a Rite of Passage: The Peculiar Funeral of Edward II" in Nicola F Macdonald and W. M. Ormrod (eds) -"Rites of Passage: Cultures of Transition in the Fourteenth Century" – ISBN 978-1903153154

Burger, G and Kruger, S.F. – "Queering the Middle Ages (Medieval Cultures)" – ISBN 978-0816634040

Burgtorf, Jochen – "With My Life His Joyes Began and Ended" in Nigel Saul (ed) "Fourteenth Century England V:5" – ISBN 978-1843833871

Chaplais, Pierre – "Piers Gaveston – Edward II's Adoptive Brother" – ISBN 978-0198204497

Chaucer, Geoffrey – "The Canterbury Tales"

Clark, James C. (ed) – "The Culture of Medieval English Monasticism" – ISBN 978-1843833215

Clarke, R D – "Some Secular Activities of the English Dominicans During the Reigns of Edward I, Edward II, and Edward III, 1272 – 1377" (MA, London, 1930)

Crompton, Louis – " Homosexuality and Civilisation" – ISBN 978-0674022331

Daniell, C – "Death and Burial in Medieval England 1066 – 1550" – ISBN 978-0415185509

Dante – "The Divine Comedy"

Dodd, Gwilym and Musson, Anthony (eds) – "Reign of Edward II : New Perspectives"- ISBN 978-1903153192

Doherty, Paul – "Isabella and the Strange Death of Edward II"- ISBN 978-1841193014

Fryde, Natalie – "The Tyranny and Fall of Edward II" – ISBN 978-052154809

Gilmour-Bryson, Anne – "Sodomy and the Knights Templar" – Journal of the History of Sexuality, October 1996, Vol 7, no 2, pp 151- 183

Greenberg, David F – "The Construction of Homosexuality" – ISBN 978-0226306285

Haines, Roy Martin – "King Edward II: Edward of Caernarfon, His Life, His Reign and its Aftermath, 1284-1330" – ISBN 978-0773531574

"Roger Mortimer's Scam" – Transactions of the Bristol and Gloucestershire Archaeological Society, Vol 126, pp 139-156

"Sumptuous Apparel for a Royal Prisoner" – English Historical Review, Vol 124, pp 885-894.

Hamilton, J S – "Menage a Roi"- History Today,Vol 49, 1999, pp 26-31

Harvey – "The Berkeleys of Berkeley" – Phd Thesis – St Andrews University.

Herbert, NM – "The Victoria History of the County of Gloucester", Vol IV, ISBN 978-0197227718

Higginbotham, Susan – "Edward II, His Friends, His Enemies, and His Death" – Internet

Huizinga, Jan – "The Waning of the Middle Ages" – ISBN 978-1849028950

Hutchison, H F – "Edward II and his Minions" – History Today, Vol 21, 1971, pp 542-9

Kathryn's website – www.edwardthesecond.com

Knowles, David – "The Religious Orders in England", Volume 1 ISBN 978-0521295666

Lawrence, Martyn – "Edward II and the Earldom of Winchester" – Historical Research, Vol 81, no 214 (November 2008)

Le Goff, Jacques – "The Birth of Purgatory" – ISBN 978-0226470832

Le Roy Ladurie, Emmanuel – "Montaillou: Cathars and Catholics in a French Village 1294-1324" – ISBN 978-0859674034

Lord, Evelyn – "The Templar's Curse" – ISBN 978-1405840385

Marchant, G – "Edward II in Gloucestershire: A King in Our Midst" (Gloucester 2007) – available at Gloucester Cathedral bookshop

McGuire, Brian Patrick – "Friendship and Community – The Monastic Experience, 350-1250" – ISBN 978-0801476723

Meyer, Ann R – "The Despensers and the Gawain Poet: A Gloucestershire Link to the Alliterative Master of the Northwest Midlands" – The Chaucer Review, Vol 35, No 4, 2001

Montford, Angela – "Health, Sickness, Medicine and the Friars in the Thirteenth and Fourteenth Centuries" – ISBN 978-0754636977.

Moore, Stuart A – "Documents Relating to the Death and Burial of Edward II" – Archaeologia, Vol 50, 1887, pp 215-221

Mortimer, Ian – "The Greatest Traitor: the Life of Sir Roger Mortimer" – ISBN 978-0099552222

Mortimer, Ian – Time-Traveller's Guide to Medieval England – ISBN 978-1845950996

Mortimer, Ian – "The Perfect King" – Appendices 2 and 3 – ISBN 978-0099527091

Mortimer, Ian – "The Death of Edward II in Berkeley Castle" – English Historical Review, Vol 120, 2005, pp 1175-1214

Mortimer, Ian – "Medieval Intrigue: Decoding Royal Conspiracies" – ISBN 978-1441102690

Neal, Derek G – "The Masculine Self in Late Medieval England" – ISBN 978-0226569550

Nicholson, Helen – "Saints or Sinners? – The Knights Templar in Medieval Europe" – History Today, Dec 1994, Vol 44, pp 30-36

Pearl Poet – "Sir Gawain and the Green Knight" and "Cleanness" in "The Complete Works of the Pearl Poet" (author: Casey Finch) – ISBN 978-0520078710

Perry, Reginald – "Edward II: Suddenly at Berkeley"- ISBN 978-0951402801

Pelikan, Jaroslav – "Mary Through the Centuries" – ISBN 978-0300069518

Phillips, Seymour – "Edward II" – ISBN 978-0300178029

Prestwich, M C – "The Three Edwards: War and State in England 1273-1377" – ISBN 978-0415303095

Tuchman, Barbara – "A Distant Mirror: The Calamitous Fourteenth Century" – ISBN 978-0140054071

Tout, T F – "The Captivity and Death of Edward of Carnarvon" – "Bulletin of the John Rylands Library", Vol 6, 1921, pp 69-113 or in "The Collected Papers of Thomas Frederick Tout", Vol 6

Saul N – "Knights and Esquires: the Gloucestershire Gentry in the Fourteenth Century"- ISBN – 978 0198218838

Saul, N – "The Despensers and the Downfall of Edward II" – English Historical Review, Jan 1984, pp 1-33

Sharpe, M – "Some Glimpses of Gloucestershire in the Early Fourteenth Century" – Transactions of the Bristol and Gloucestershire Archaeological Society Vol 93, 1974, pp 5-14

Smith, W J – "The Rise of the Berkeleys: an Account of the Berkeleys of Berkeley Castle 1243-1361" – Transactions of the Bristol and Gloucestershire Archaeological Society, 1951, pp 76-78

Smyth, J – "Lives of the Berkeleys" – Vol 1 of the Berkeley Manuscripts – ed Sir John Maclean – Gloucester 1883-5

Southern, R W – "Western Society and the Church in the Middle Ages" – ISBN 978-0140137552

Tanqueray, F J – "The Conspiracy of Thomas Dunsheved 1327" – English Historical Review, Vol 31, 1916, pp 119-24

Thurlow, G – "Gloucester and Berkeley and the Story of Edward II Martyr King" - Norwich 1977

Verey, David and Brooks, Alan – Pevsner Architectural Guides – "Gloucestershire 2: The Vale and the Forest of Dean" – ISBN 978-0300097337

Valente, Claire – "The Deposition and Abdication of Edward II" – English Historical Review, 1998, p 852

Waugh S L – "The Profits of Violence: the Minor Gentry in the Rebellion of 1321-1322 in Gloucestershire and Herefordshire" – Speculum, Vol 52, 1977, pp 843-69

Weir, Alison – "Isabella, She Wolf of France"- ISBN 978-0099578390

Westerhof, Danielle – "Deconstructing Identities on the Scaffold: the Execution of Hugh Despenser the Younger, 1326" – Journal of Medieval History, Vol 33, Issue 1, March 2007

Westerhof, Danielle – "Death and the Noble Body in Medieval England"-

ISBN 978-1843834168

Wood, Charles T. – "Joan of Arc & Richard III: Sex, Saints, and Government in the Middle Ages" – ISBN 978-0195069518

C.M. Woolgar – "The Senses in Late Medieval England"- ISBN 978-0300118711

C. Woolgar, D. Serjeantson, T. Waldron (eds) – "Food in Medieval England – Diet and Nutrition"- ISBN 978-0199563357

Zeikowitz , R E – "Homoeroticism and Chivalry: Discourses of Male Same-Sex Desire n the Fourteenth Century", pp 1-15, 27-43.– ISBN978-1403960429